THE SWISS FAMILY ROBINSON

Johann David Wyss

CAMPFIRE™

KALYANI NAVYUG MEDIA PVT. LTD

New Delhi

Sitting around the Campfire, telling the story, were:

Wordsmith	:	Richard Blandford
Illustrator	:	Amit Tayal
Illustrations Editor	:	Jayshree Das
Colorist	:	Pradeep Sherawat
Art Director	:	Kamal Sarkar
Letterer	:	Bhavnath Chaudhary
Editors	:	Suparna Deb
		Divya Dubey
Editor (Informative Content)	:	Pushpanjali Borooah
Production Controller	:	Vishal Sharma

Cover Artists:

Illustrator	:	Amit Tayal
Colorist	:	Jayakrishnan K. P.
Designer	:	Pushpa Verma

Published by Kalyani Navyug Media Pvt. Ltd
101 C, Shiv House, Hari Nagar Ashram
New Delhi 110014
India
www.campfire.co.in

ISBN: 978-93-80741-31-4

Printed in India at Rave India

About the Author

Johann David Wyss was born in Berne, Switzerland, in 1743. A pastor, Wyss spoke four different languages, and loved nature. Not much is known about Wyss's early life, but we do know that he was greatly inspired by Daniel Defoe's famous shipwreck adventure story, *Robinson Crusoe*.

Though it is said that *Robinson Crusoe* played quite an influential role in the writing of *The Swiss Family Robinson*, few know that it was originally written to educate and entertain Wyss's four sons.

The book was edited by one of his sons, Johann Rudolf Wyss, a scholar, who also wrote the Swiss national anthem. *The Swiss Family Robinson* was published in German in 1812, and translated into English two years later. It has since become an internationally popular classic for children. Even after Wyss's death in 1818, his timeless tale lives on in nearly two hundred versions of the novel, as well as two films and a telefilm.

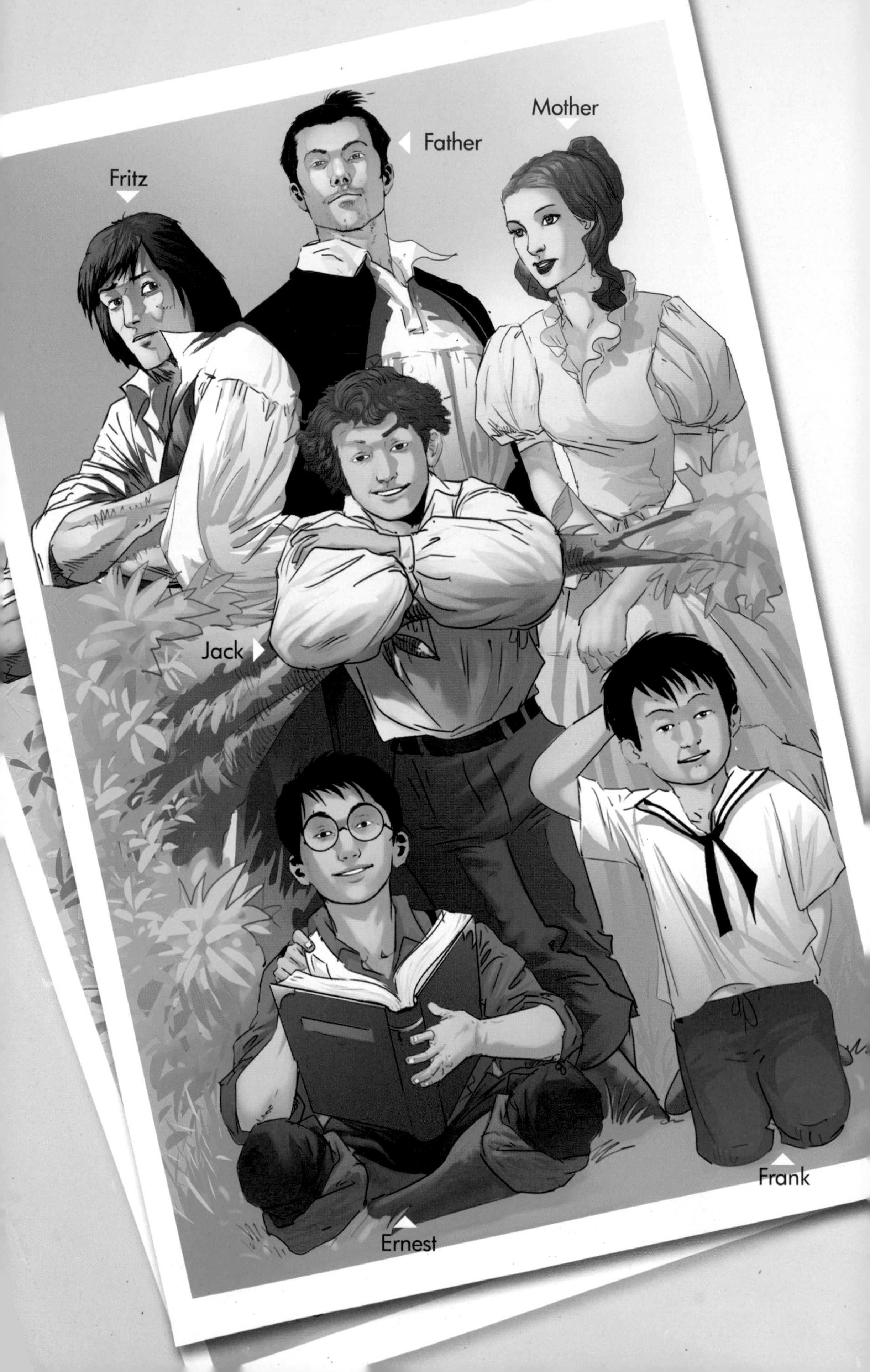
Mother
Father
Fritz
Jack
Frank
Ernest

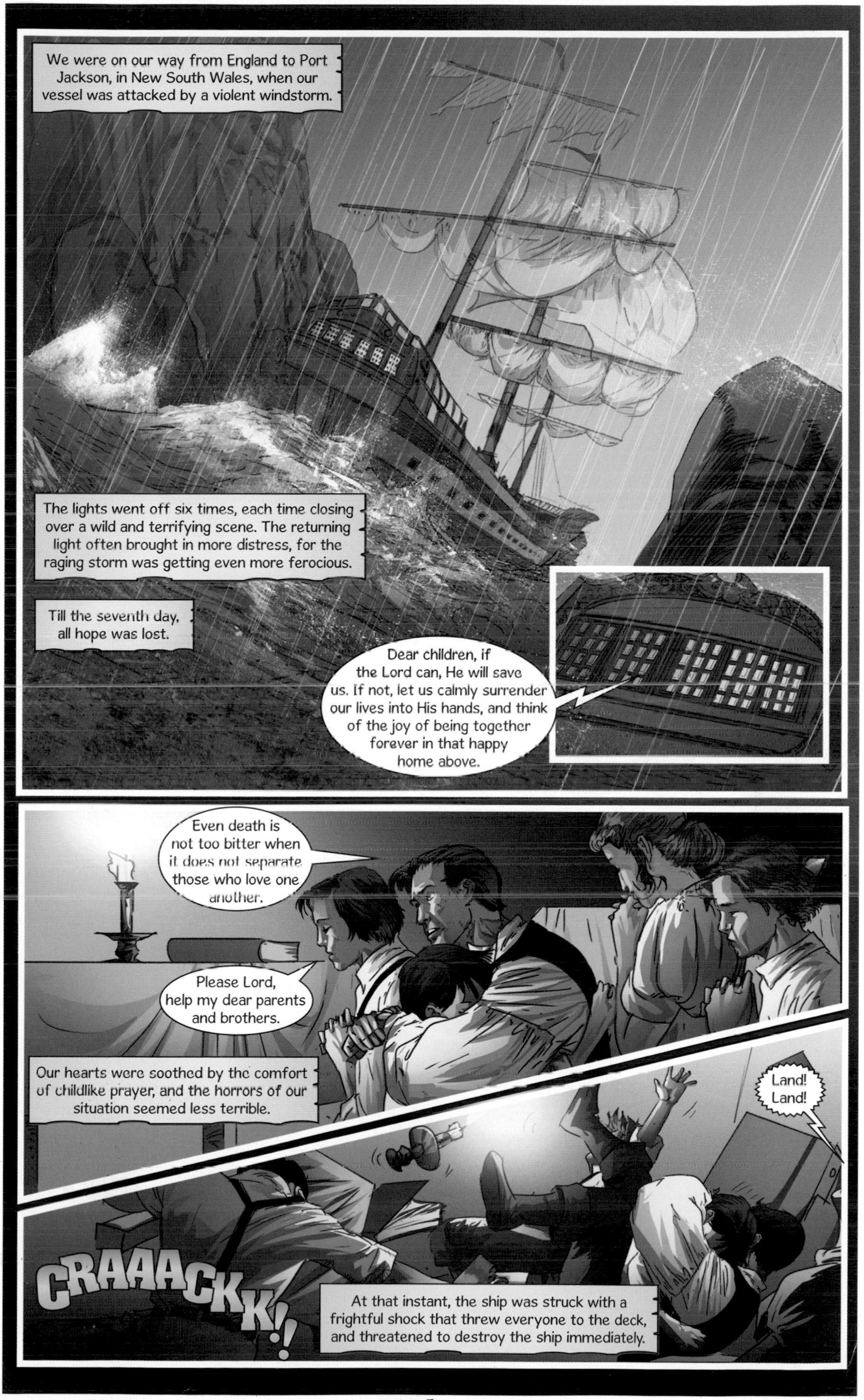
We were on our way from England to Port Jackson, in New South Wales, when our vessel was attacked by a violent windstorm.
The lights went off six times, each time closing over a wild and terrifying scene. The returning light often brought in more distress, for the raging storm was getting even more ferocious.
Till the seventh day, all hope was lost.
Dear children, if the Lord can, He will save us. If not, let us calmly surrender our lives into His hands, and think of the joy of being together forever in that happy home above.
Even death is not too bitter when it does not separate those who love one another.
Please Lord, help my dear parents and brothers.
Our hearts were soothed by the comfort of childlike prayer, and the horrors of our situation seemed less terrible.
Land! Land!
CRAAACKK!!
At that instant, the ship was struck with a frightful shock that threw everyone to the deck, and threatened to destroy the ship immediately.

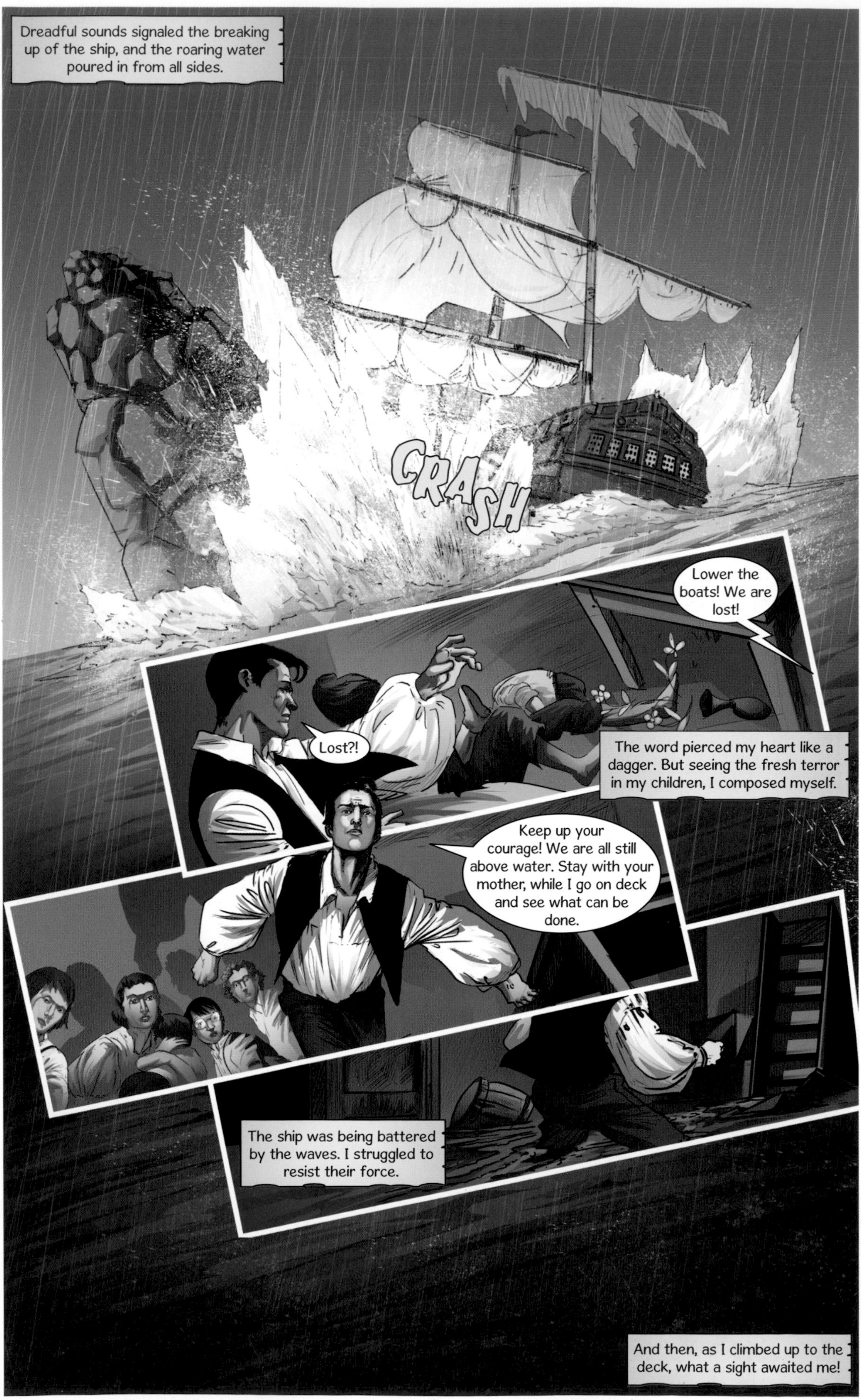
Dreadful sounds signaled the breaking up of the ship, and the roaring water poured in from all sides.
CRASH
Lower the boats! We are lost!
Lost?!
The word pierced my heart like a dagger. But seeing the fresh terror in my children, I composed myself.
Keep up your courage! We are all still above water. Stay with your mother, while I go on deck and see what can be done.
The ship was being battered by the waves. I struggled to resist their force.
And then, as I climbed up to the deck, what a sight awaited me!

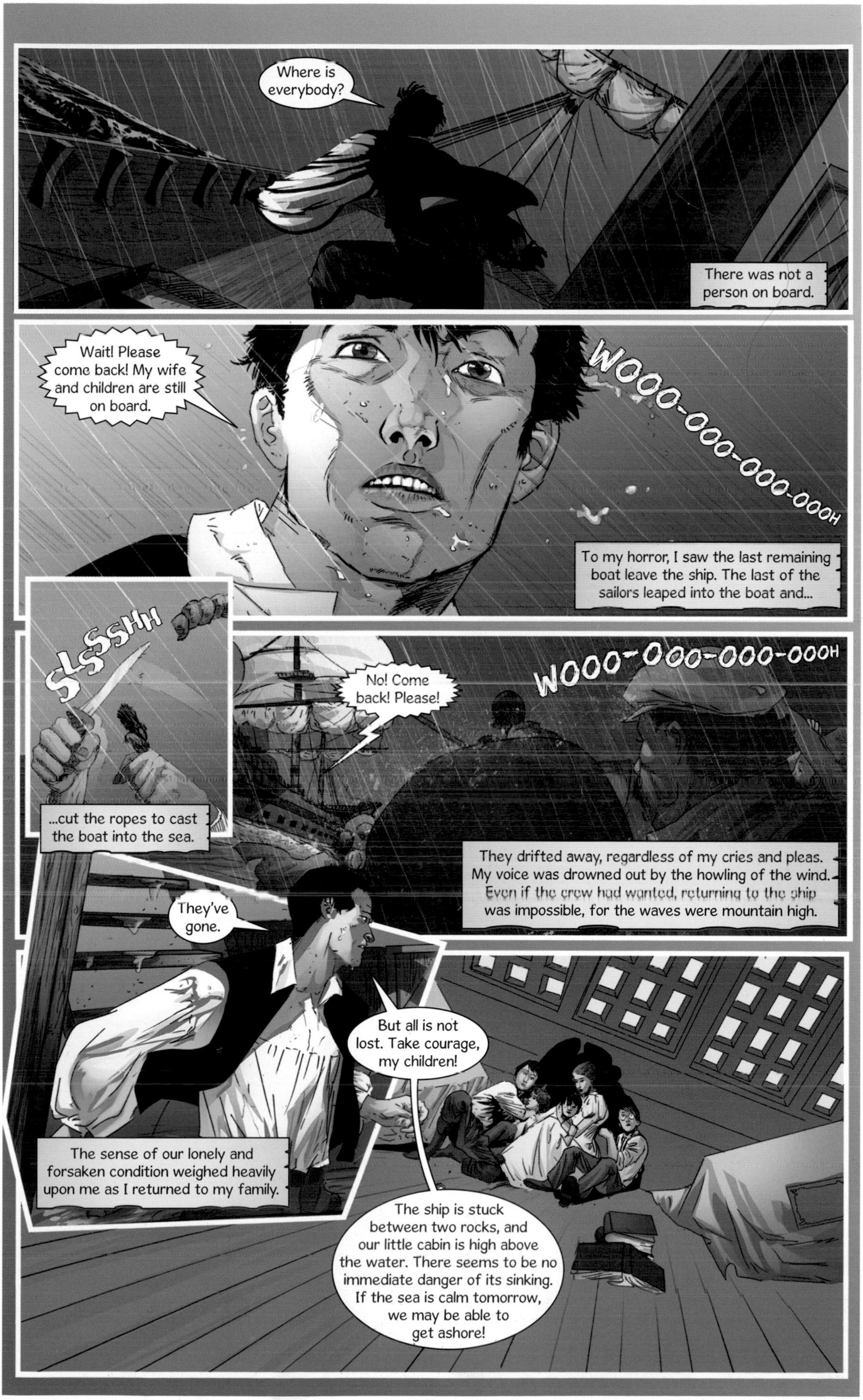
Where is everybody?
There was not a person on board.
Wait! Please come back! My wife and children are still on board.
WOOO-OOO-OOO-OOOH
To my horror, I saw the last remaining boat leave the ship. The last of the sailors leaped into the boat and...
SLSSSHH
...cut the ropes to cast the boat into the sea.
No! Come back! Please!
WOOO-OOO-OOO-OOOH
They drifted away, regardless of my cries and pleas. My voice was drowned out by the howling of the wind. Even if the crew had wanted, returning to the ship was impossible, for the waves were mountain high.
They've gone.
But all is not lost. Take courage, my children!
The sense of our lonely and forsaken condition weighed heavily upon me as I returned to my family.
The ship is stuck between two rocks, and our little cabin is high above the water. There seems to be no immediate danger of its sinking. If the sea is calm tomorrow, we may be able to get ashore!

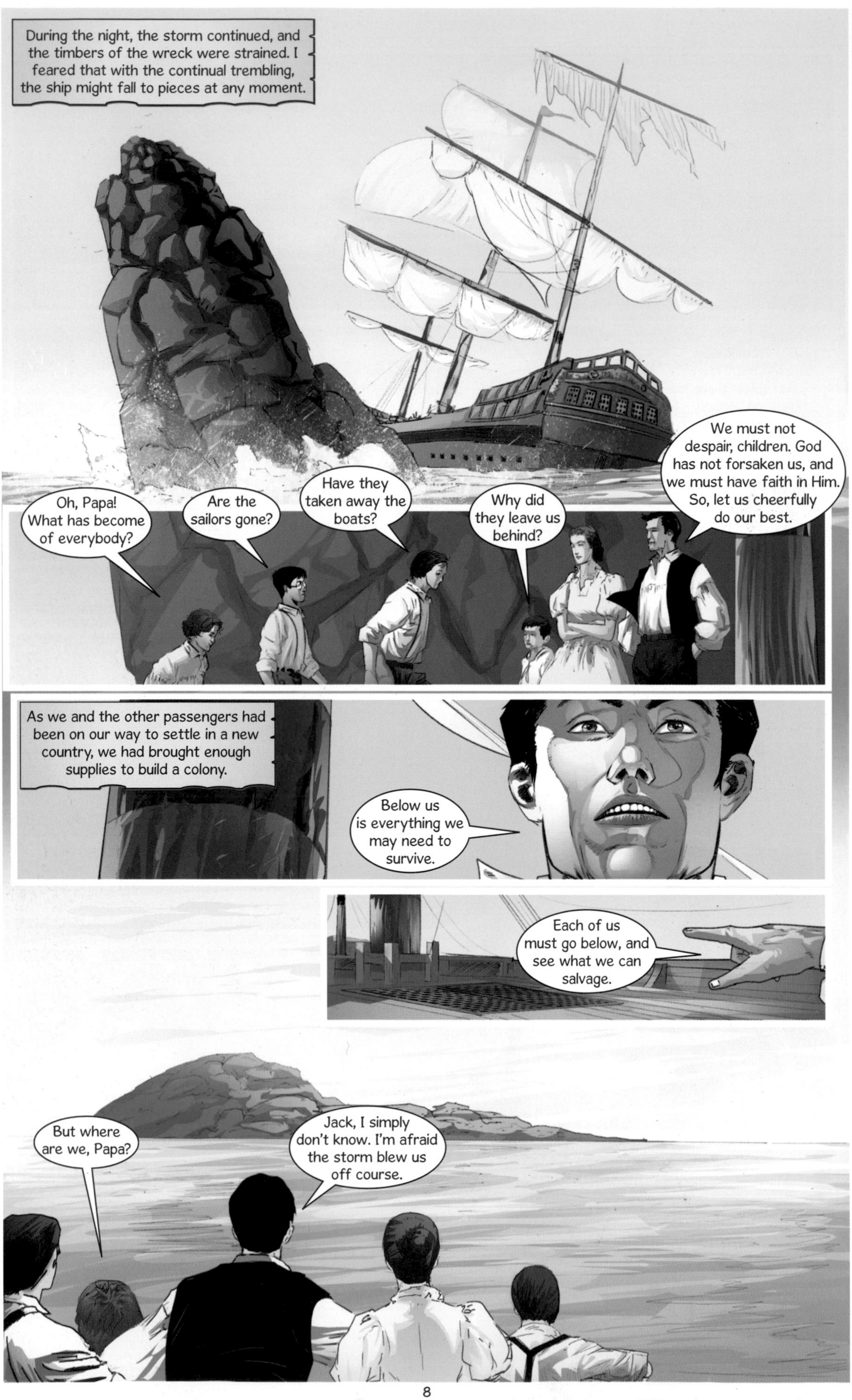
During the night, the storm continued, and the timbers of the wreck were strained. I feared that with the continual trembling, the ship might fall to pieces at any moment.
Oh, Papa! What has become of everybody?
Are the sailors gone?
Have they taken away the boats?
Why did they leave us behind?
We must not despair, children. God has not forsaken us, and we must have faith in Him. So, let us cheerfully do our best.
As we and the other passengers had been on our way to settle in a new country, we had brought enough supplies to build a colony.
Below us is everything we may need to survive.
Each of us must go below, and see what we can salvage.
But where are we, Papa?
Jack, I simply don't know. I'm afraid the storm blew us off course.

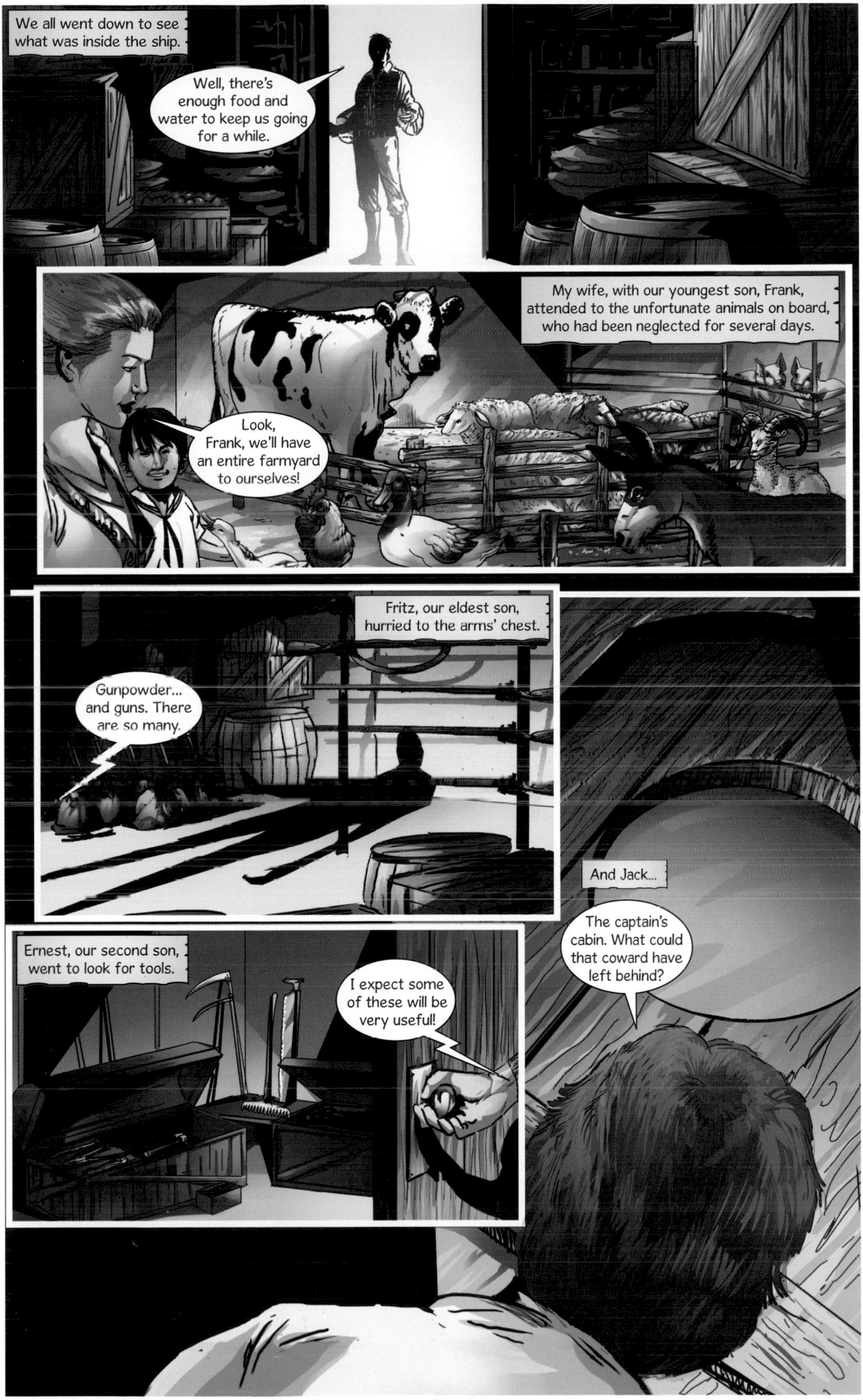
We all went down to see what was inside the ship.
Well, there's enough food and water to keep us going for a while.
My wife, with our youngest son, Frank, attended to the unfortunate animals on board, who had been neglected for several days.
Look, Frank, we'll have an entire farmyard to ourselves!
Fritz, our eldest son, hurried to the arms' chest.
Gunpowder... and guns. There are so many.
Ernest, our second son, went to look for tools.
I expect some of these will be very useful!
And Jack...
The captain's cabin. What could that coward have left behind?

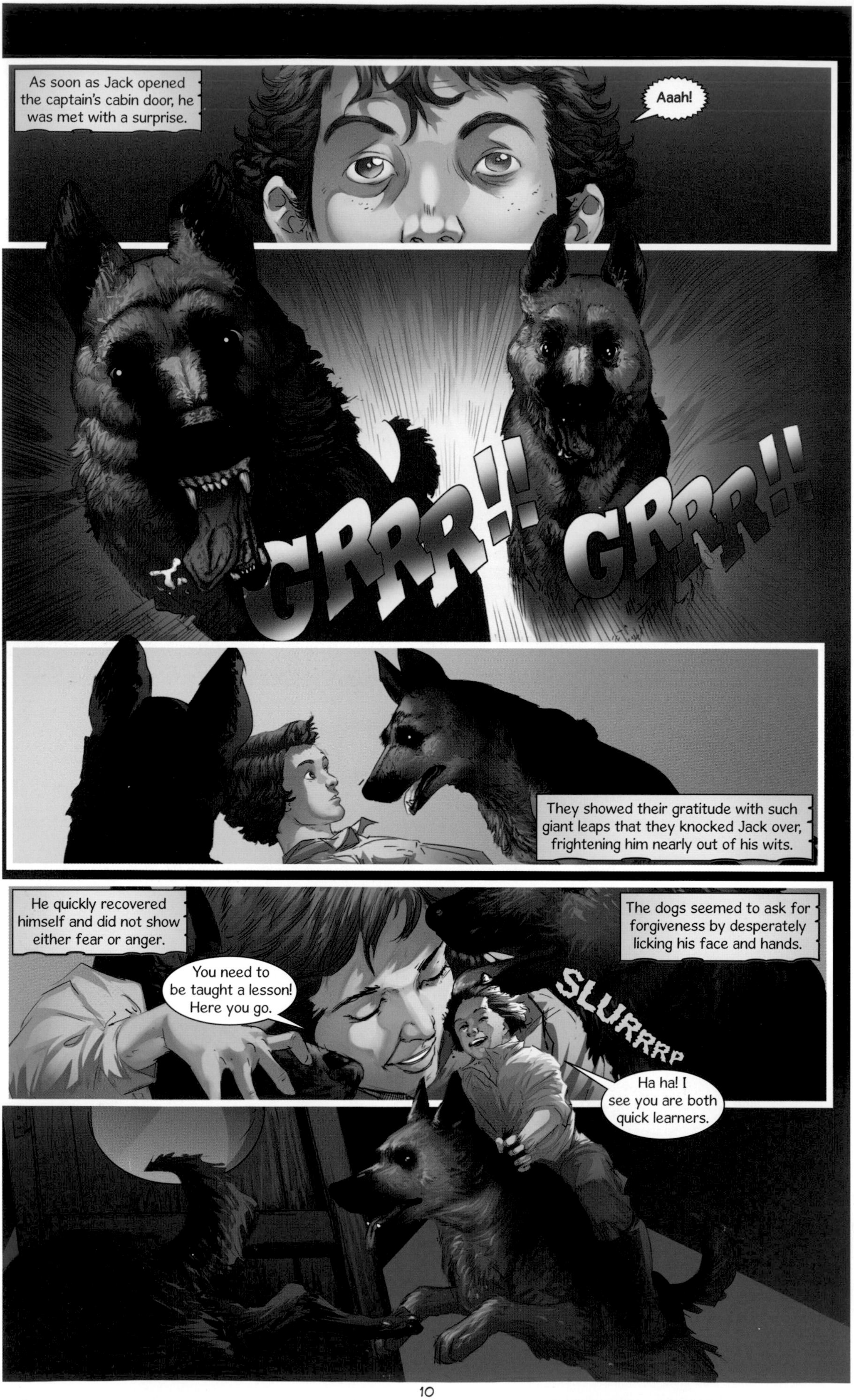
As soon as Jack opened the captain's cabin door, he was met with a surprise.
Aaah!
GRRR!!
GRRR!!
They showed their gratitude with such giant leaps that they knocked Jack over, frightening him nearly out of his wits.
He quickly recovered himself and did not show either fear or anger.
The dogs seemed to ask for forgiveness by desperately licking his face and hands.
You need to be taught a lesson! Here you go.
SLURRRP
Ha ha! I see you are both quick learners.

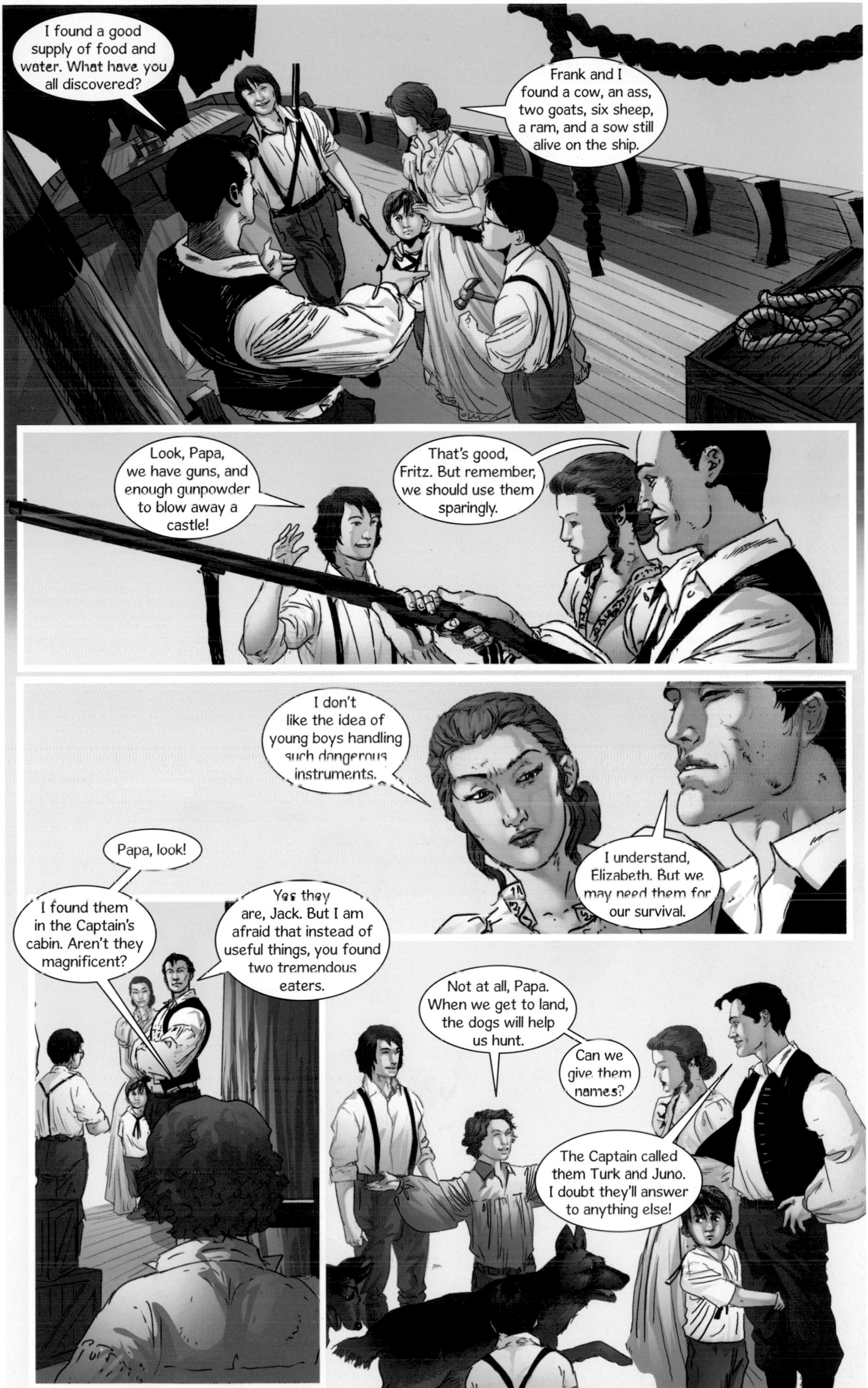
I found a good supply of food and water. What have you all discovered?
Frank and I found a cow, an ass, two goats, six sheep, a ram, and a sow still alive on the ship.
Look, Papa, we have guns, and enough gunpowder to blow away a castle!
That's good, Fritz. But remember, we should use them sparingly.
I don't like the idea of young boys handling such dangerous instruments.
I understand, Elizabeth. But we may need them for our survival.
Papa, look!
I found them in the Captain's cabin. Aren't they magnificent?
Yes they are, Jack. But I am afraid that instead of useful things, you found two tremendous eaters.
Not at all, Papa. When we get to land, the dogs will help us hunt.
Can we give them names?
The Captain called them Turk and Juno. I doubt they'll answer to anything else!

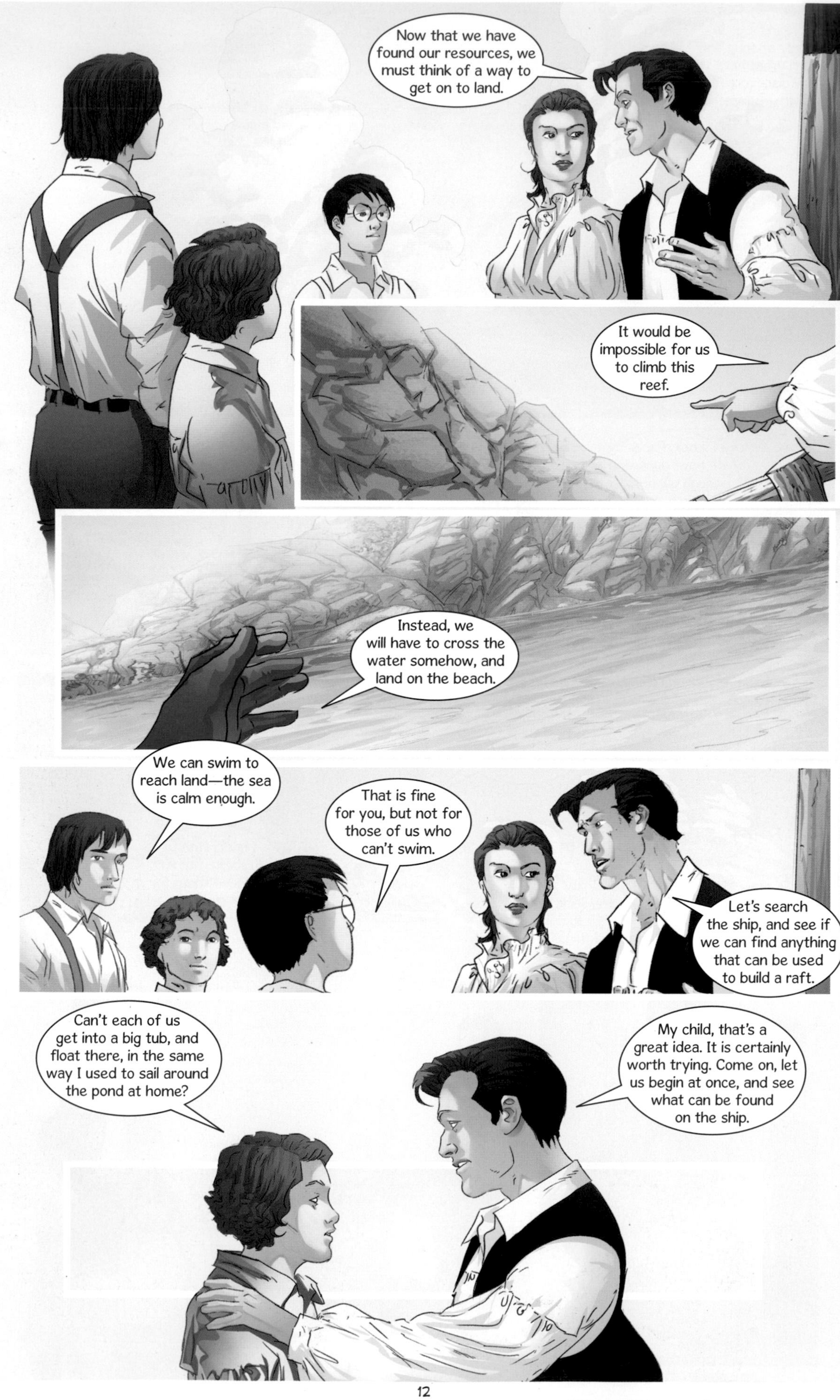
Now that we have found our resources, we must think of a way to get on to land.
It would be impossible for us to climb this reef.
Instead, we will have to cross the water somehow, and land on the beach.
We can swim to reach land—the sea is calm enough.
That is fine for you, but not for those of us who can't swim.
Let's search the ship, and see if we can find anything that can be used to build a raft.
Can't each of us get into a big tub, and float there, in the same way I used to sail around the pond at home?
My child, that's a great idea. It is certainly worth trying. Come on, let us begin at once, and see what can be found on the ship.

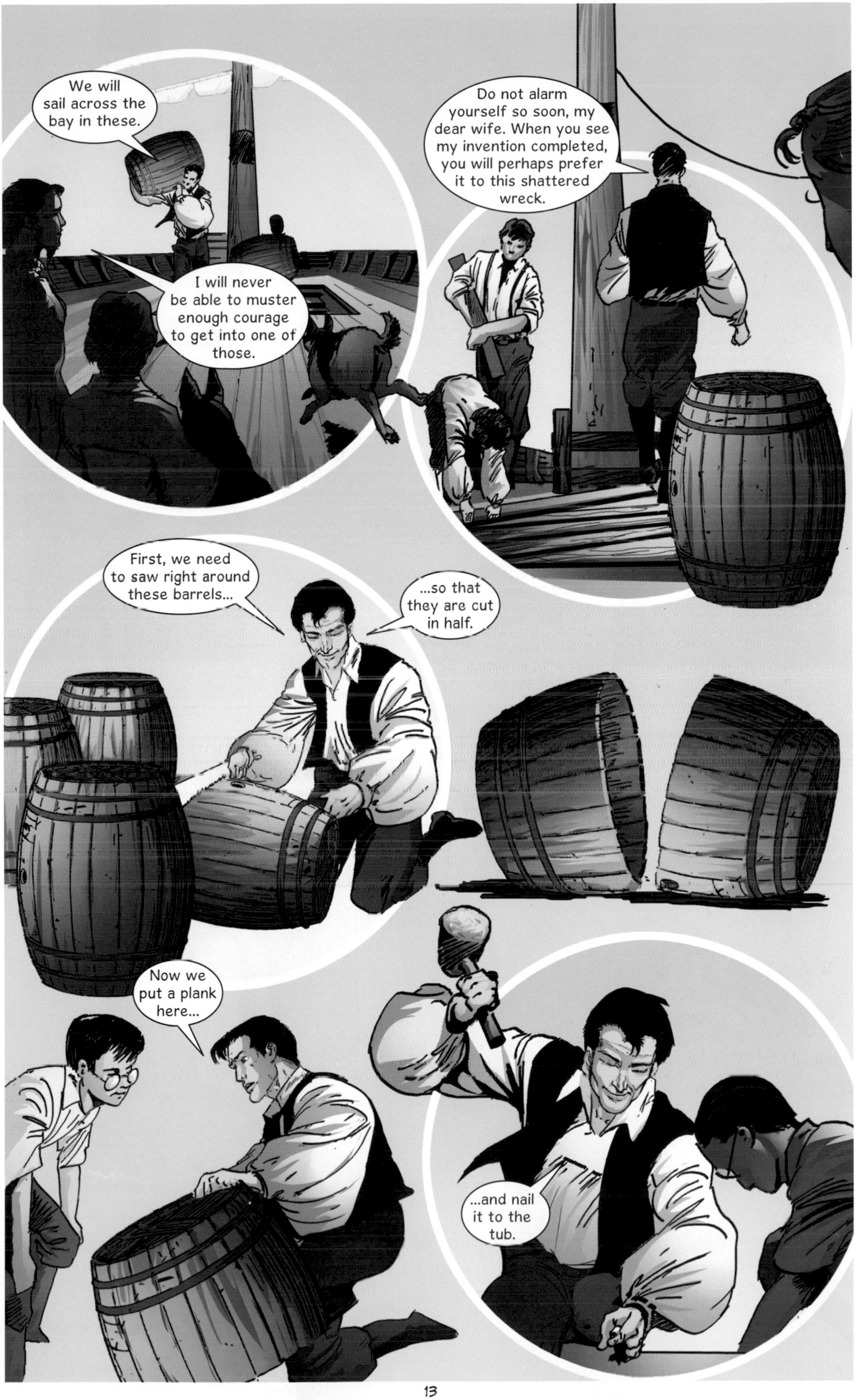
We will sail across the bay in these.
I will never be able to muster enough courage to get into one of those.
Do not alarm yourself so soon, my dear wife. When you see my invention completed, you will perhaps prefer it to this shattered wreck.
First, we need to saw right around these barrels...
...so that they are cut in half.
Now we put a plank here...
...and nail it to the tub.

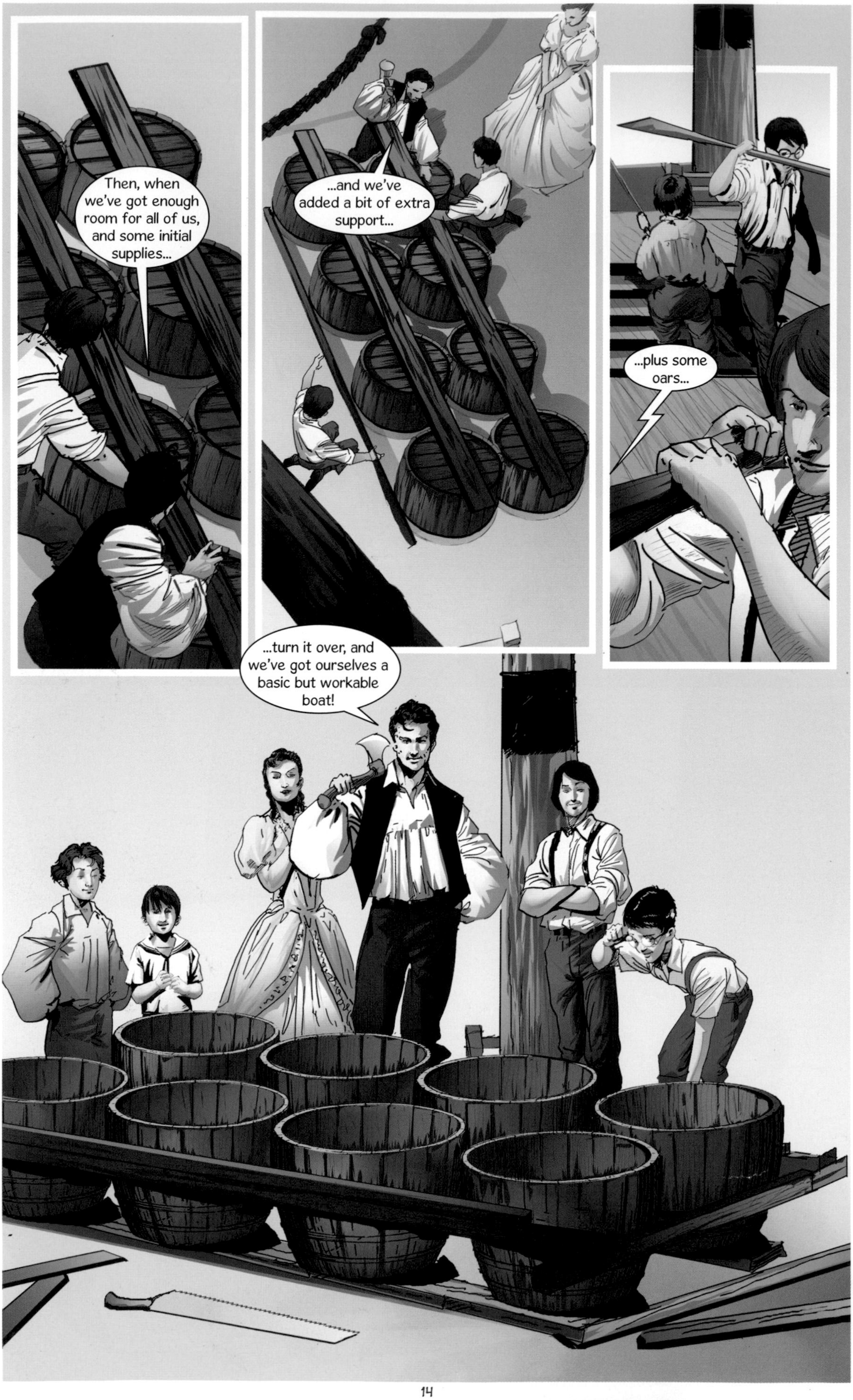
Then, when we've got enough room for all of us, and some initial supplies...
...and we've added a bit of extra support...
...plus some oars...
...turn it over, and we've got ourselves a basic but workable boat!

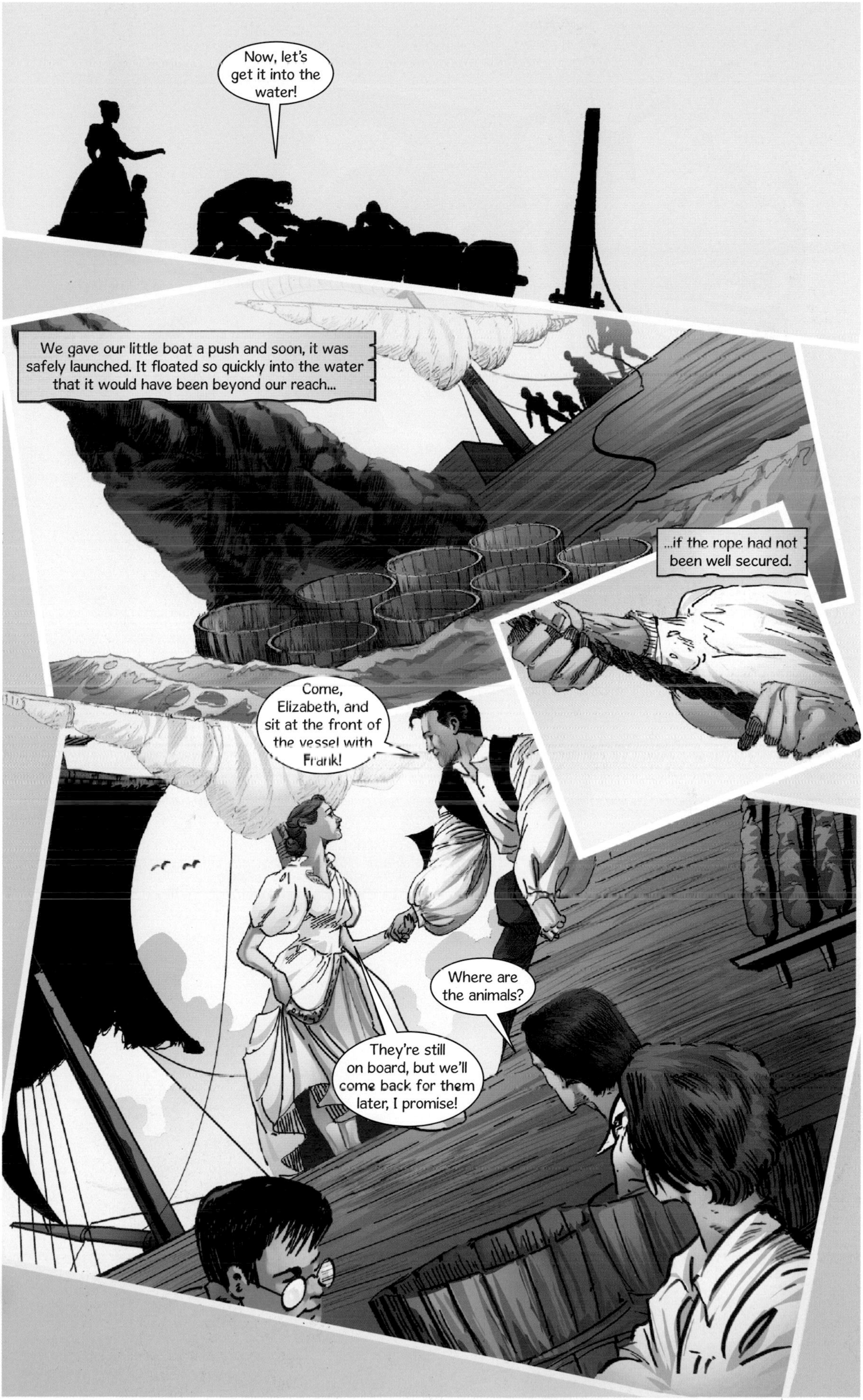
Now, let's get it into the water!
We gave our little boat a push and soon, it was safely launched. It floated so quickly into the water that it would have been beyond our reach...
...if the rope had not been well secured.
Come, Elizabeth, and sit at the front of the vessel with Frank!
Where are the animals?
They're still on board, but we'll come back for them later, I promise!

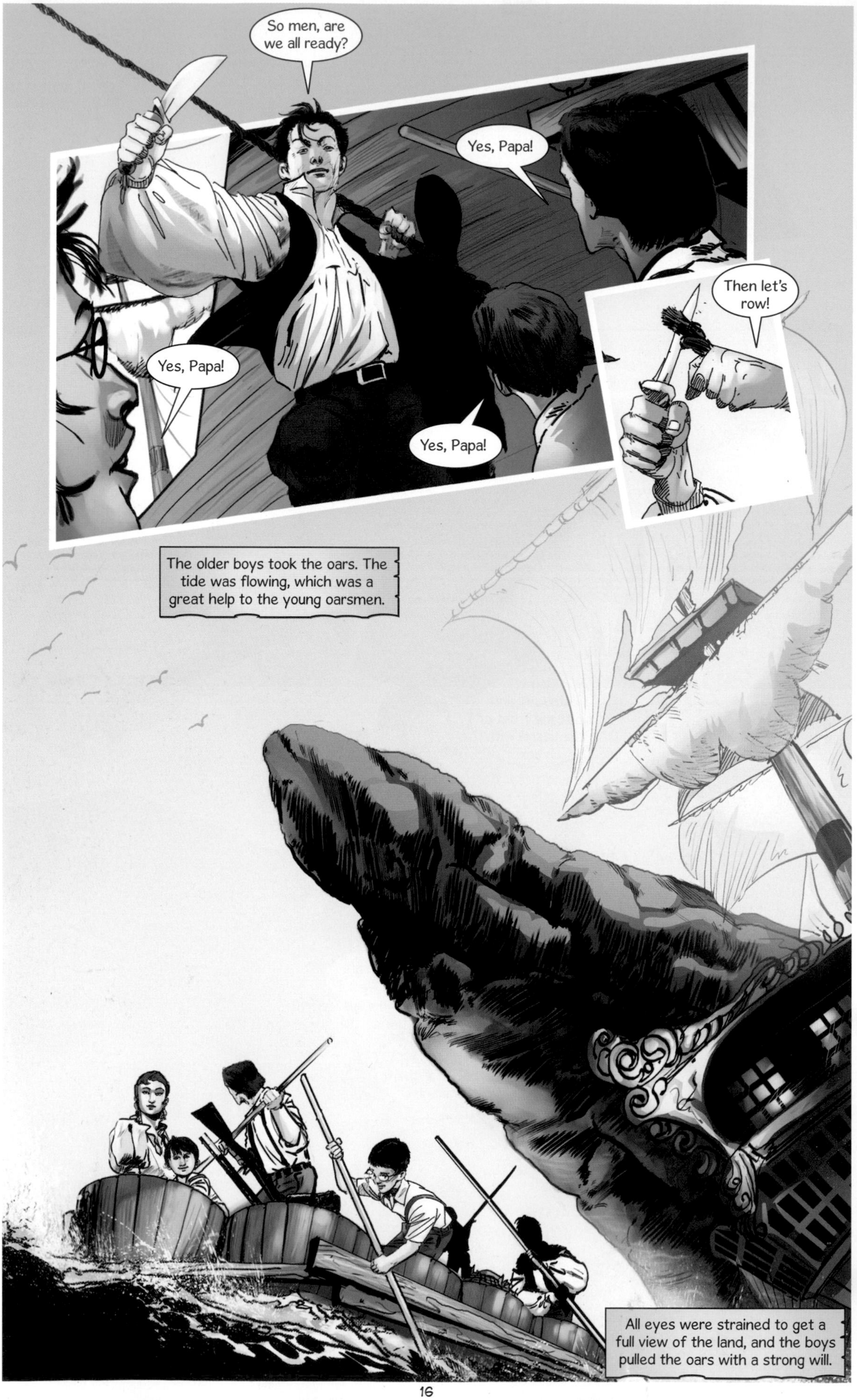
So men, are we all ready?
Yes, Papa!
Yes, Papa!
Yes, Papa!
Then let's row!
The older boys took the oars. The tide was flowing, which was a great help to the young oarsmen.
All eyes were strained to get a full view of the land, and the boys pulled the oars with a strong will.

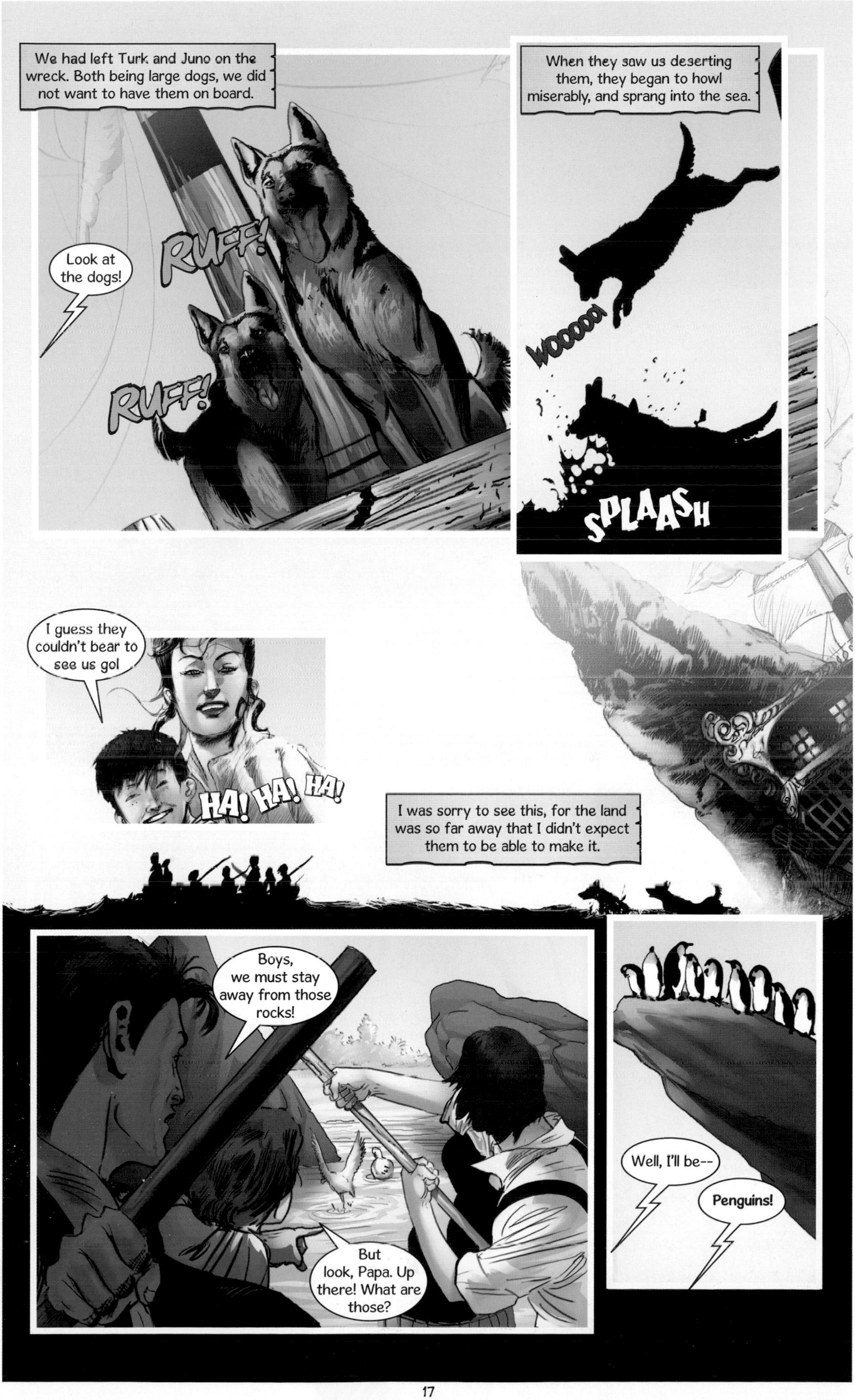

We had left Turk and Juno on the wreck. Both being large dogs, we did not want to have them on board.
Look at the dogs!
RUFF!
RUFF!
When they saw us deserting them, they began to howl miserably, and sprang into the sea.
WOOOOO!
SPLAASH
I guess they couldn't bear to see us go!
HA! HA! HA!
I was sorry to see this, for the land was so far away that I didn't expect them to be able to make it.
Boys, we must stay away from those rocks!
But look, Papa. Up there! What are those?
Well, I'll be--
Penguins!

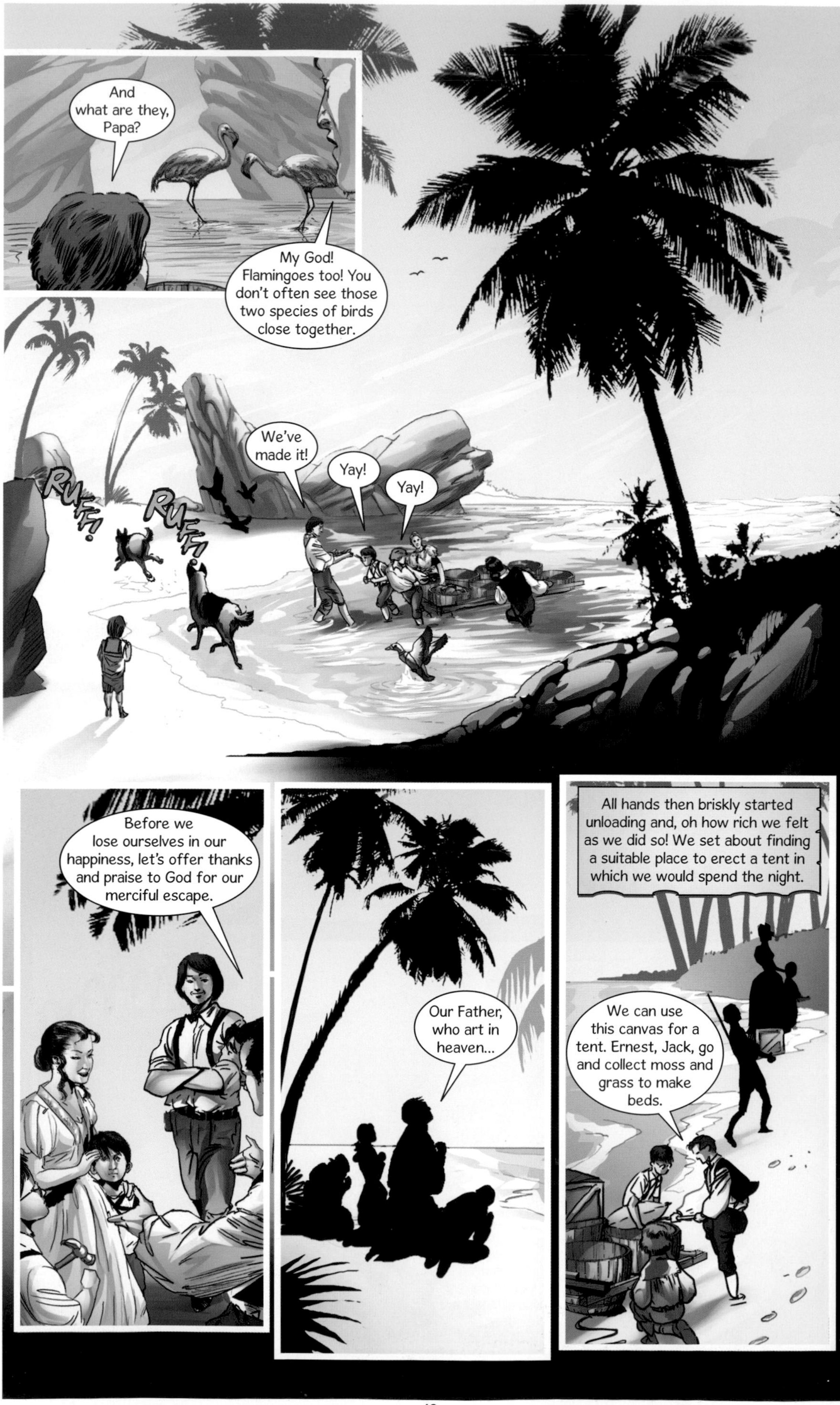
And what are they, Papa?
My God! Flamingoes too! You don't often see those two species of birds close together.
RUFF!
RUFF!
We've made it!
Yay!
Yay!
Before we lose ourselves in our happiness, let's offer thanks and praise to God for our merciful escape.
Our Father, who art in heaven...
All hands then briskly started unloading and, oh how rich we felt as we did so! We set about finding a suitable place to erect a tent in which we would spend the night.
We can use this canvas for a tent. Ernest, Jack, go and collect moss and grass to make beds.

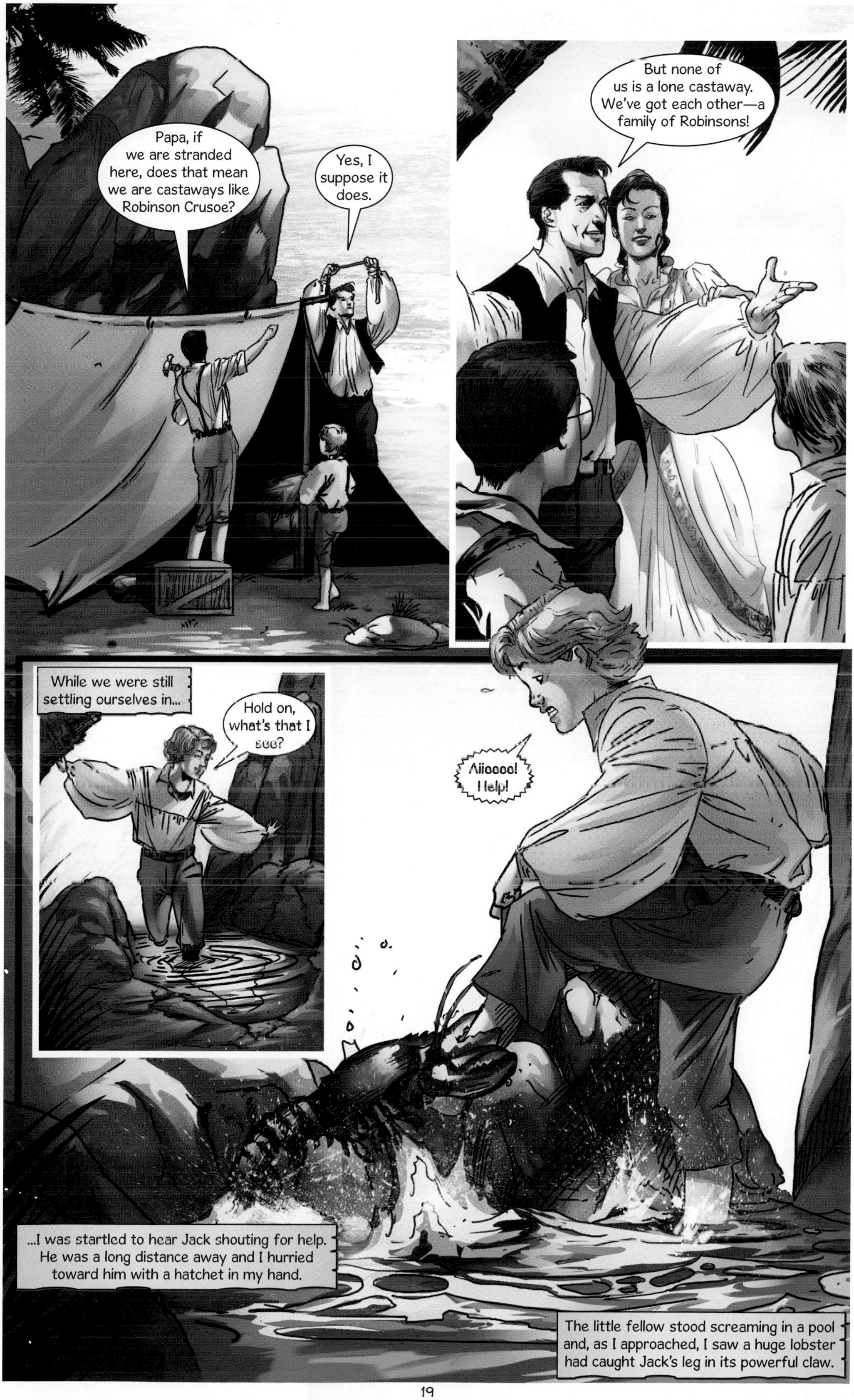

Papa, if we are stranded here, does that mean we are castaways like Robinson Crusoe?
Yes, I suppose it does.
But none of us is a lone castaway. We've got each other—a family of Robinsons!
While we were still settling ourselves in...
Hold on, what's that I see?
Aiiooo! Help!
...I was startled to hear Jack shouting for help. He was a long distance away and I hurried toward him with a hatchet in my hand.
The little fellow stood screaming in a pool and, as I approached, I saw a huge lobster had caught Jack's leg in its powerful claw.

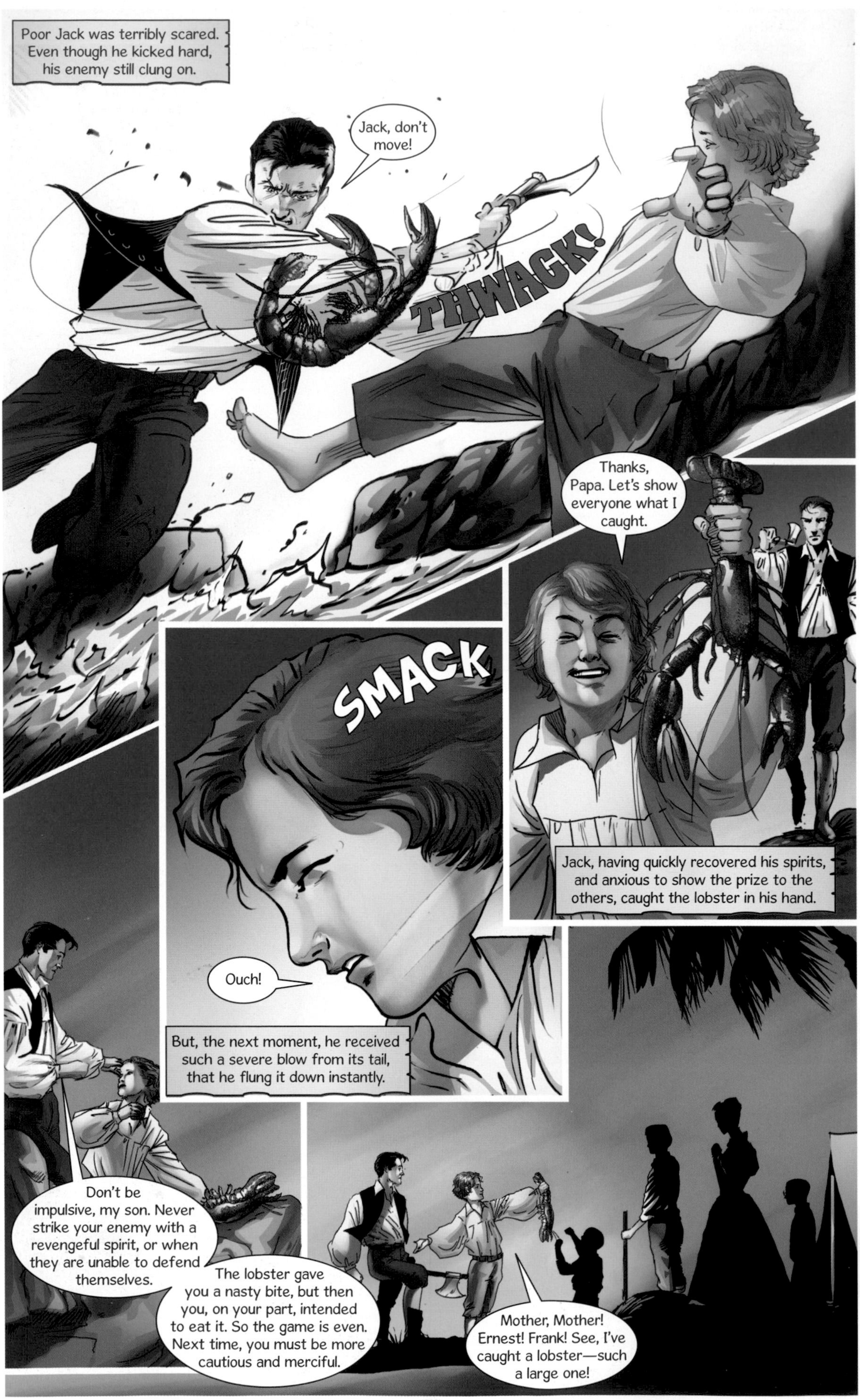
Poor Jack was terribly scared. Even though he kicked hard, his enemy still clung on.
Jack, don't move!
THWACK!
Thanks, Papa. Let's show everyone what I caught.
SMACK
Jack, having quickly recovered his spirits, and anxious to show the prize to the others, caught the lobster in his hand.
Ouch!
But, the next moment, he received such a severe blow from its tail, that he flung it down instantly.
Don't be impulsive, my son. Never strike your enemy with a revengeful spirit, or when they are unable to defend themselves.
The lobster gave you a nasty bite, but then you, on your part, intended to eat it. So the game is even. Next time, you must be more cautious and merciful.
Mother, Mother! Ernest! Frank! See, I've caught a lobster—such a large one!

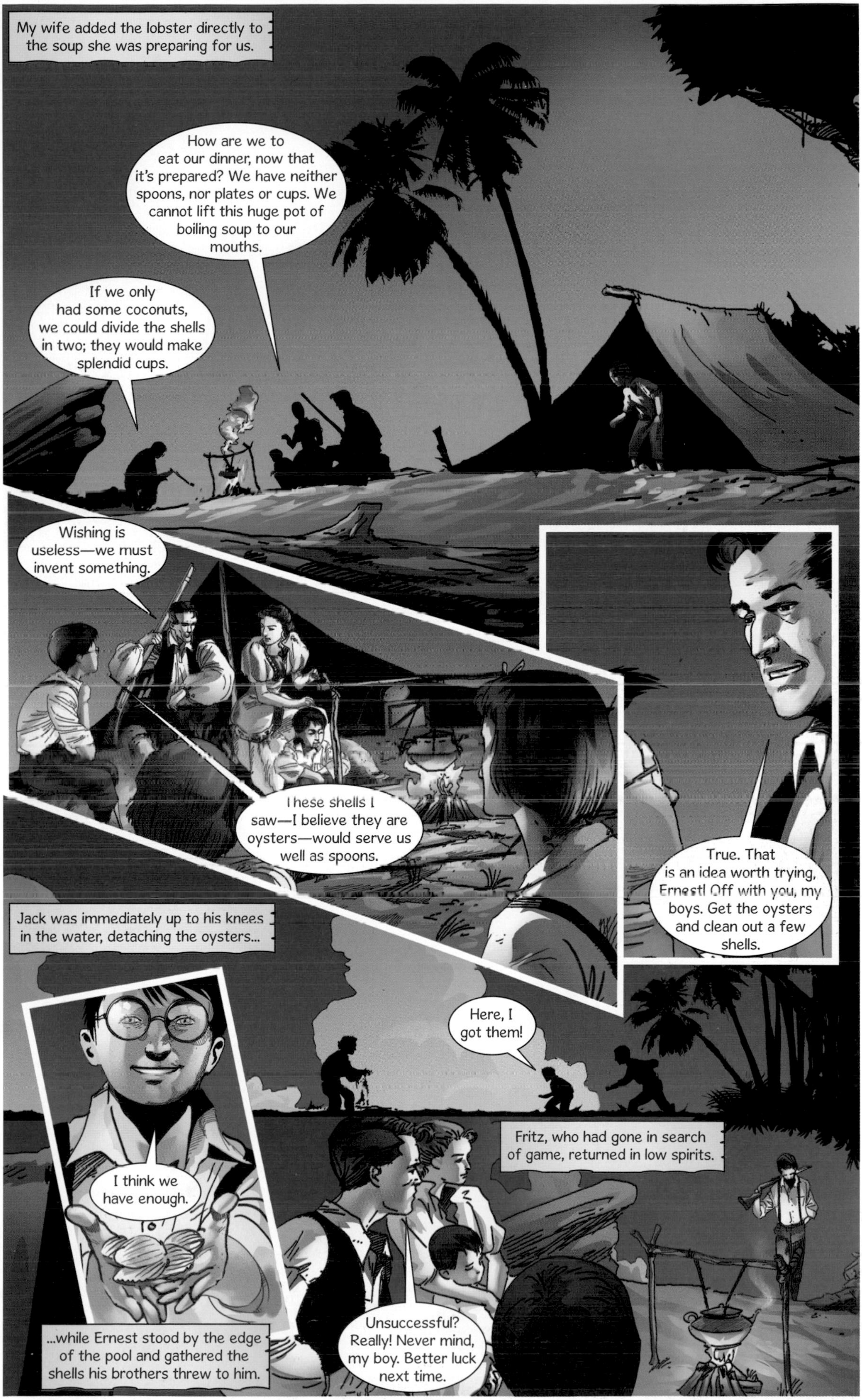

My wife added the lobster directly to the soup she was preparing for us.
How are we to eat our dinner, now that it's prepared? We have neither spoons, nor plates or cups. We cannot lift this huge pot of boiling soup to our mouths.
If we only had some coconuts, we could divide the shells in two; they would make splendid cups.
Wishing is useless—we must invent something.
These shells I saw—I believe they are oysters—would serve us well as spoons.
True. That is an idea worth trying, Ernest! Off with you, my boys. Get the oysters and clean out a few shells.
Jack was immediately up to his knees in the water, detaching the oysters...
Here, I got them!
I think we have enough.
...while Ernest stood by the edge of the pool and gathered the shells his brothers threw to him.
Fritz, who had gone in search of game, returned in low spirits.
Unsuccessful? Really! Never mind, my boy. Better luck next time.

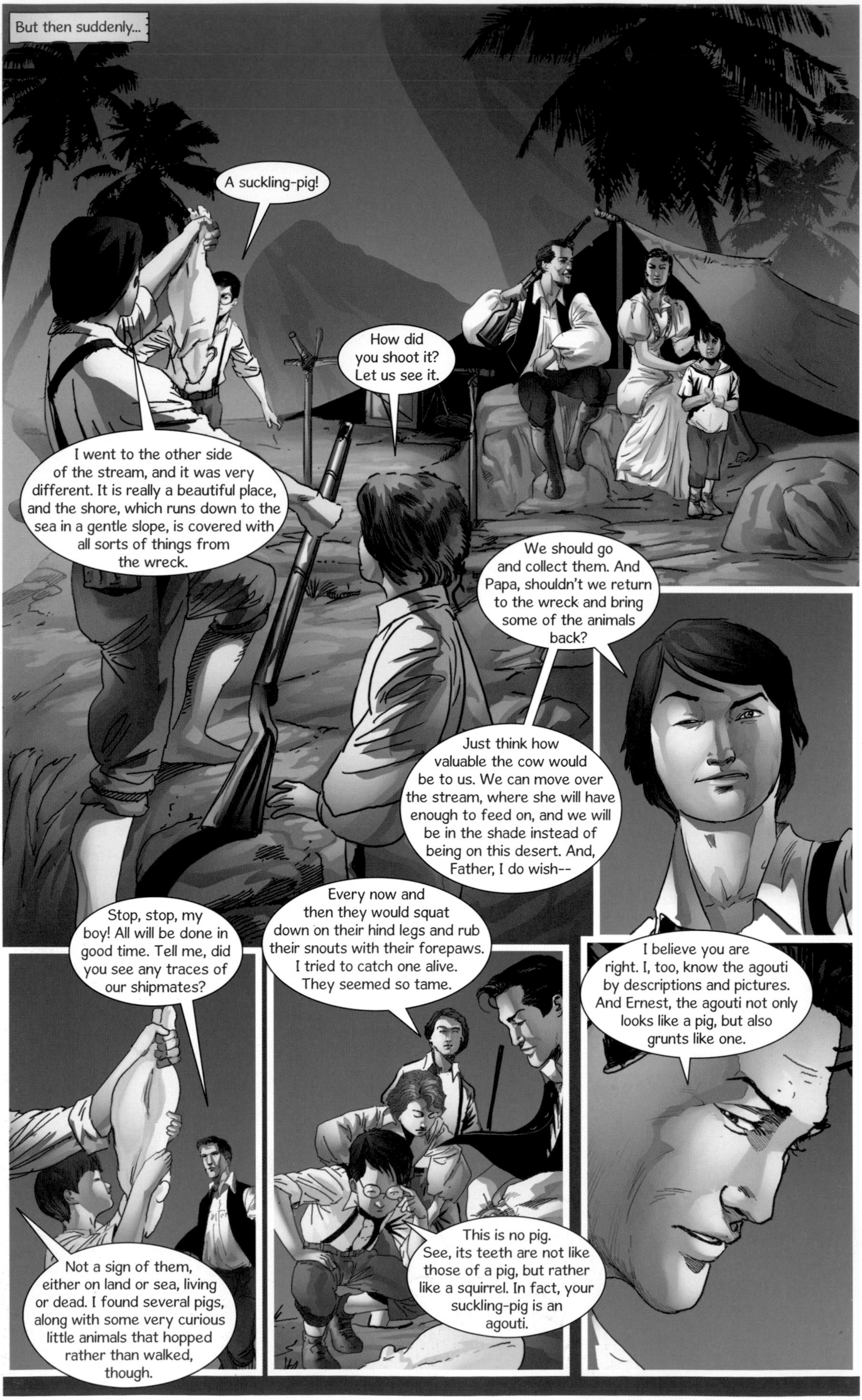
But then suddenly...
A suckling-pig!
How did you shoot it? Let us see it.
I went to the other side of the stream, and it was very different. It is really a beautiful place, and the shore, which runs down to the sea in a gentle slope, is covered with all sorts of things from the wreck.
We should go and collect them. And Papa, shouldn't we return to the wreck and bring some of the animals back?
Just think how valuable the cow would be to us. We can move over the stream, where she will have enough to feed on, and we will be in the shade instead of being on this desert. And, Father, I do wish--
Stop, stop, my boy! All will be done in good time. Tell me, did you see any traces of our shipmates?
Not a sign of them, either on land or sea, living or dead. I found several pigs, along with some very curious little animals that hopped rather than walked, though.
Every now and then they would squat down on their hind legs and rub their snouts with their forepaws. I tried to catch one alive. They seemed so tame.
This is no pig. See, its teeth are not like those of a pig, but rather like a squirrel. In fact, your suckling-pig is an agouti.
I believe you are right. I, too, know the agouti by descriptions and pictures. And Ernest, the agouti not only looks like a pig, but also grunts like one.

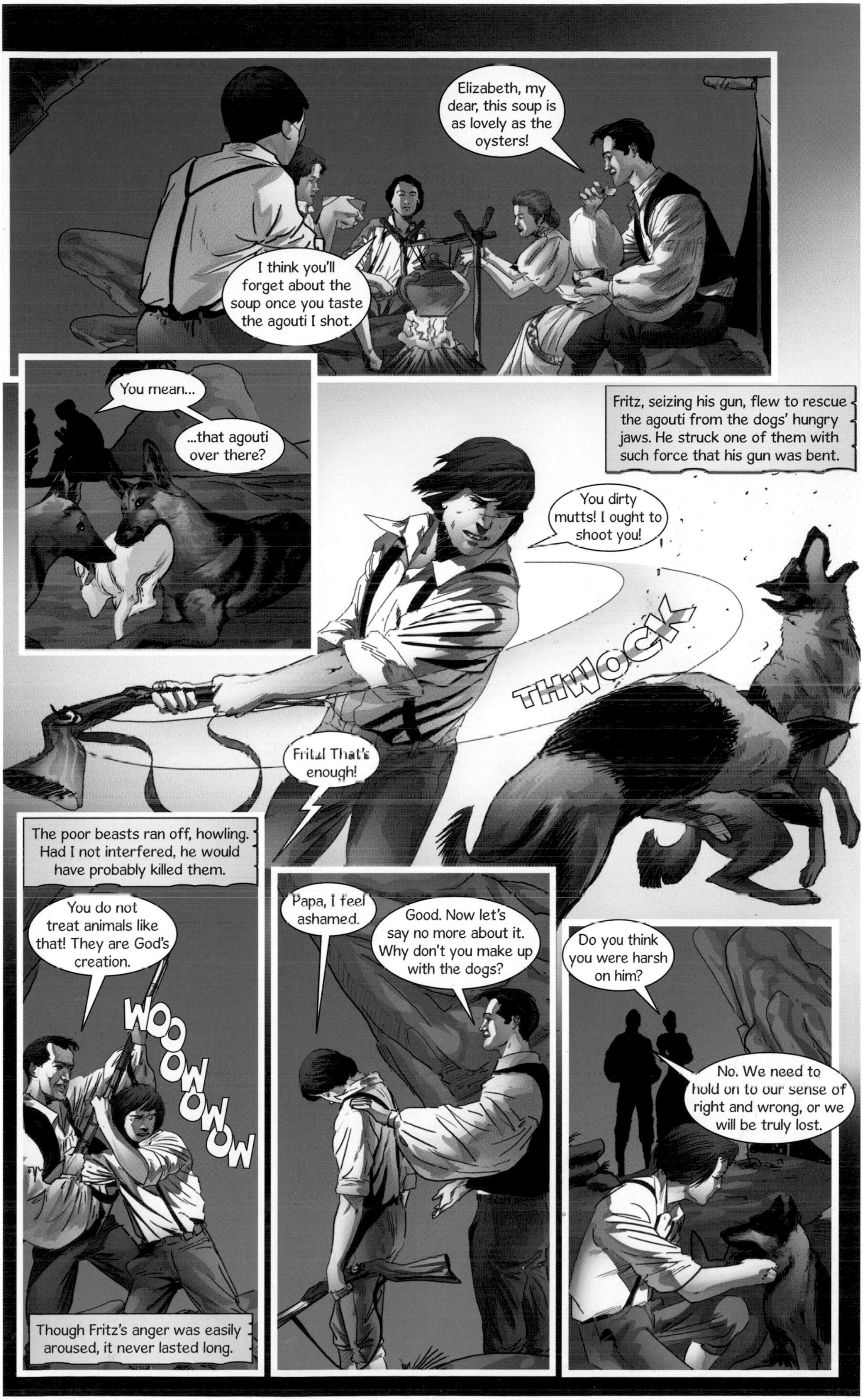

Elizabeth, my dear, this soup is as lovely as the oysters!
I think you'll forget about the soup once you taste the agouti I shot.
You mean...
...that agouti over there?
Fritz, seizing his gun, flew to rescue the agouti from the dogs' hungry jaws. He struck one of them with such force that his gun was bent.
You dirty mutts! I ought to shoot you!
THWOCK
Fritz! That's enough!
The poor beasts ran off, howling. Had I not interfered, he would have probably killed them.
You do not treat animals like that! They are God's creation.
WOOOWOWOW
Though Fritz's anger was easily aroused, it never lasted long.
Papa, I feel ashamed.
Good. Now let's say no more about it. Why don't you make up with the dogs?
Do you think you were harsh on him?
No. We need to hold on to our sense of right and wrong, or we will be truly lost.

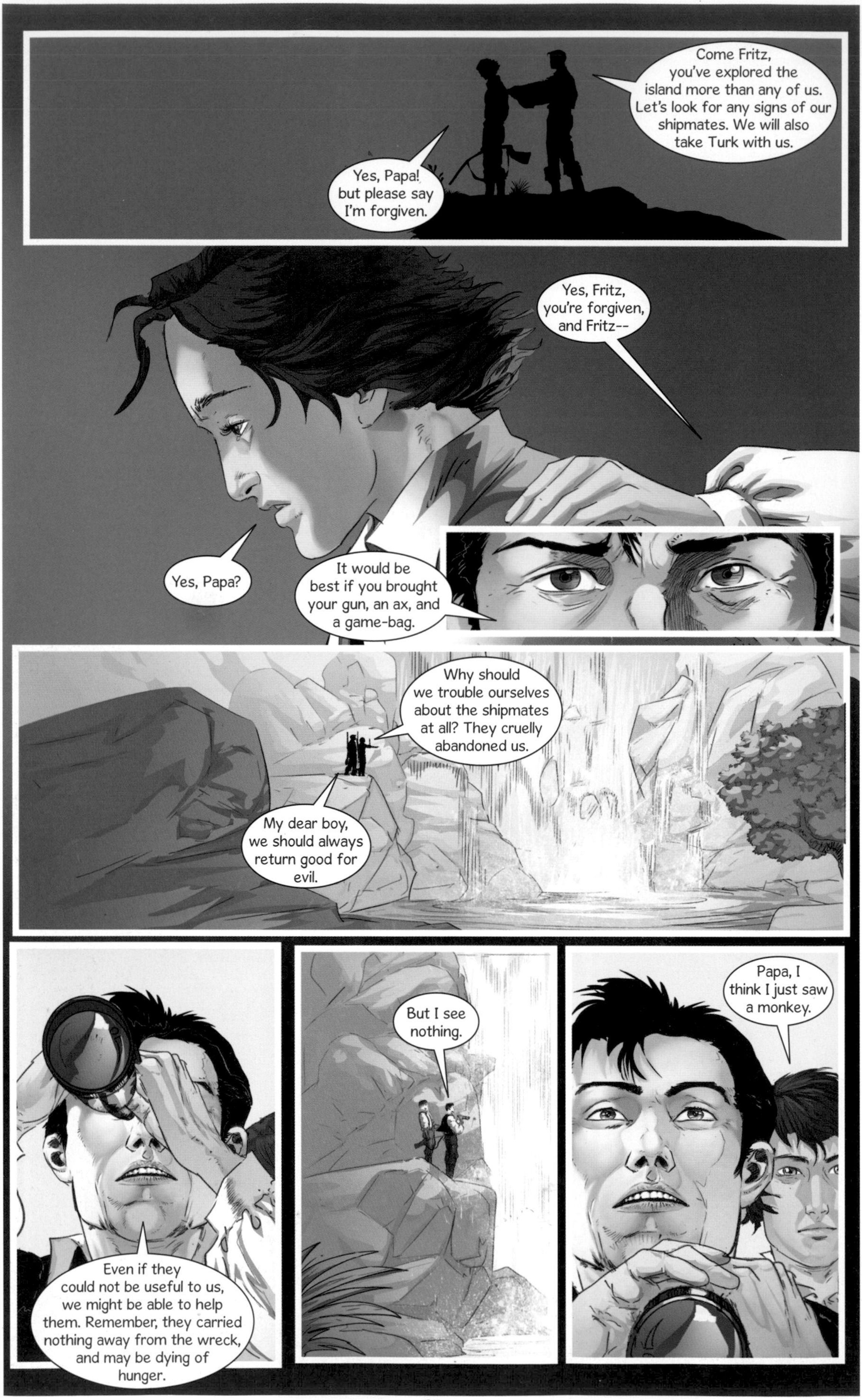
Come Fritz, you've explored the island more than any of us. Let's look for any signs of our shipmates. We will also take Turk with us.
Yes, Papa! but please say I'm forgiven.
Yes, Fritz, you're forgiven, and Fritz--
Yes, Papa?
It would be best if you brought your gun, an ax, and a game-bag.
Why should we trouble ourselves about the shipmates at all? They cruelly abandoned us.
My dear boy, we should always return good for evil.
Even if they could not be useful to us, we might be able to help them. Remember, they carried nothing away from the wreck, and may be dying of hunger.
But I see nothing.
Papa, I think I just saw a monkey.

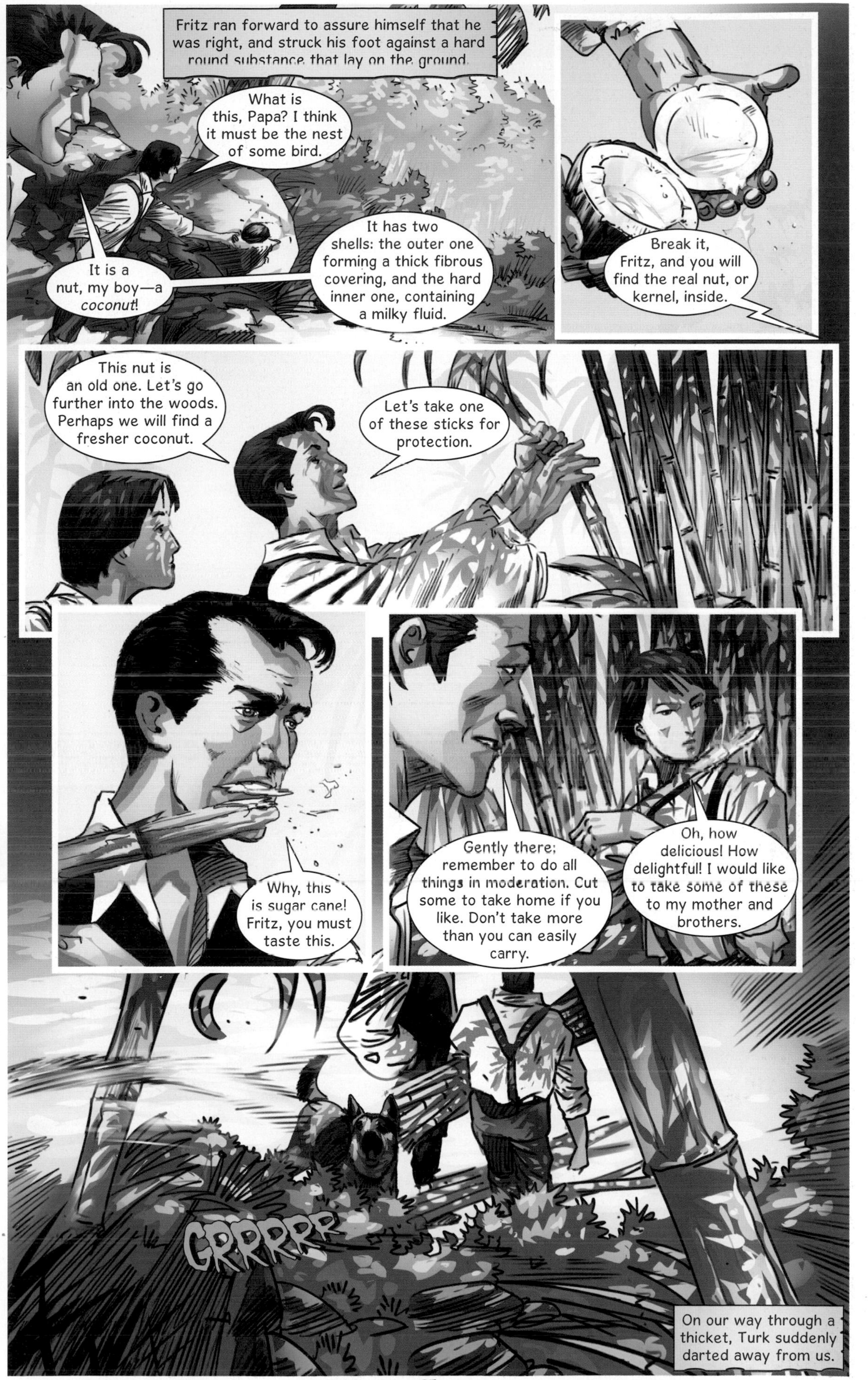

Fritz ran forward to assure himself that he was right, and struck his foot against a hard round substance that lay on the ground.
What is this, Papa? I think it must be the nest of some bird.
It is a nut, my boy—a *coconut*!
It has two shells: the outer one forming a thick fibrous covering, and the hard inner one, containing a milky fluid.
Break it, Fritz, and you will find the real nut, or kernel, inside.
This nut is an old one. Let's go further into the woods. Perhaps we will find a fresher coconut.
Let's take one of these sticks for protection.
Why, this is sugar cane! Fritz, you must taste this.
Gently there; remember to do all things in moderation. Cut some to take home if you like. Don't take more than you can easily carry.
Oh, how delicious! How delightful! I would like to take some of these to my mother and brothers.
GRRRRR
On our way through a thicket, Turk suddenly darted away from us.

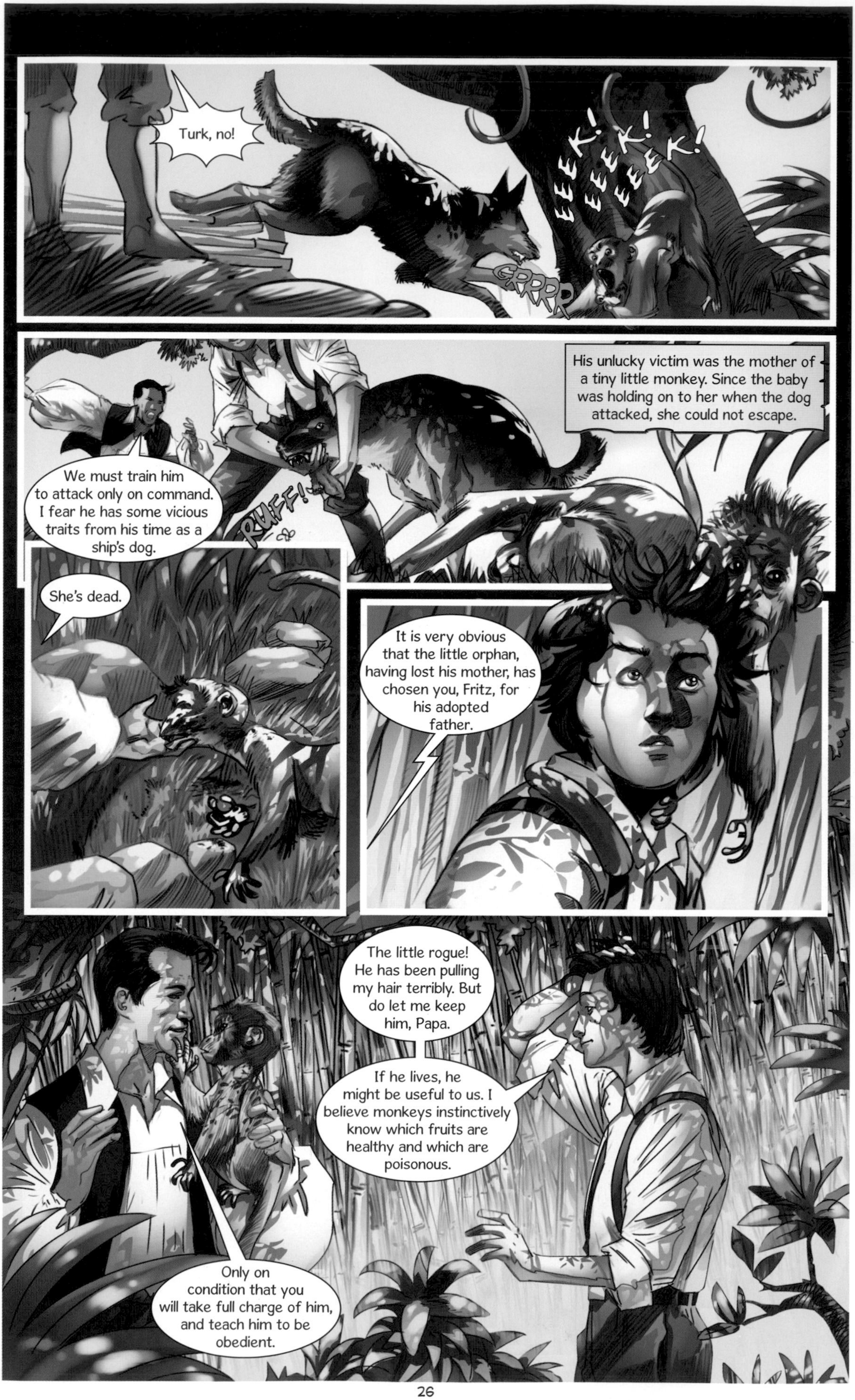

Turk, no!
EEEK! EEEK! EEEK!
GRRRR
His unlucky victim was the mother of a tiny little monkey. Since the baby was holding on to her when the dog attacked, she could not escape.
We must train him to attack only on command. I fear he has some vicious traits from his time as a ship's dog.
RUFF!
She's dead.
It is very obvious that the little orphan, having lost his mother, has chosen you, Fritz, for his adopted father.
The little rogue! He has been pulling my hair terribly. But do let me keep him, Papa.
If he lives, he might be useful to us. I believe monkeys instinctively know which fruits are healthy and which are poisonous.
Only on condition that you will take full charge of him, and teach him to be obedient.

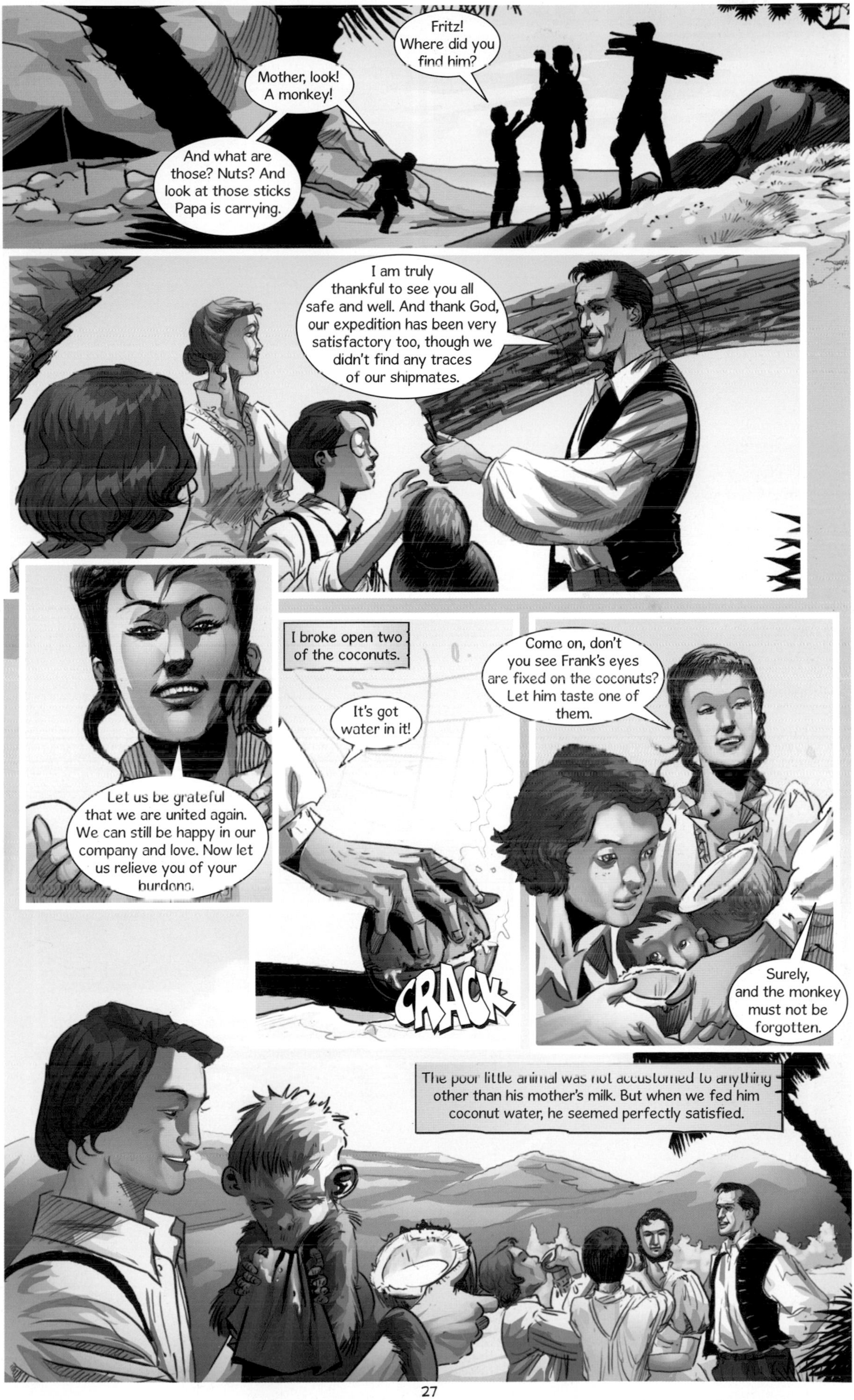
Mother, look! A monkey!
Fritz! Where did you find him?
And what are those? Nuts? And look at those sticks Papa is carrying.
I am truly thankful to see you all safe and well. And thank God, our expedition has been very satisfactory too, though we didn't find any traces of our shipmates.
Let us be grateful that we are united again. We can still be happy in our company and love. Now let us relieve you of your burdens.
I broke open two of the coconuts.
It's got water in it!
CRACK
Come on, don't you see Frank's eyes are fixed on the coconuts? Let him taste one of them.
Surely, and the monkey must not be forgotten.
The poor little animal was not accustomed to anything other than his mother's milk. But when we fed him coconut water, he seemed perfectly satisfied.

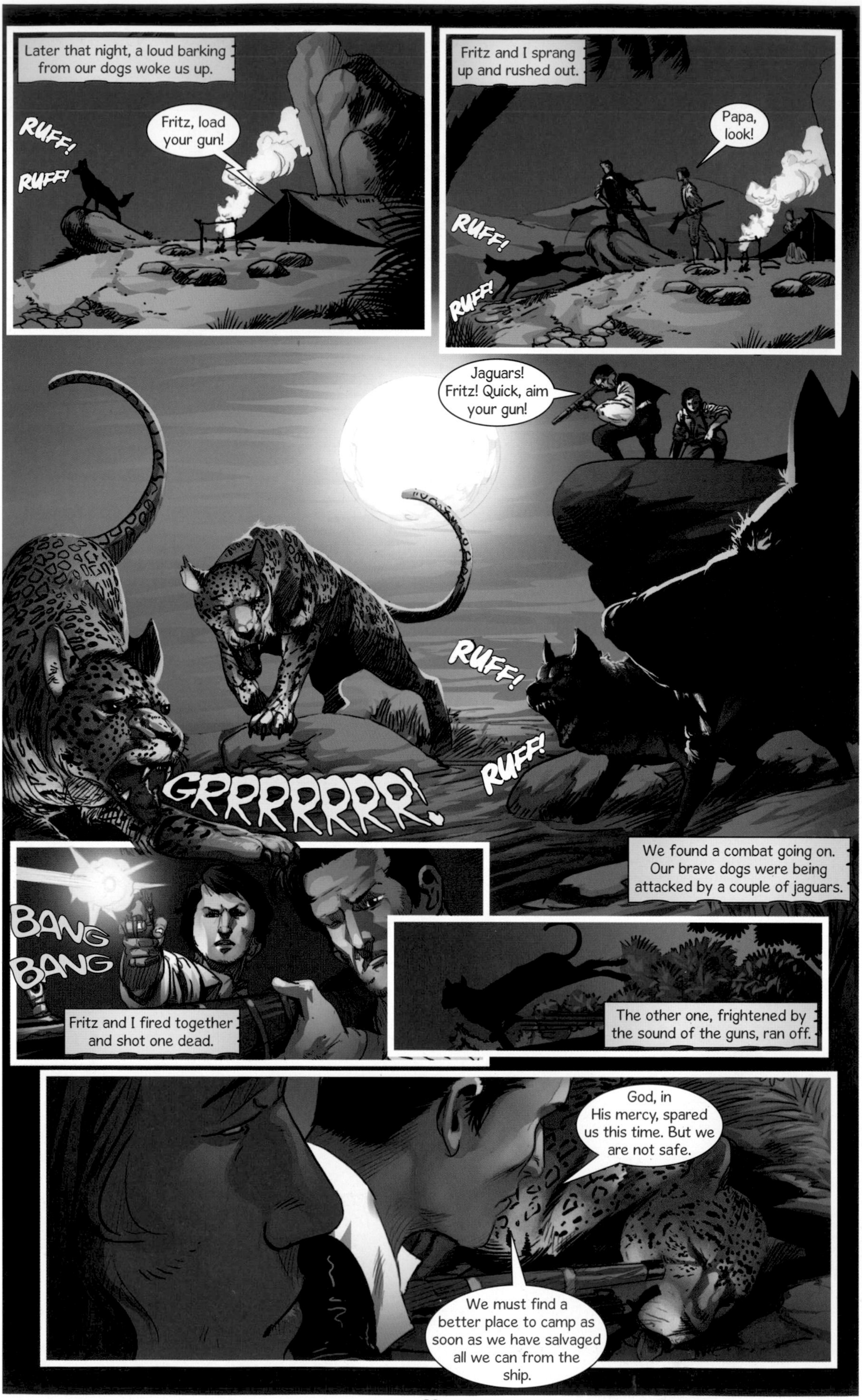
Later that night, a loud barking from our dogs woke us up.
RUFF!
RUFF!
Fritz, load your gun!
Fritz and I sprang up and rushed out.
Papa, look!
RUFF!
RUFF!
Jaguars! Fritz! Quick, aim your gun!
RUFF!
RUFF!
GRRRRRRR!
We found a combat going on. Our brave dogs were being attacked by a couple of jaguars.
BANG
BANG
Fritz and I fired together and shot one dead.
The other one, frightened by the sound of the guns, ran off.
God, in His mercy, spared us this time. But we are not safe.
We must find a better place to camp as soon as we have salvaged all we can from the ship.

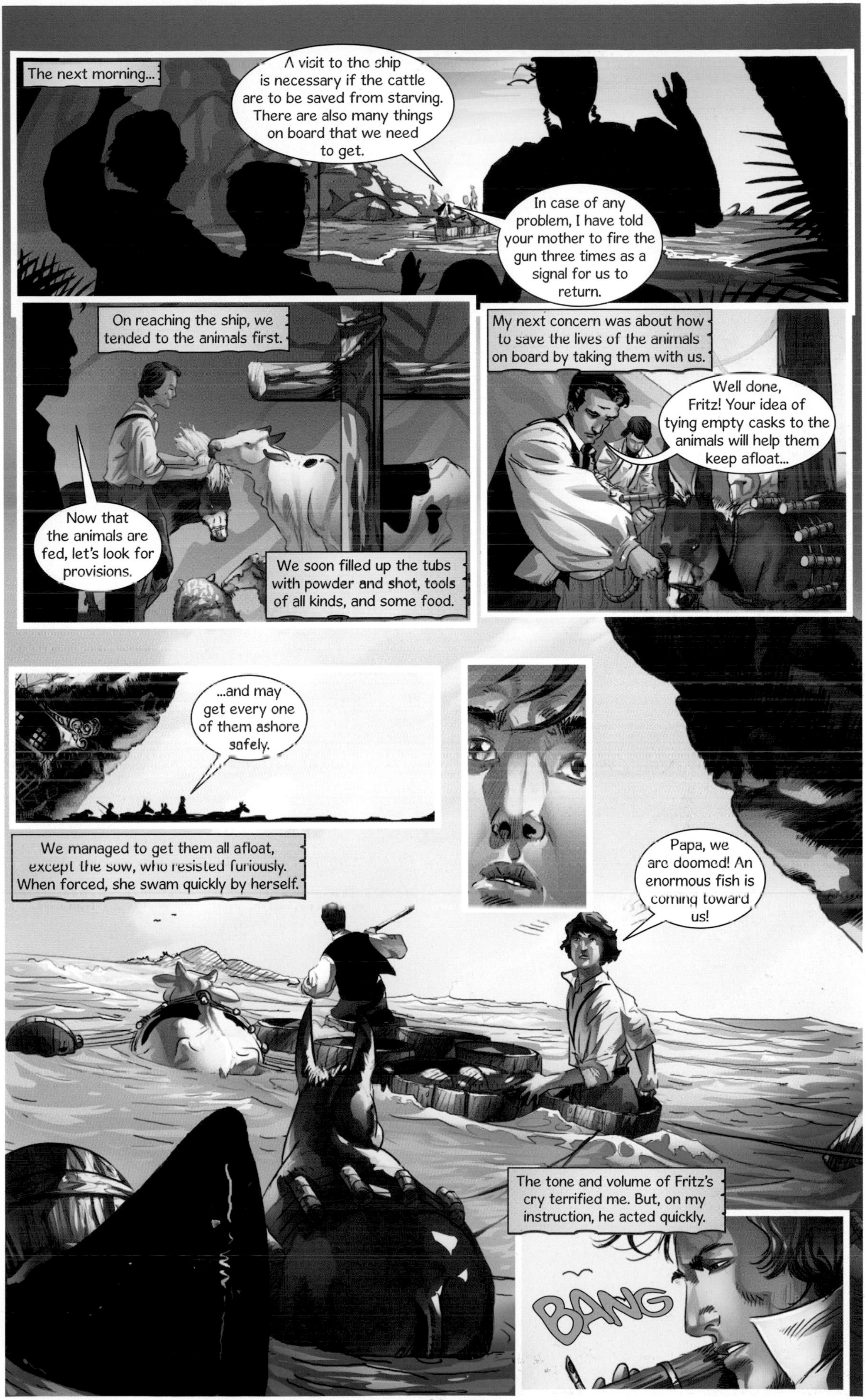
The next morning...
A visit to the ship is necessary if the cattle are to be saved from starving. There are also many things on board that we need to get.
In case of any problem, I have told your mother to fire the gun three times as a signal for us to return.
On reaching the ship, we tended to the animals first.
Now that the animals are fed, let's look for provisions.
We soon filled up the tubs with powder and shot, tools of all kinds, and some food.
My next concern was about how to save the lives of the animals on board by taking them with us.
Well done, Fritz! Your idea of tying empty casks to the animals will help them keep afloat...
...and may get every one of them ashore safely.
We managed to get them all afloat, except the sow, who resisted furiously. When forced, she swam quickly by herself.
Papa, we are doomed! An enormous fish is coming toward us!
The tone and volume of Fritz's cry terrified me. But, on my instruction, he acted quickly.
BANG

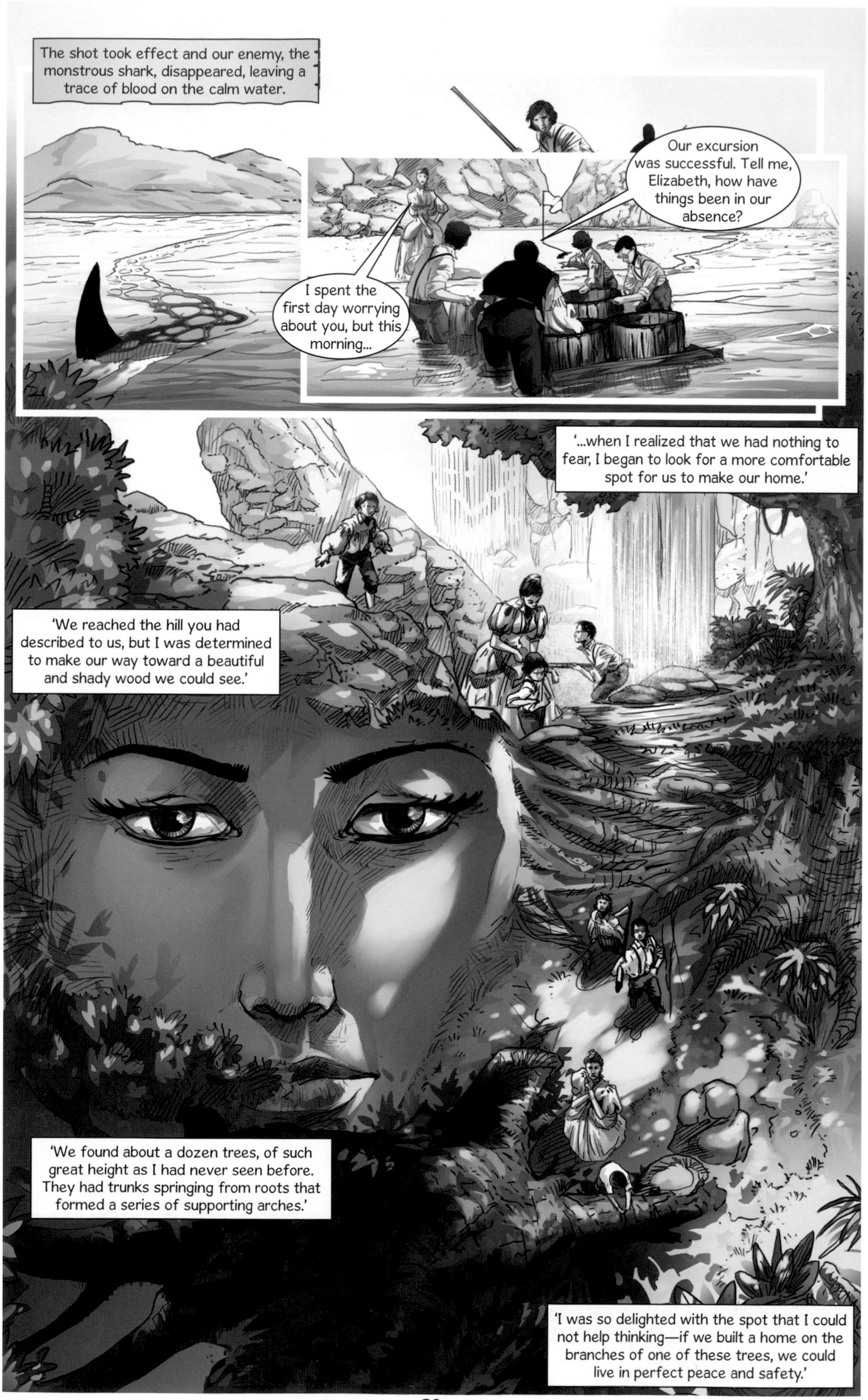
The shot took effect and our enemy, the monstrous shark, disappeared, leaving a trace of blood on the calm water.
Our excursion was successful. Tell me, Elizabeth, how have things been in our absence?
I spent the first day worrying about you, but this morning...
'...when I realized that we had nothing to fear, I began to look for a more comfortable spot for us to make our home.'
'We reached the hill you had described to us, but I was determined to make our way toward a beautiful and shady wood we could see.'
'We found about a dozen trees, of such great height as I had never seen before. They had trunks springing from roots that formed a series of supporting arches.'
'I was so delighted with the spot that I could not help thinking—if we built a home on the branches of one of these trees, we could live in perfect peace and safety.'

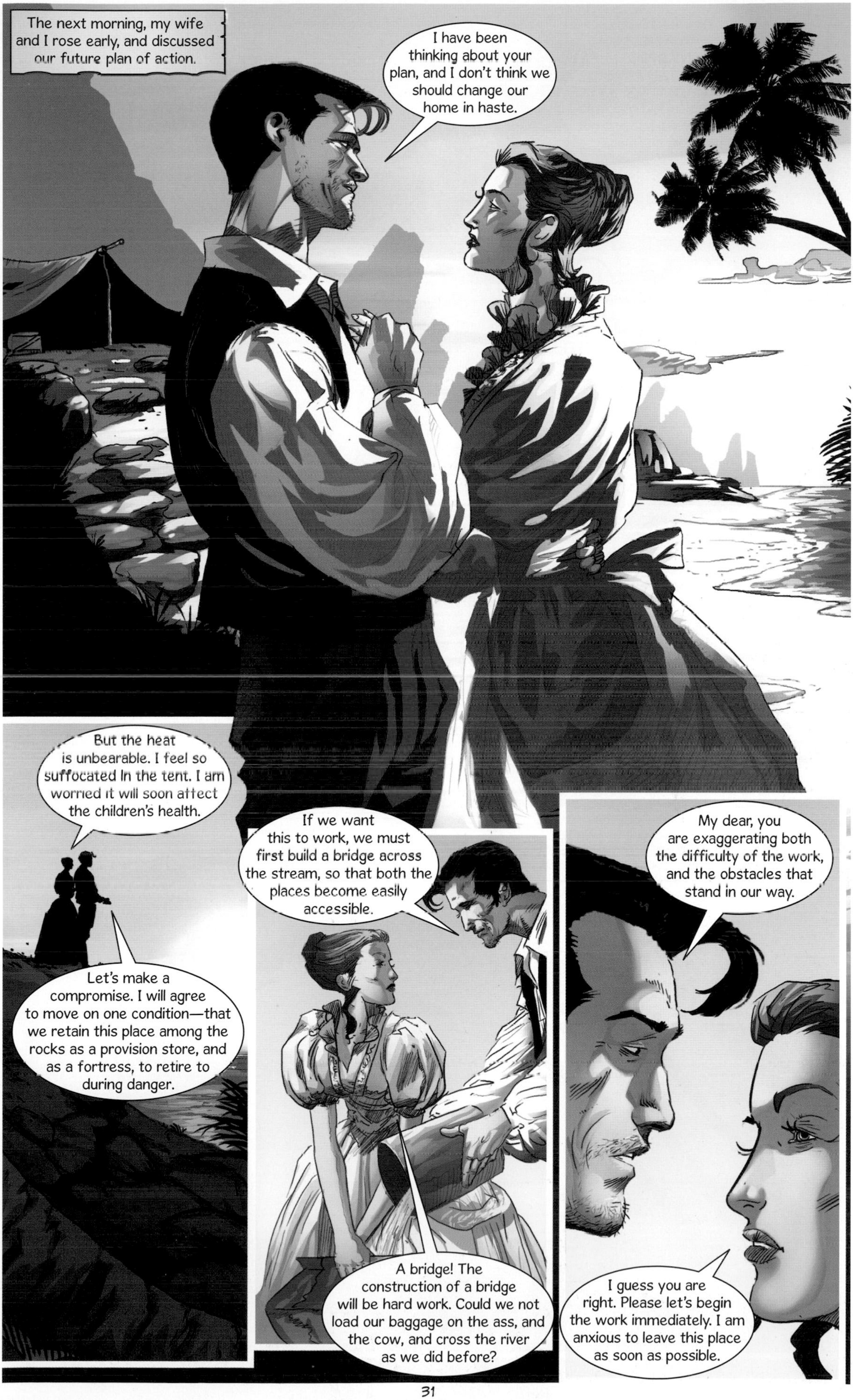
The next morning, my wife and I rose early, and discussed our future plan of action.
I have been thinking about your plan, and I don't think we should change our home in haste.
But the heat is unbearable. I feel so suffocated in the tent. I am worried it will soon affect the children's health.
Let's make a compromise. I will agree to move on one condition—that we retain this place among the rocks as a provision store, and as a fortress, to retire to during danger.
If we want this to work, we must first build a bridge across the stream, so that both the places become easily accessible.
A bridge! The construction of a bridge will be hard work. Could we not load our baggage on the ass, and the cow, and cross the river as we did before?
My dear, you are exaggerating both the difficulty of the work, and the obstacles that stand in our way.
I guess you are right. Please let's begin the work immediately. I am anxious to leave this place as soon as possible.

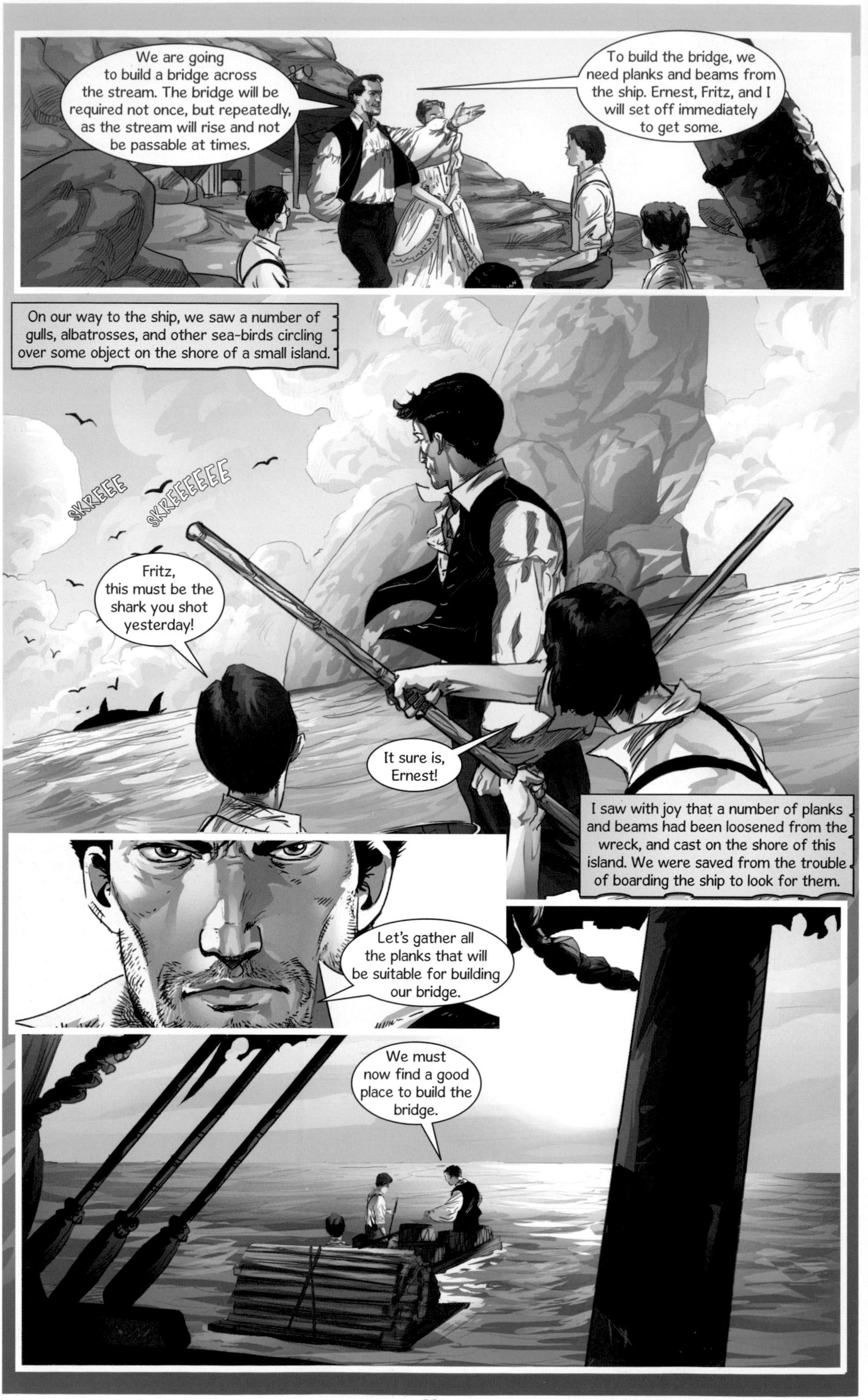
We are going to build a bridge across the stream. The bridge will be required not once, but repeatedly, as the stream will rise and not be passable at times.
To build the bridge, we need planks and beams from the ship. Ernest, Fritz, and I will set off immediately to get some.
On our way to the ship, we saw a number of gulls, albatrosses, and other sea-birds circling over some object on the shore of a small island.
SKREEE
SKREEEEEE
Fritz, this must be the shark you shot yesterday!
It sure is, Ernest!
I saw with joy that a number of planks and beams had been loosened from the wreck, and cast on the shore of this island. We were saved from the trouble of boarding the ship to look for them.
Let's gather all the planks that will be suitable for building our bridge.
We must now find a good place to build the bridge.

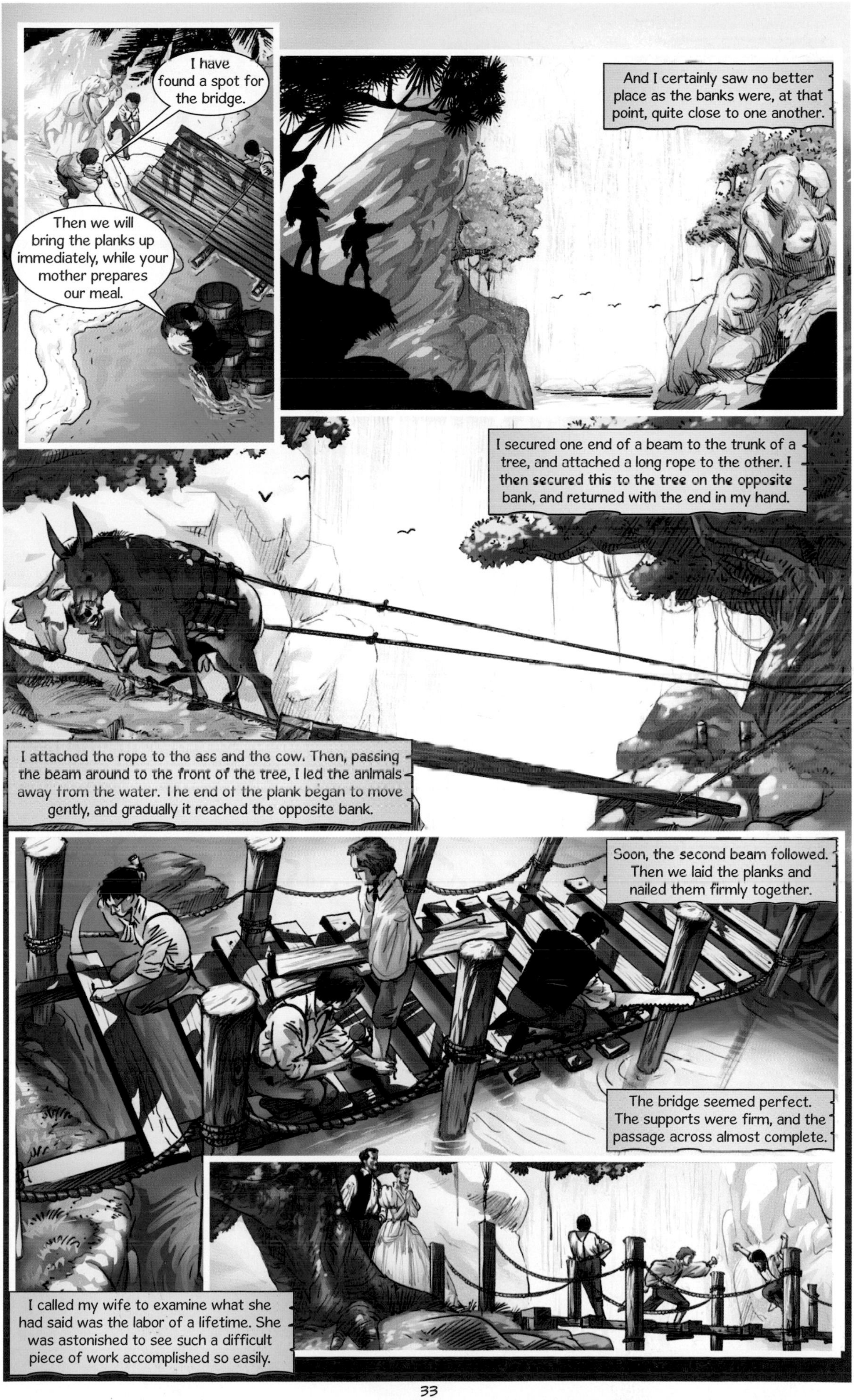
I have found a spot for the bridge.
Then we will bring the planks up immediately, while your mother prepares our meal.
And I certainly saw no better place as the banks were, at that point, quite close to one another.
I secured one end of a beam to the trunk of a tree, and attached a long rope to the other. I then secured this to the tree on the opposite bank, and returned with the end in my hand.
I attached the rope to the ass and the cow. Then, passing the beam around to the front of the tree, I led the animals away from the water. The end of the plank began to move gently, and gradually it reached the opposite bank.
Soon, the second beam followed. Then we laid the planks and nailed them firmly together.
The bridge seemed perfect. The supports were firm, and the passage across almost complete.
I called my wife to examine what she had said was the labor of a lifetime. She was astonished to see such a difficult piece of work accomplished so easily.

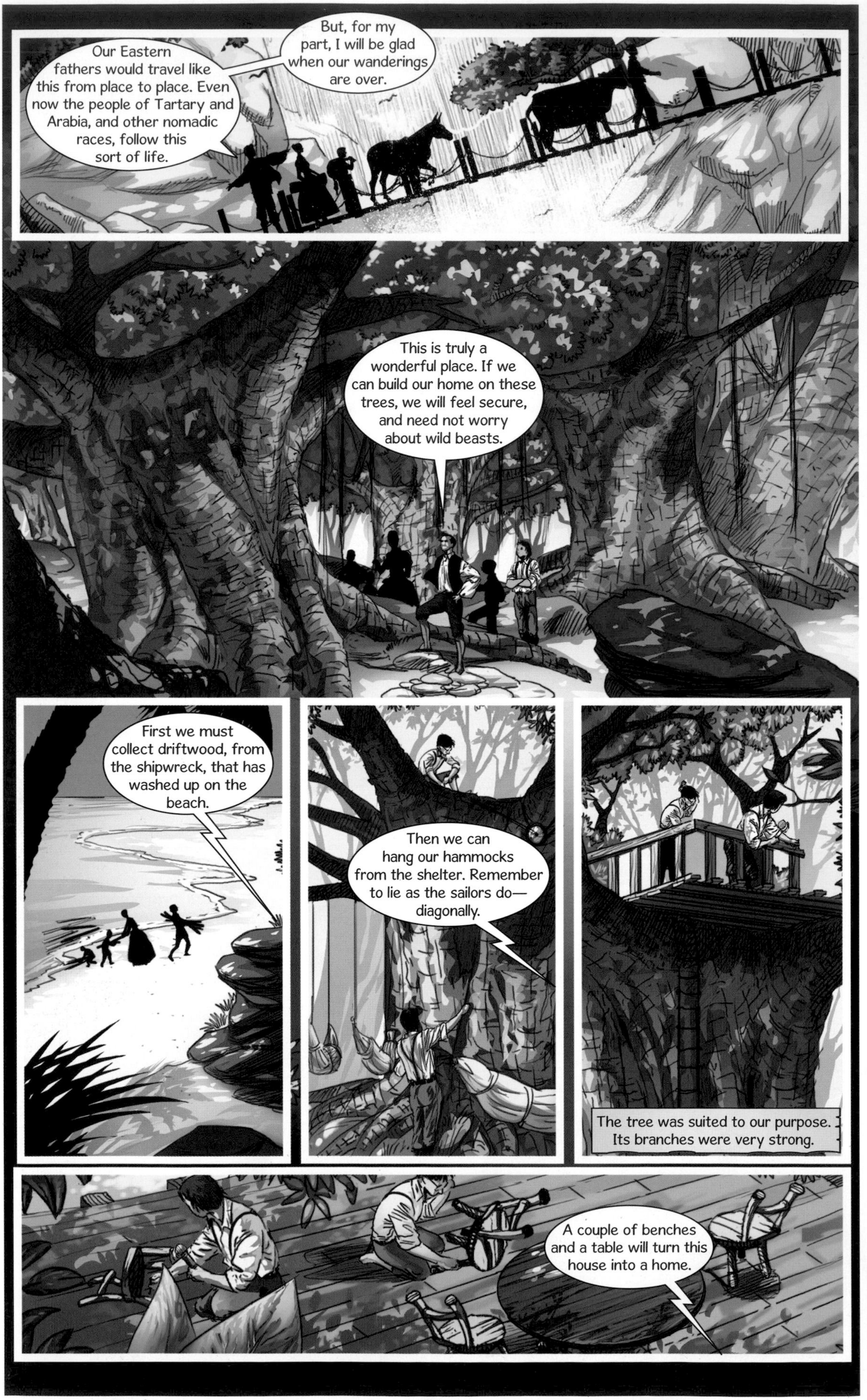
Our Eastern fathers would travel like this from place to place. Even now the people of Tartary and Arabia, and other nomadic races, follow this sort of life.
But, for my part, I will be glad when our wanderings are over.
This is truly a wonderful place. If we can build our home on these trees, we will feel secure, and need not worry about wild beasts.
First we must collect driftwood, from the shipwreck, that has washed up on the beach.
Then we can hang our hammocks from the shelter. Remember to lie as the sailors do—diagonally.
The tree was suited to our purpose. Its branches were very strong.
A couple of benches and a table will turn this house into a home.

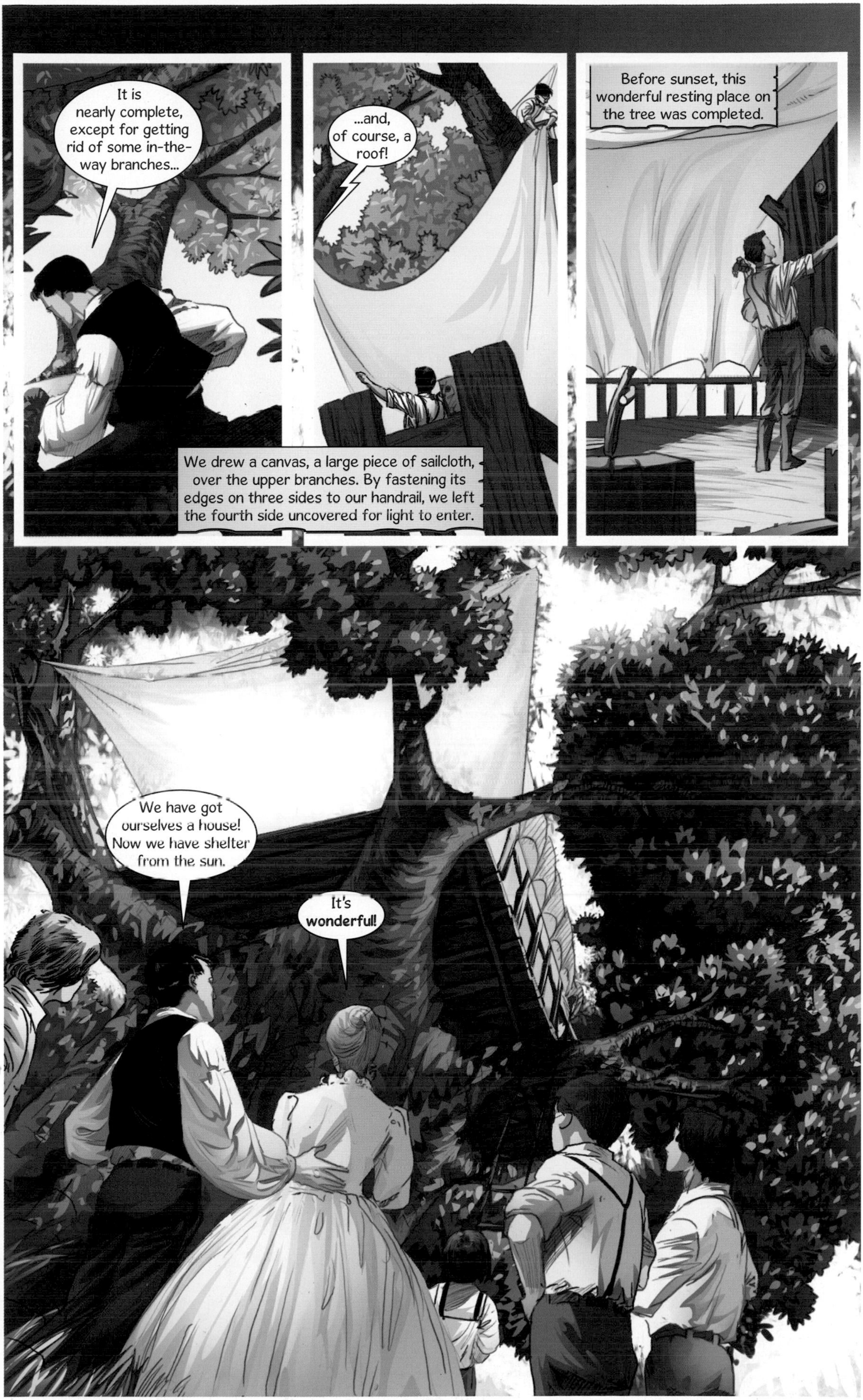
It is nearly complete, except for getting rid of some in-the-way branches...
...and, of course, a roof!
We drew a canvas, a large piece of sailcloth, over the upper branches. By fastening its edges on three sides to our handrail, we left the fourth side uncovered for light to enter.
Before sunset, this wonderful resting place on the tree was completed.
We have got ourselves a house! Now we have shelter from the sun.
It's wonderful!

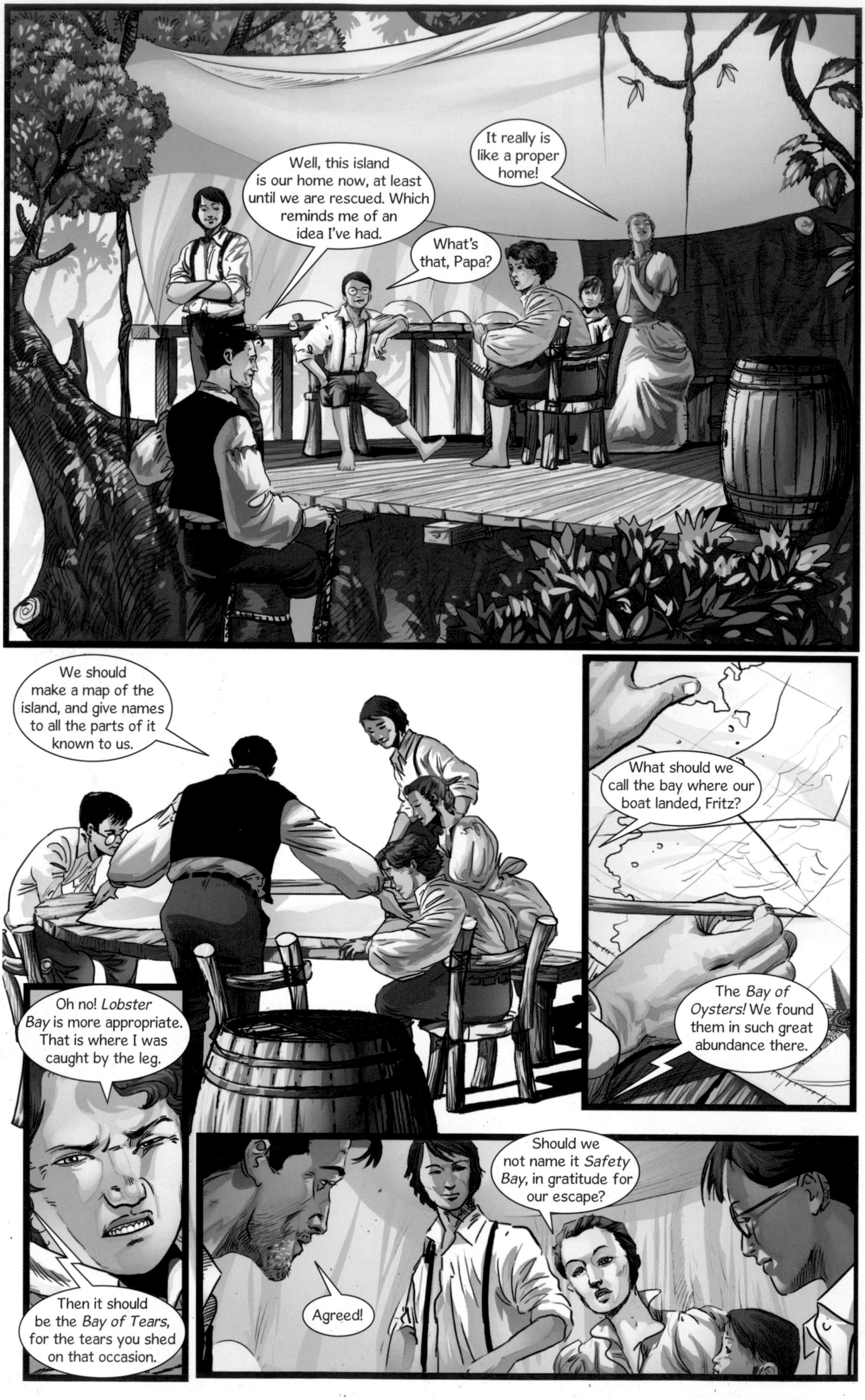
Well, this island is our home now, at least until we are rescued. Which reminds me of an idea I've had.
What's that, Papa?
It really is like a proper home!
We should make a map of the island, and give names to all the parts of it known to us.
What should we call the bay where our boat landed, Fritz?
The *Bay of Oysters!* We found them in such great abundance there.
Oh no! *Lobster Bay* is more appropriate. That is where I was caught by the leg.
Then it should be the *Bay of Tears*, for the tears you shed on that occasion.
Should we not name it *Safety Bay*, in gratitude for our escape?
Agreed!

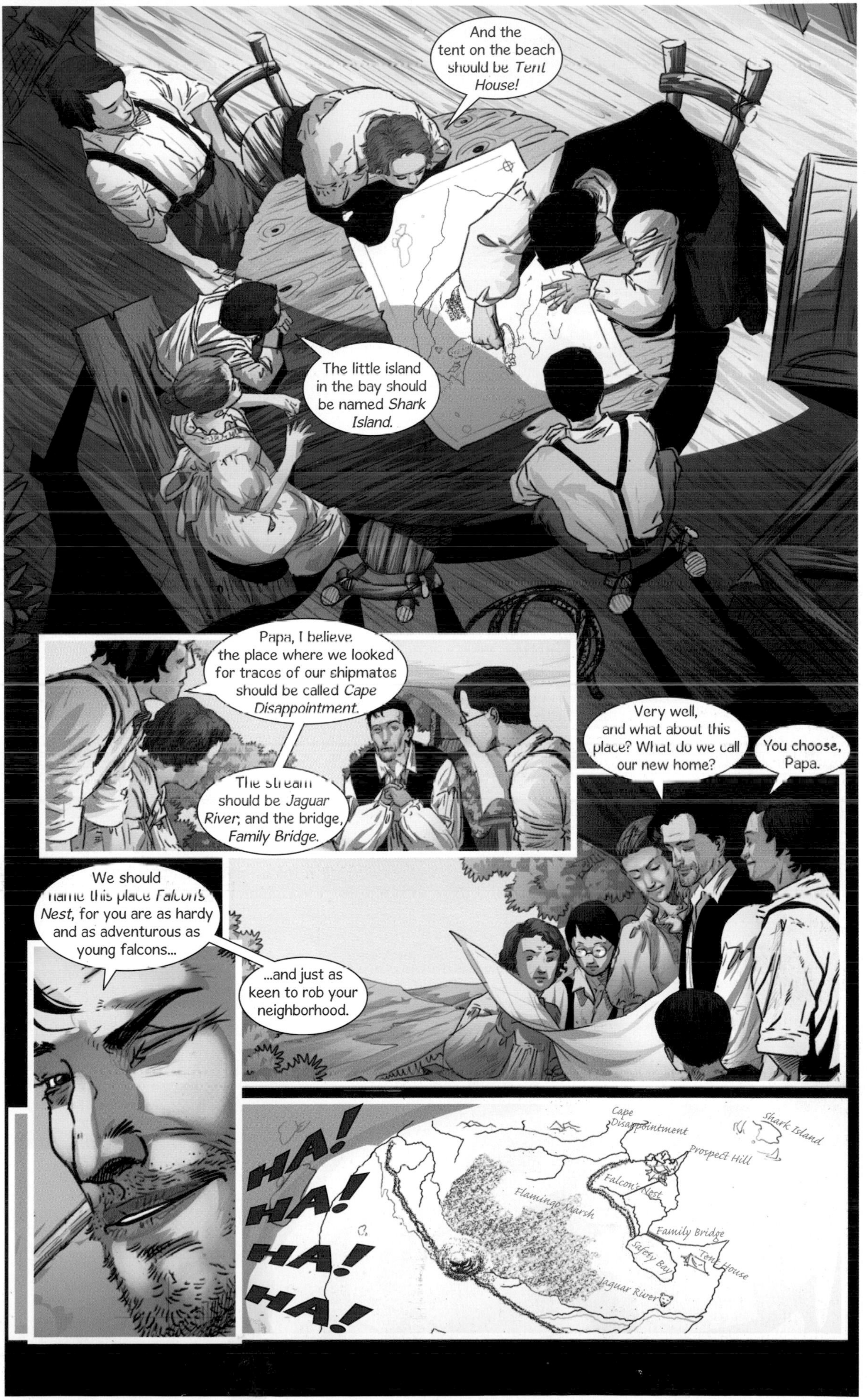
And the tent on the beach should be *Tent House!*
The little island in the bay should be named *Shark Island.*
Papa, I believe the place where we looked for traces of our shipmates should be called *Cape Disappointment.*
The stream should be *Jaguar River*, and the bridge, *Family Bridge.*
Very well, and what about this place? What do we call our new home?
You choose, Papa.
We should name this place *Falcon's Nest*, for you are as hardy and as adventurous as young falcons...
...and just as keen to rob your neighborhood.
HA! HA! HA! HA!
Cape Disappointment
Shark Island
Prospect Hill
Falcon's Nest
Flamingo Marsh
Family Bridge
Safety Bay
Tent House
Jaguar River

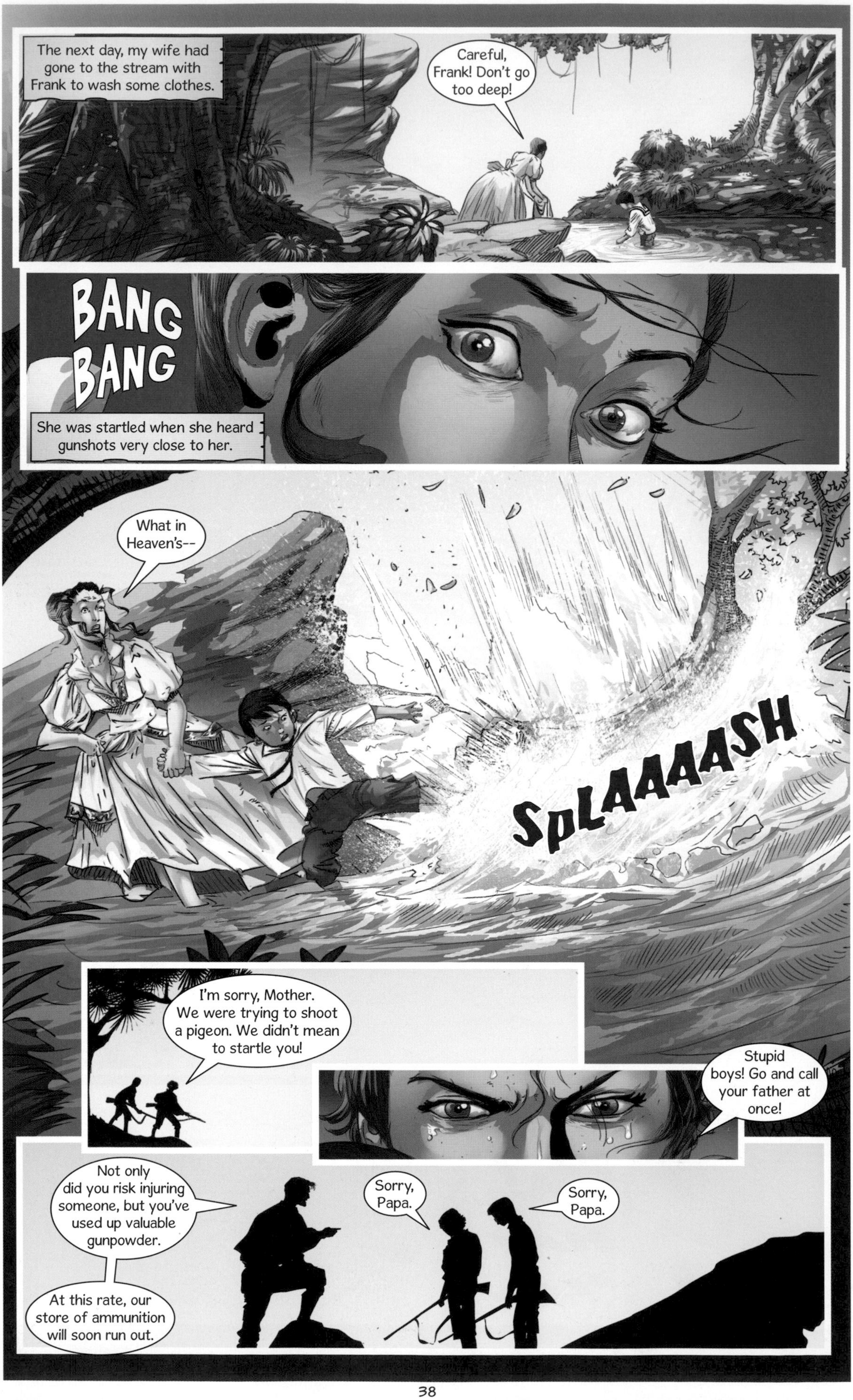
The next day, my wife had gone to the stream with Frank to wash some clothes.
Careful, Frank! Don't go too deep!
BANG
BANG
She was startled when she heard gunshots very close to her.
What in Heaven's--
SPLAAAAASH
I'm sorry, Mother. We were trying to shoot a pigeon. We didn't mean to startle you!
Stupid boys! Go and call your father at once!
Not only did you risk injuring someone, but you've used up valuable gunpowder.
At this rate, our store of ammunition will soon run out.
Sorry, Papa.
Sorry, Papa.

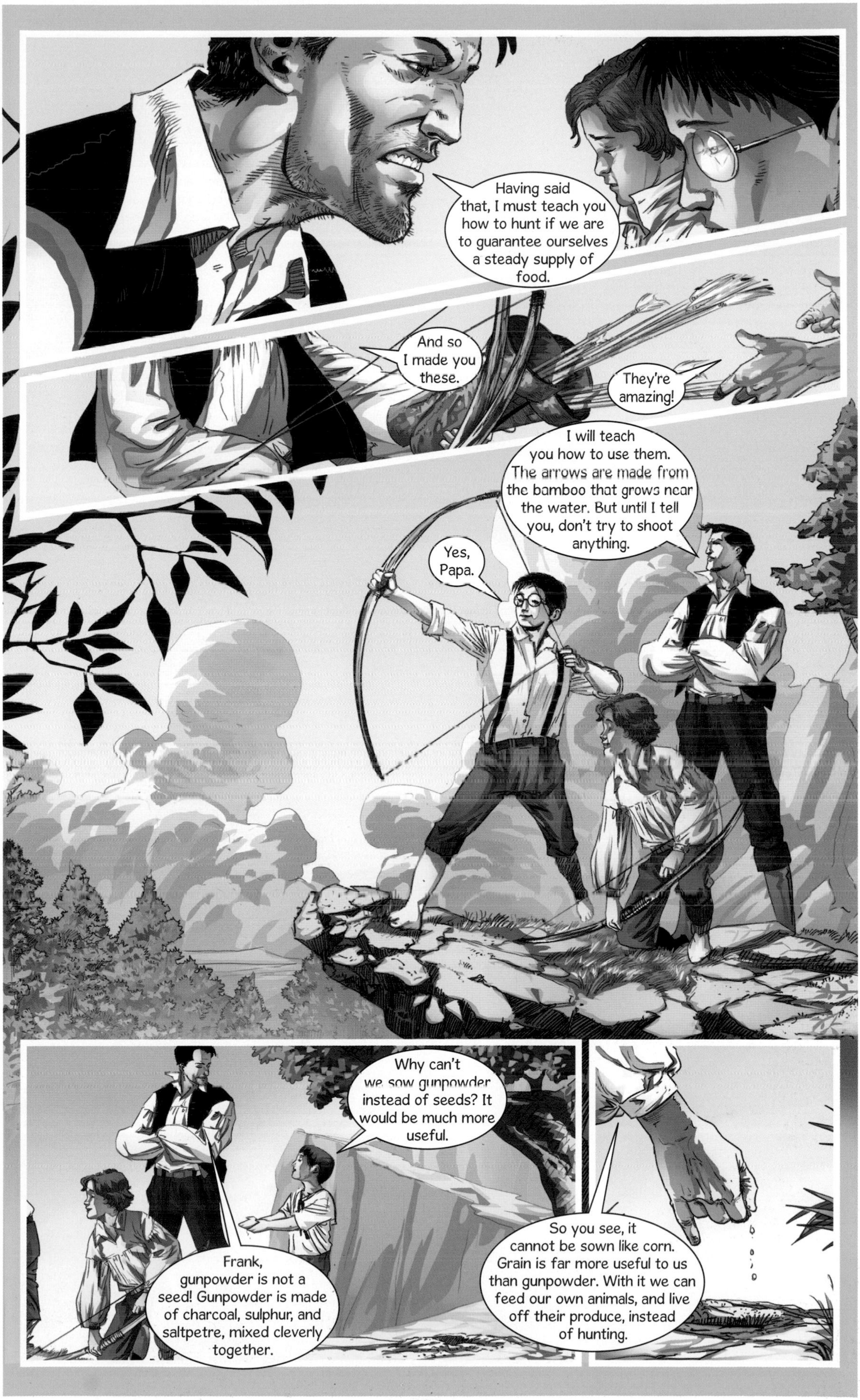
Having said that, I must teach you how to hunt if we are to guarantee ourselves a steady supply of food.
And so I made you these.
They're amazing!
I will teach you how to use them. The arrows are made from the bamboo that grows near the water. But until I tell you, don't try to shoot anything.
Yes, Papa.
Why can't we sow gunpowder instead of seeds? It would be much more useful.
Frank, gunpowder is not a seed! Gunpowder is made of charcoal, sulphur, and saltpetre, mixed cleverly together.
So you see, it cannot be sown like corn. Grain is far more useful to us than gunpowder. With it we can feed our own animals, and live off their produce, instead of hunting.

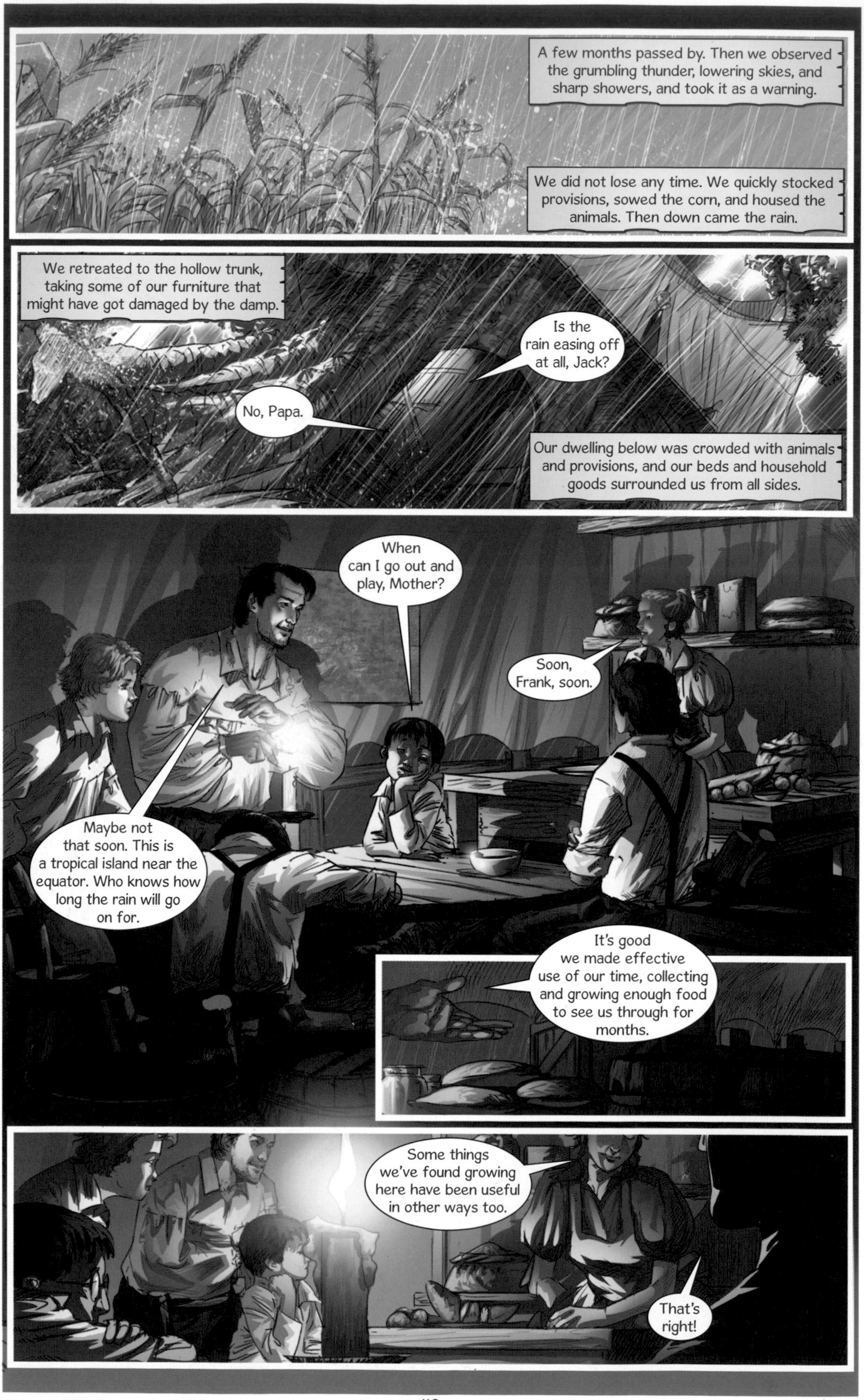
A few months passed by. Then we observed the grumbling thunder, lowering skies, and sharp showers, and took it as a warning.
We did not lose any time. We quickly stocked provisions, sowed the corn, and housed the animals. Then down came the rain.
We retreated to the hollow trunk, taking some of our furniture that might have got damaged by the damp.
Is the rain easing off at all, Jack?
No, Papa.
Our dwelling below was crowded with animals and provisions, and our beds and household goods surrounded us from all sides.
When can I go out and play, Mother?
Soon, Frank, soon.
Maybe not that soon. This is a tropical island near the equator. Who knows how long the rain will go on for.
It's good we made effective use of our time, collecting and growing enough food to see us through for months.
Some things we've found growing here have been useful in other ways too.
That's right!

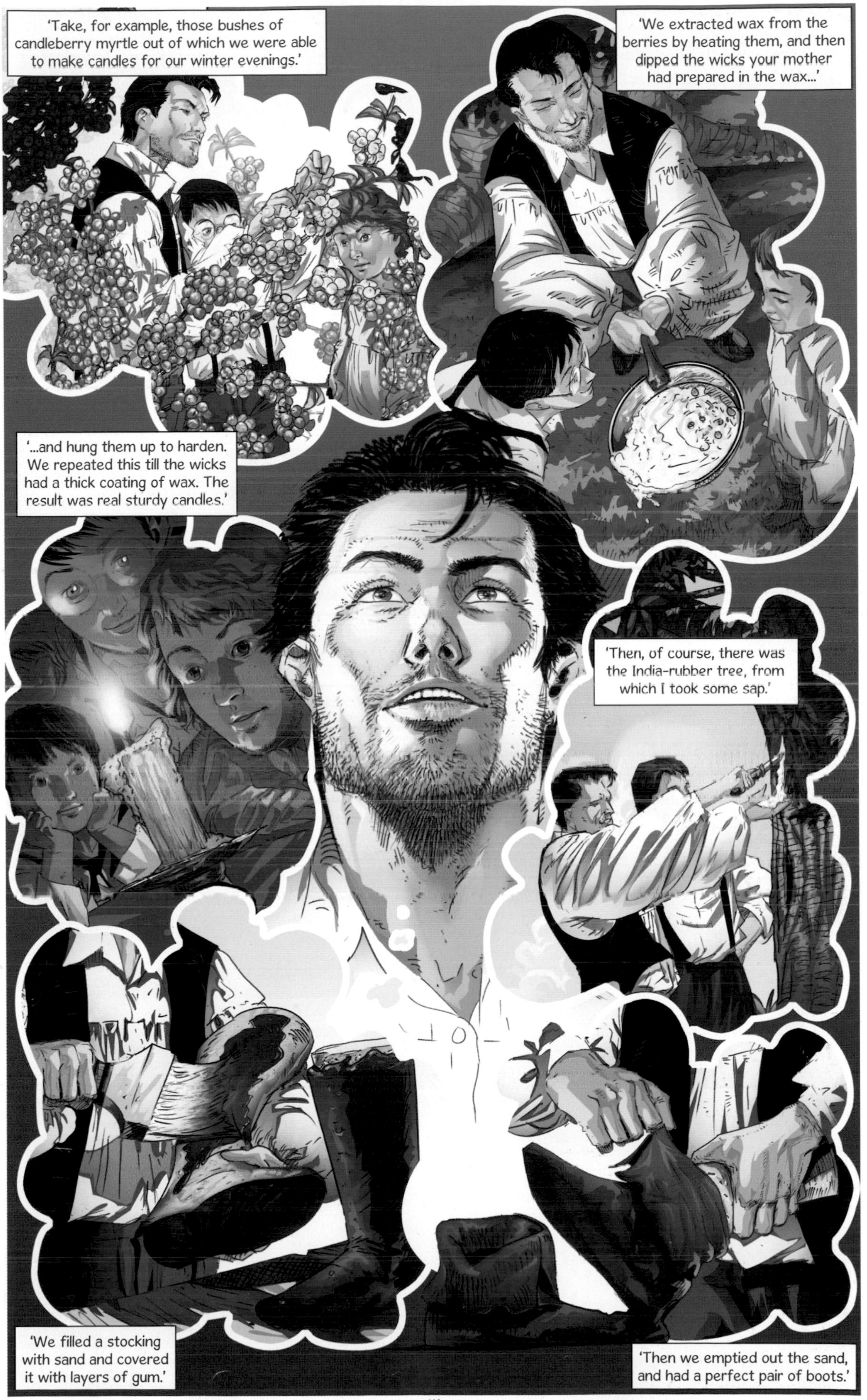
'Take, for example, those bushes of candleberry myrtle out of which we were able to make candles for our winter evenings.'
'We extracted wax from the berries by heating them, and then dipped the wicks your mother had prepared in the wax...'
'...and hung them up to harden. We repeated this till the wicks had a thick coating of wax. The result was real sturdy candles.'
'Then, of course, there was the India-rubber tree, from which I took some sap.'
'We filled a stocking with sand and covered it with layers of gum.'
'Then we emptied out the sand, and had a perfect pair of boots.'

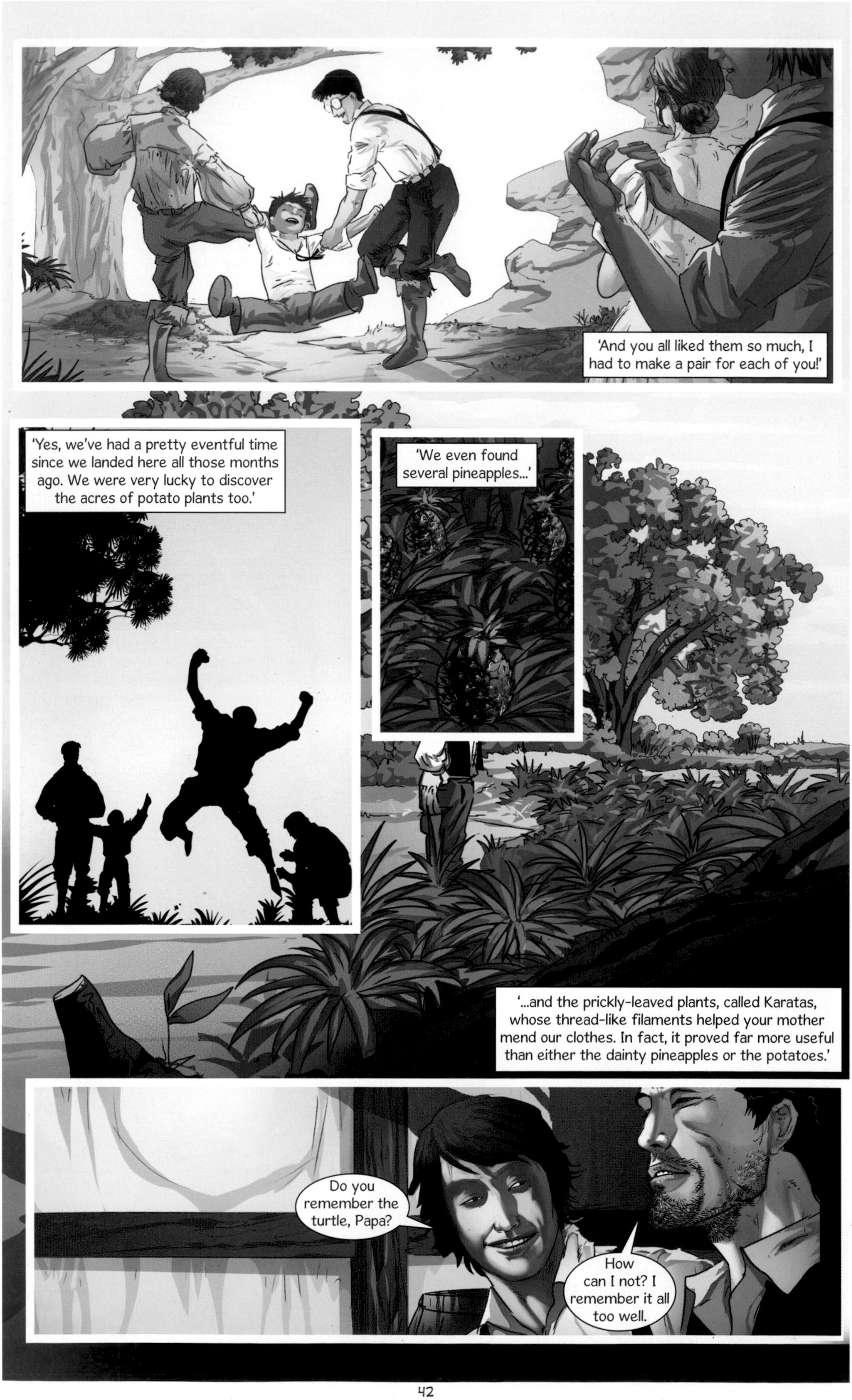
'And you all liked them so much, I had to make a pair for each of you!'
'Yes, we've had a pretty eventful time since we landed here all those months ago. We were very lucky to discover the acres of potato plants too.'
'We even found several pineapples...'
'...and the prickly-leaved plants, called Karatas, whose thread-like filaments helped your mother mend our clothes. In fact, it proved far more useful than either the dainty pineapples or the potatoes.'
Do you remember the turtle, Papa?
How can I not? I remember it all too well.

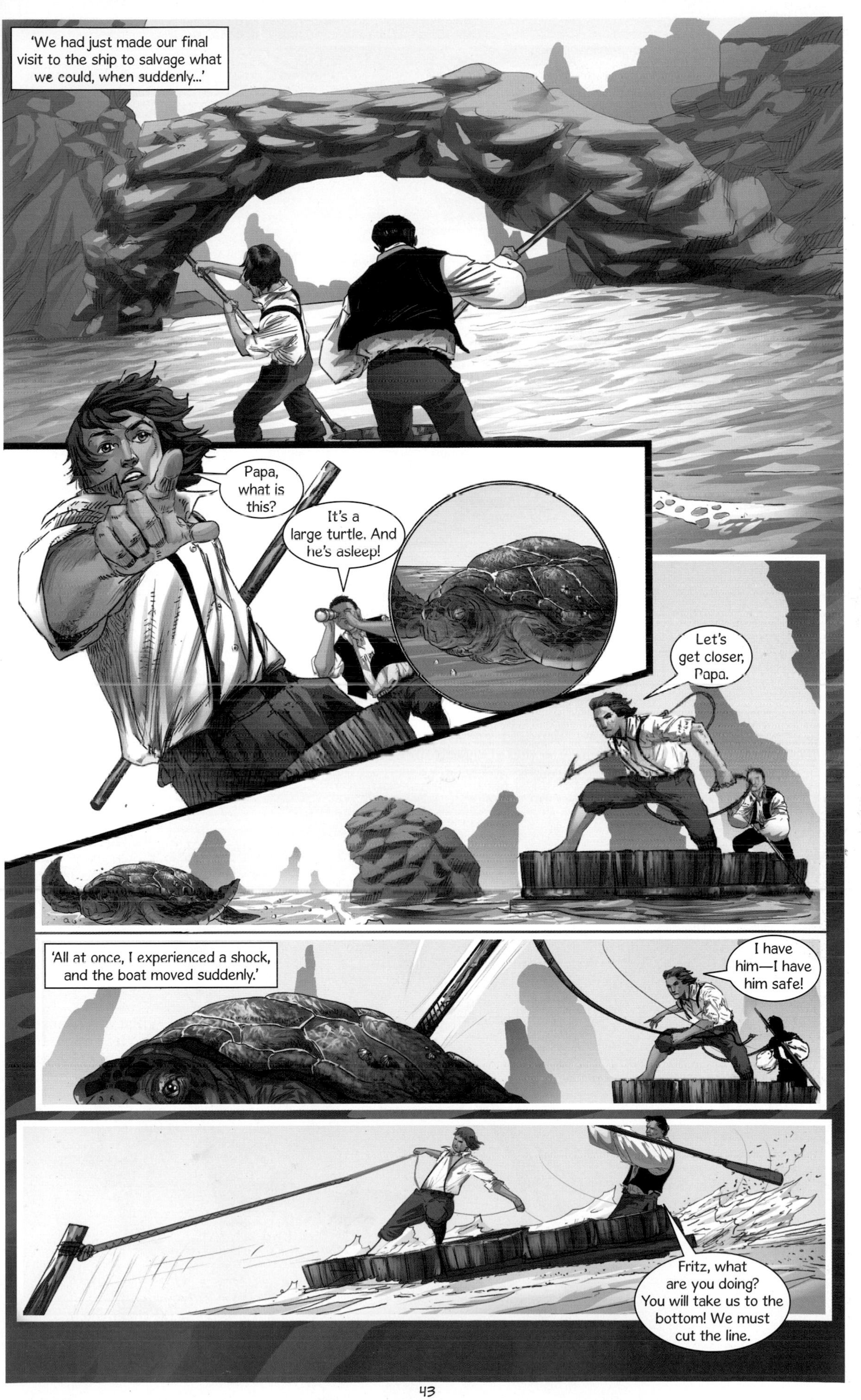
'We had just made our final visit to the ship to salvage what we could, when suddenly...'
Papa, what is this?
It's a large turtle. And he's asleep!
Let's get closer, Papa.
'All at once, I experienced a shock, and the boat moved suddenly.'
I have him—I have him safe!
Fritz, what are you doing? You will take us to the bottom! We must cut the line.

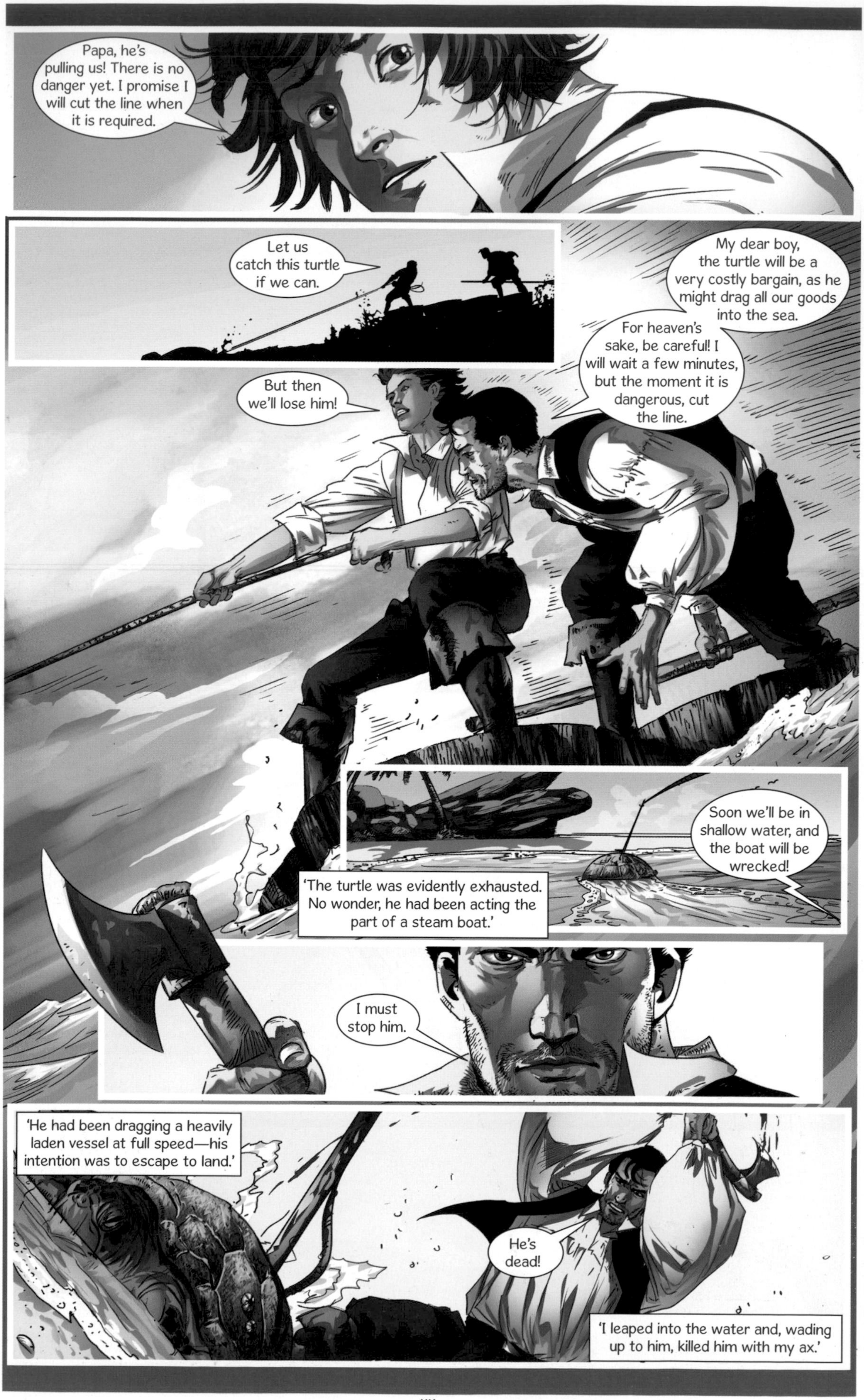

Papa, he's pulling us! There is no danger yet. I promise I will cut the line when it is required.
Let us catch this turtle if we can.
My dear boy, the turtle will be a very costly bargain, as he might drag all our goods into the sea.
For heaven's sake, be careful! I will wait a few minutes, but the moment it is dangerous, cut the line.
But then we'll lose him!
Soon we'll be in shallow water, and the boat will be wrecked!
'The turtle was evidently exhausted. No wonder, he had been acting the part of a steam boat.'
I must stop him.
'He had been dragging a heavily laden vessel at full speed—his intention was to escape to land.'
He's dead!
'I leaped into the water and, wading up to him, killed him with my ax.'

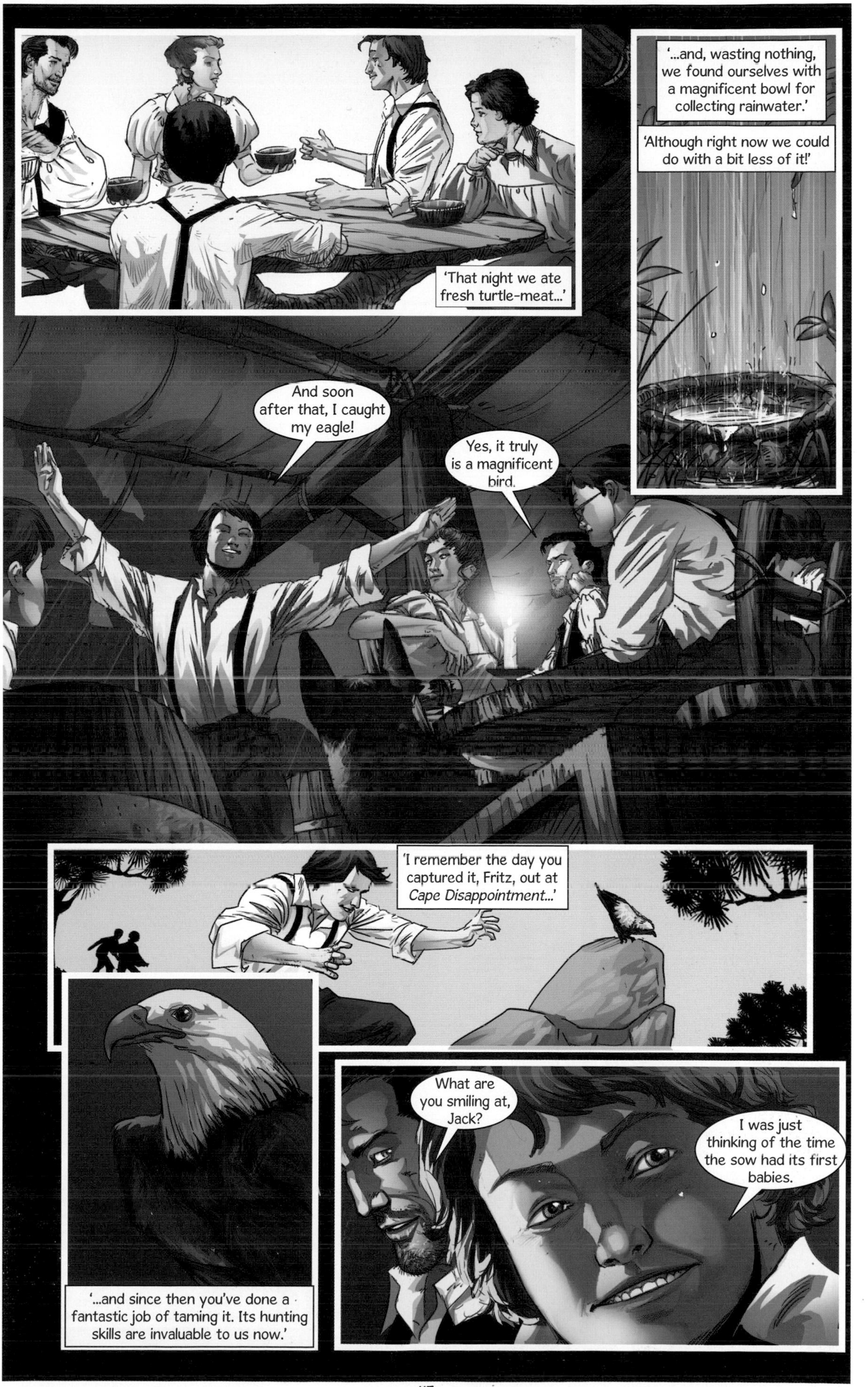
'That night we ate fresh turtle-meat...'
'...and, wasting nothing, we found ourselves with a magnificent bowl for collecting rainwater.'
'Although right now we could do with a bit less of it!'
And soon after that, I caught my eagle!
Yes, it truly is a magnificent bird.
'I remember the day you captured it, Fritz, out at *Cape Disappointment*...'
'...and since then you've done a fantastic job of taming it. Its hunting skills are invaluable to us now.'
What are you smiling at, Jack?
I was just thinking of the time the sow had its first babies.

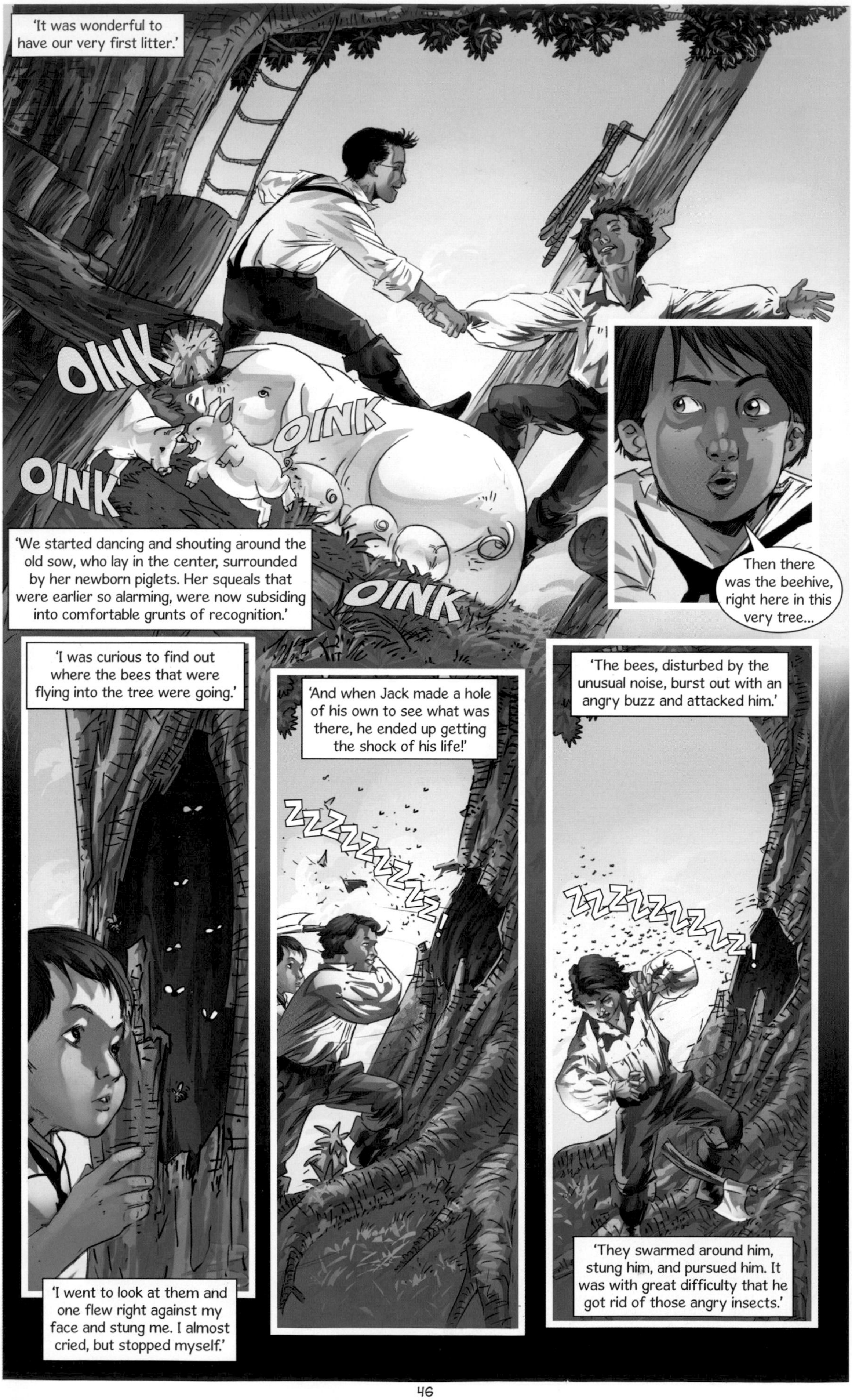

'It was wonderful to have our very first litter.'
OINK
OINK
OINK
'We started dancing and shouting around the old sow, who lay in the center, surrounded by her newborn piglets. Her squeals that were earlier so alarming, were now subsiding into comfortable grunts of recognition.'
OINK
Then there was the beehive, right here in this very tree...
'I was curious to find out where the bees that were flying into the tree were going.'
'I went to look at them and one flew right against my face and stung me. I almost cried, but stopped myself.'
'And when Jack made a hole of his own to see what was there, he ended up getting the shock of his life!'
ZZZZZZZZZZ!
'The bees, disturbed by the unusual noise, burst out with an angry buzz and attacked him.'
ZZZZZZZZZZ!
'They swarmed around him, stung him, and pursued him. It was with great difficulty that he got rid of those angry insects.'

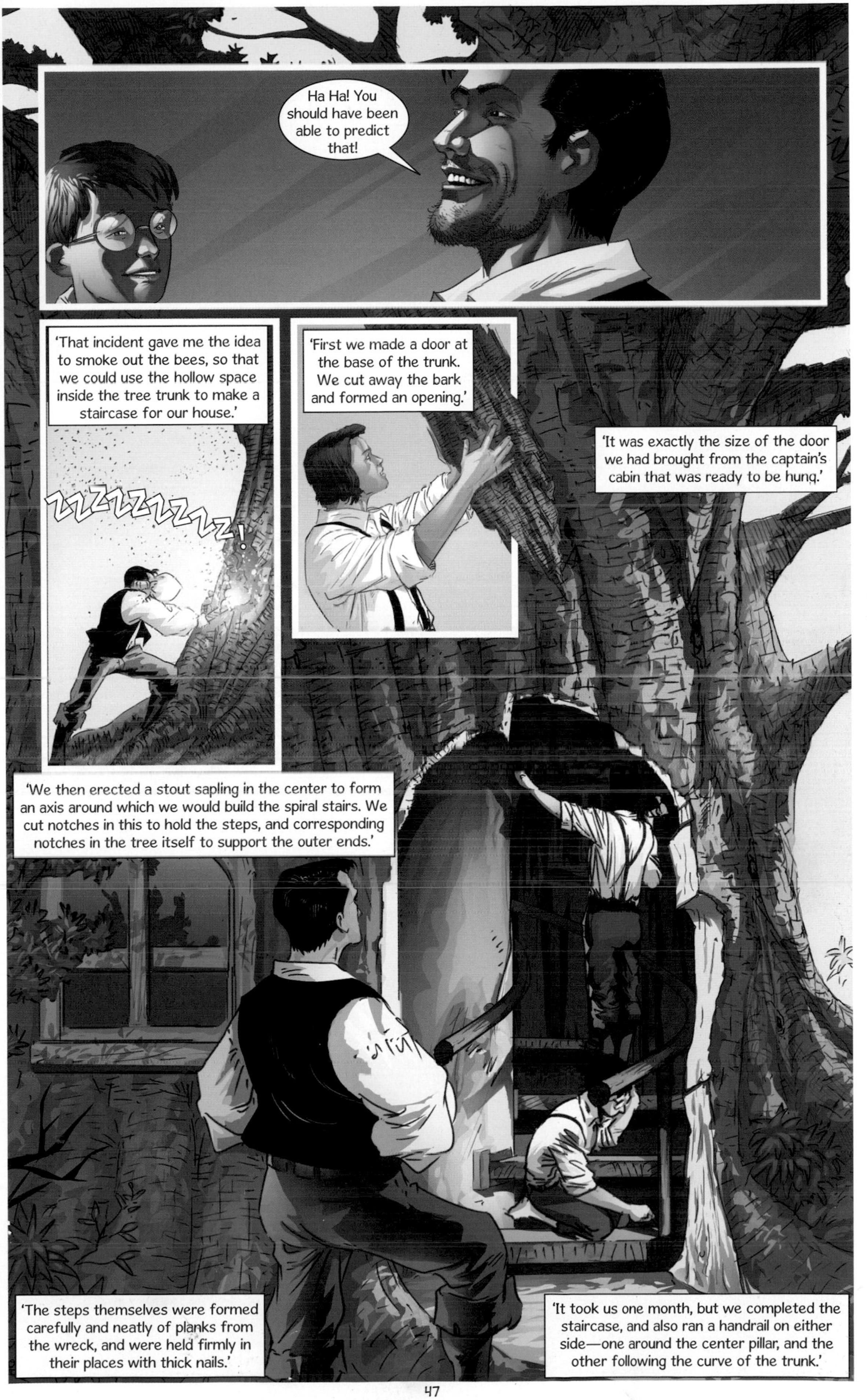
Ha Ha! You should have been able to predict that!
'That incident gave me the idea to smoke out the bees, so that we could use the hollow space inside the tree trunk to make a staircase for our house.'
ZZZZZZZZZZZ!
'First we made a door at the base of the trunk. We cut away the bark and formed an opening.'
'It was exactly the size of the door we had brought from the captain's cabin that was ready to be hung.'
'We then erected a stout sapling in the center to form an axis around which we would build the spiral stairs. We cut notches in this to hold the steps, and corresponding notches in the tree itself to support the outer ends.'
'The steps themselves were formed carefully and neatly of planks from the wreck, and were held firmly in their places with thick nails.'
'It took us one month, but we completed the staircase, and also ran a handrail on either side—one around the center pillar, and the other following the curve of the trunk.'

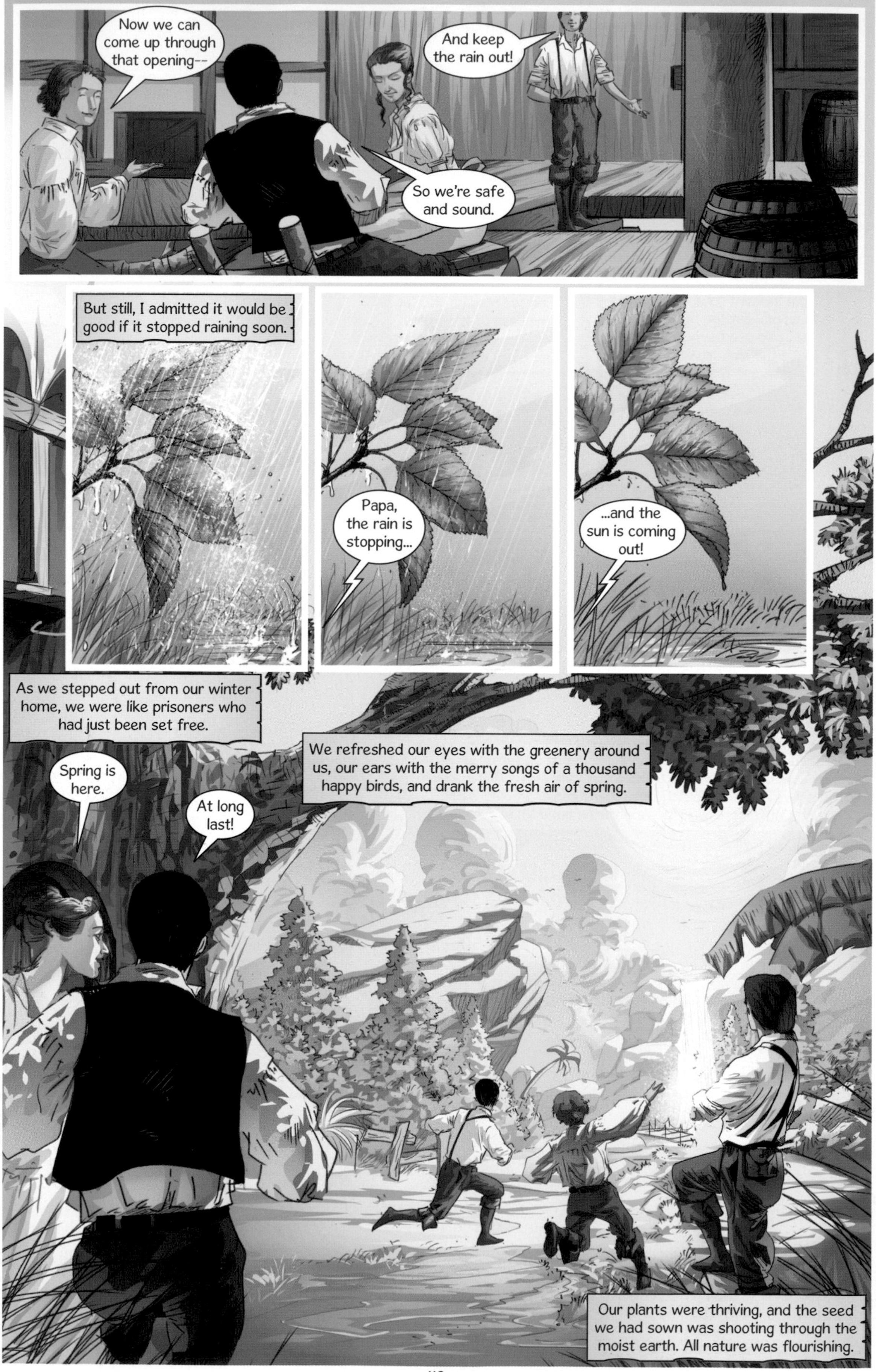
Now we can come up through that opening--
So we're safe and sound.
And keep the rain out!
But still, I admitted it would be good if it stopped raining soon.
Papa, the rain is stopping...
...and the sun is coming out!
As we stepped out from our winter home, we were like prisoners who had just been set free.
Spring is here.
At long last!
We refreshed our eyes with the greenery around us, our ears with the merry songs of a thousand happy birds, and drank the fresh air of spring.
Our plants were thriving, and the seed we had sown was shooting through the moist earth. All nature was flourishing.

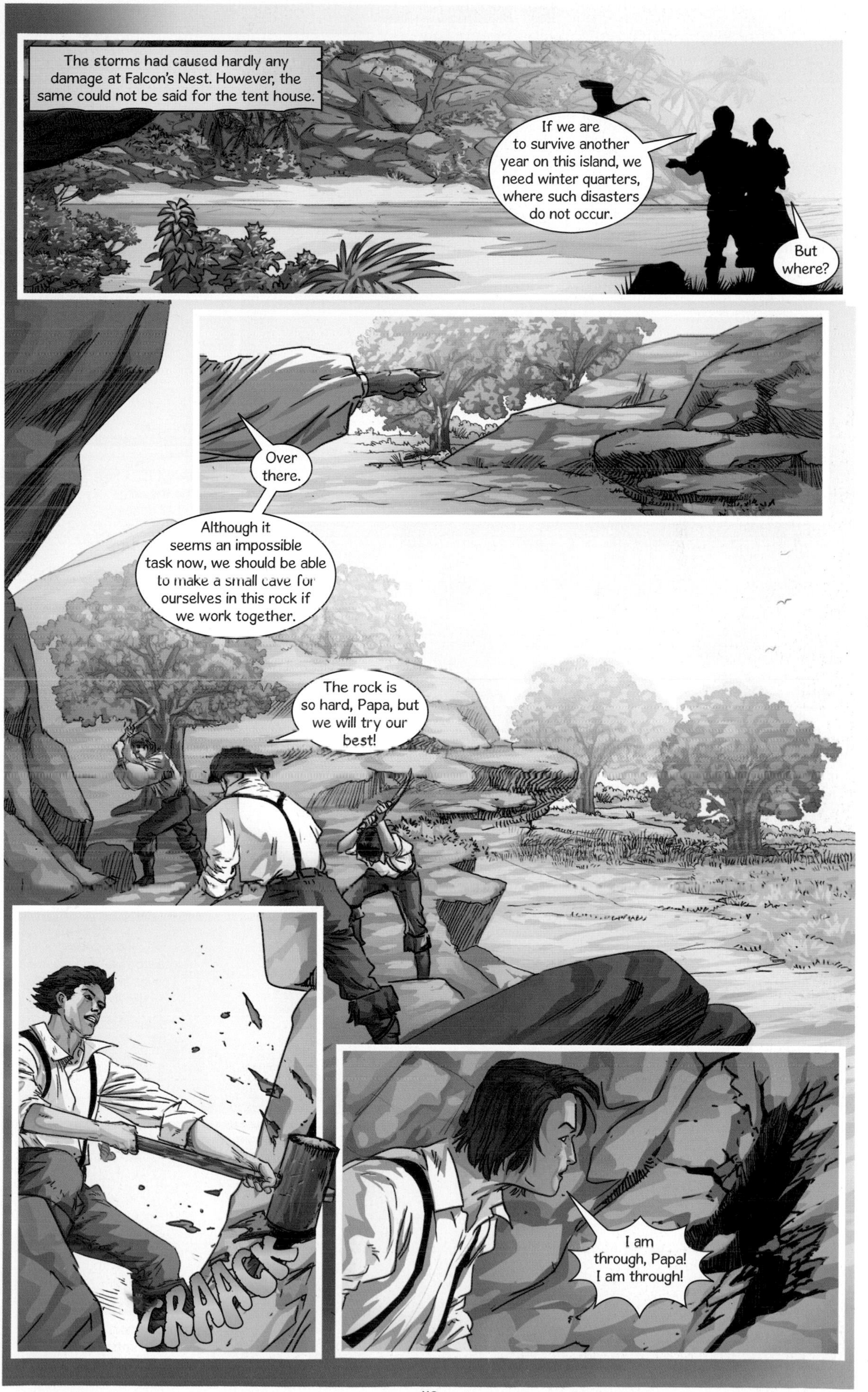
The storms had caused hardly any damage at Falcon's Nest. However, the same could not be said for the tent house.
If we are to survive another year on this island, we need winter quarters, where such disasters do not occur.
But where?
Over there.
Although it seems an impossible task now, we should be able to make a small cave for ourselves in this rock if we work together.
The rock is so hard, Papa, but we will try our best!
CRAACK
I am through, Papa! I am through!

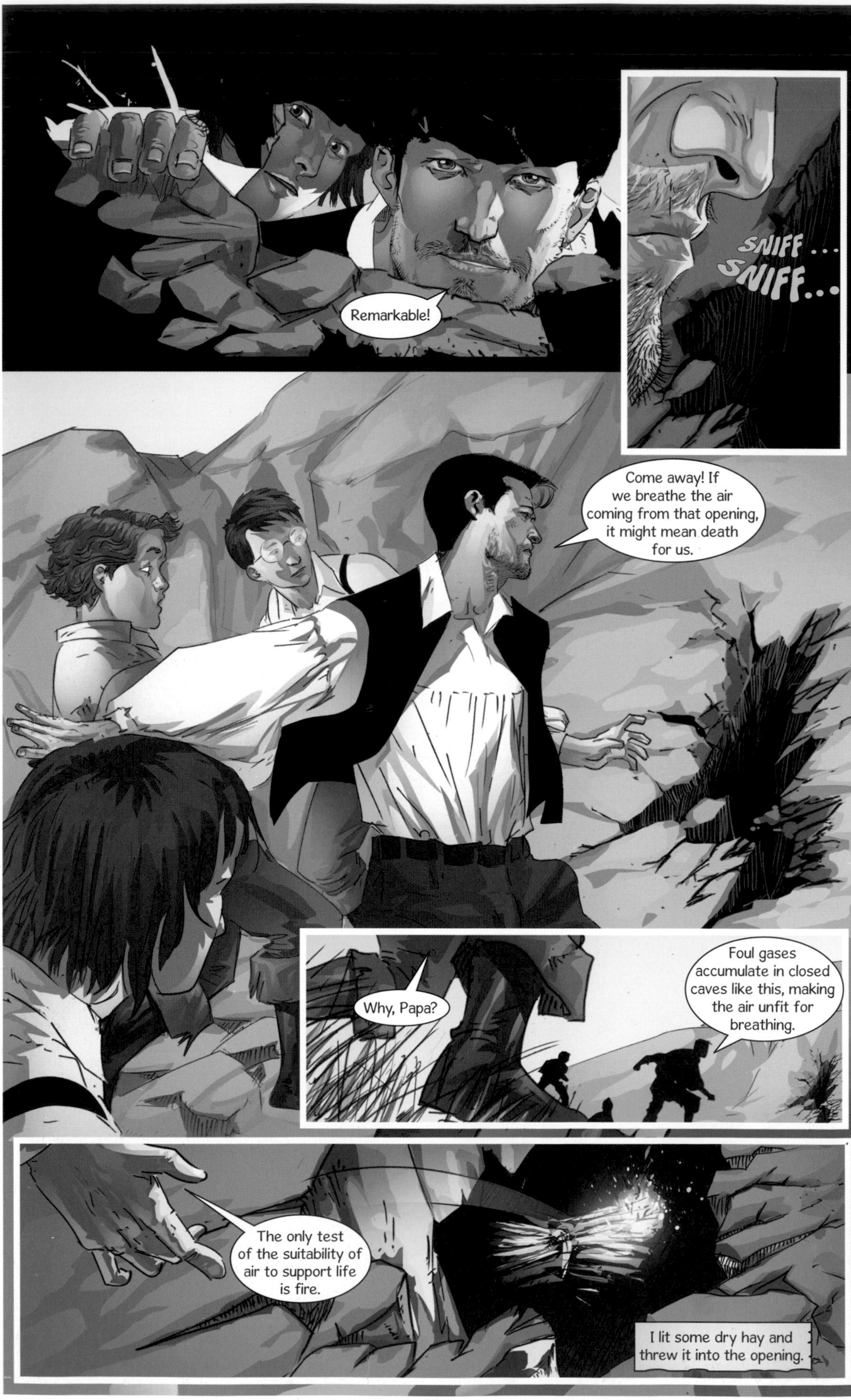
Remarkable!
SNIFF...
SNIFF...
Come away! If we breathe the air coming from that opening, it might mean death for us.
Why, Papa?
Foul gases accumulate in closed caves like this, making the air unfit for breathing.
The only test of the suitability of air to support life is fire.
I lit some dry hay and threw it into the opening.

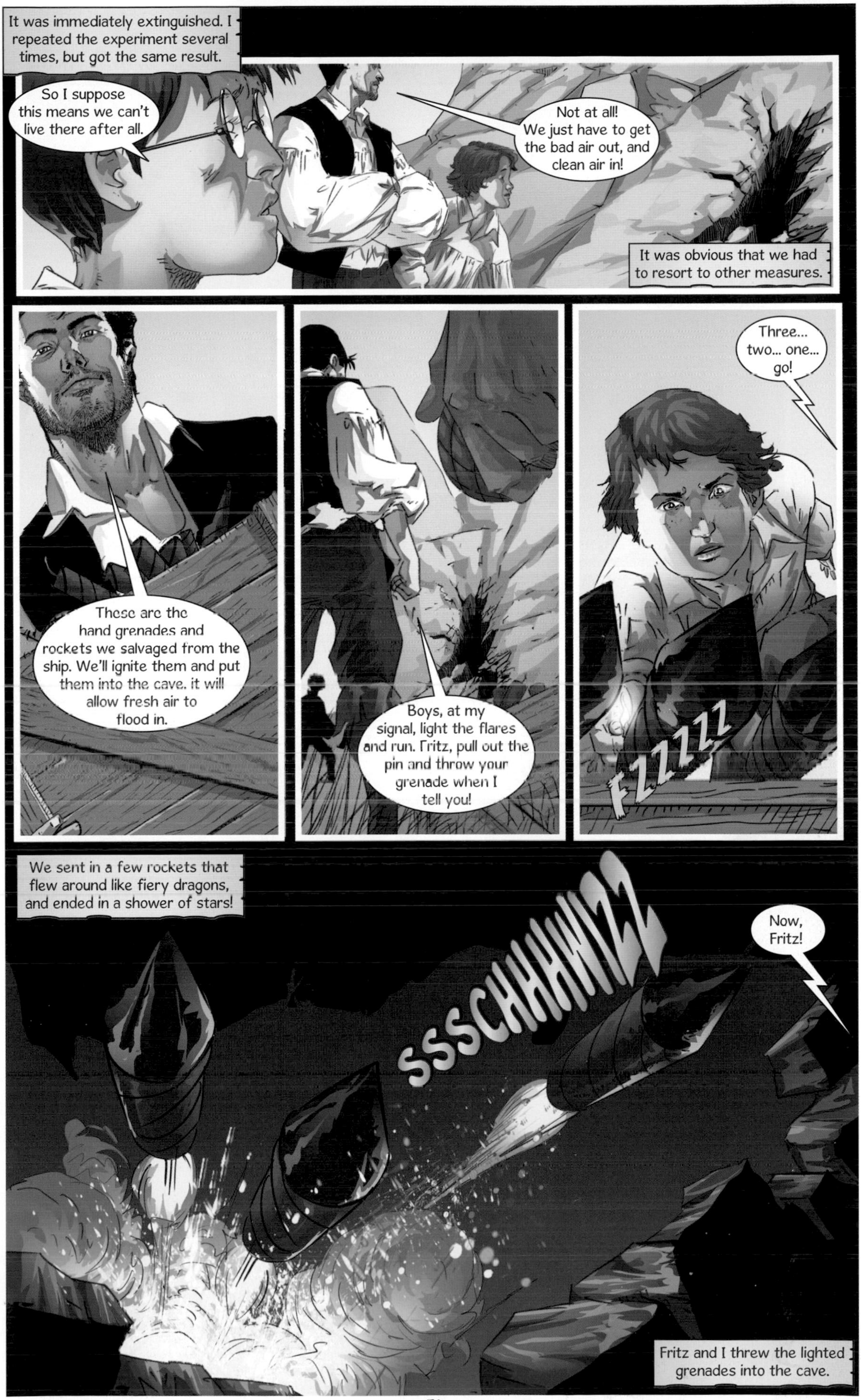
It was immediately extinguished. I repeated the experiment several times, but got the same result.
So I suppose this means we can't live there after all.
Not at all! We just have to get the bad air out, and clean air in!
It was obvious that we had to resort to other measures.
These are the hand grenades and rockets we salvaged from the ship. We'll ignite them and put them into the cave. it will allow fresh air to flood in.
Boys, at my signal, light the flares and run. Fritz, pull out the pin and throw your grenade when I tell you!
Three... two... one... go!
FZZZZZ
We sent in a few rockets that flew around like fiery dragons, and ended in a shower of stars!
SSSCHHHWIZZ
Now, Fritz!
Fritz and I threw the lighted grenades into the cave.

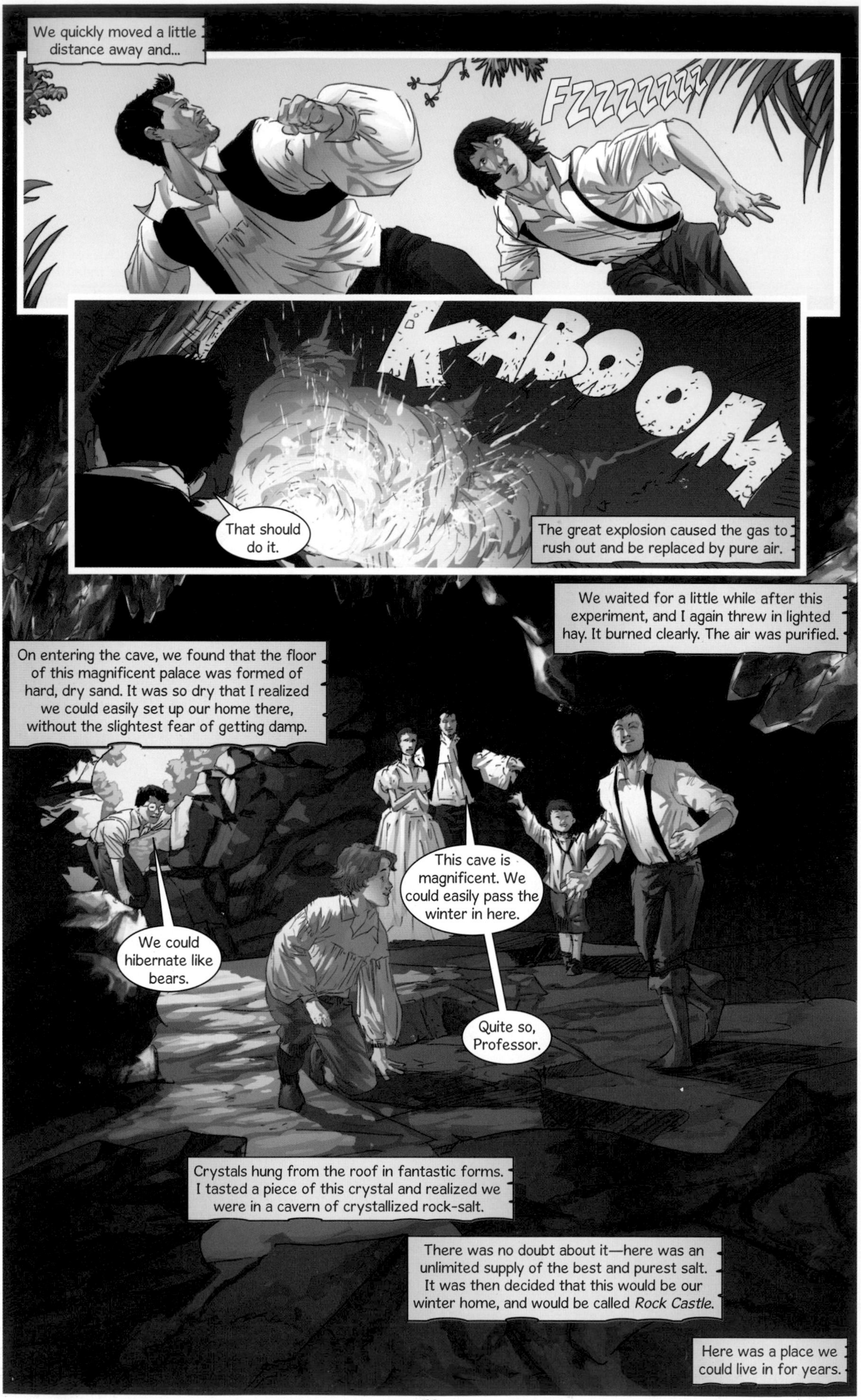
We quickly moved a little distance away and...
FZZZZZZZ
KABOOM
That should do it.
The great explosion caused the gas to rush out and be replaced by pure air.
We waited for a little while after this experiment, and I again threw in lighted hay. It burned clearly. The air was purified.
On entering the cave, we found that the floor of this magnificent palace was formed of hard, dry sand. It was so dry that I realized we could easily set up our home there, without the slightest fear of getting damp.
This cave is magnificent. We could easily pass the winter in here.
We could hibernate like bears.
Quite so, Professor.
Crystals hung from the roof in fantastic forms. I tasted a piece of this crystal and realized we were in a cavern of crystallized rock-salt.
There was no doubt about it—here was an unlimited supply of the best and purest salt. It was then decided that this would be our winter home, and would be called *Rock Castle*.
Here was a place we could live in for years.

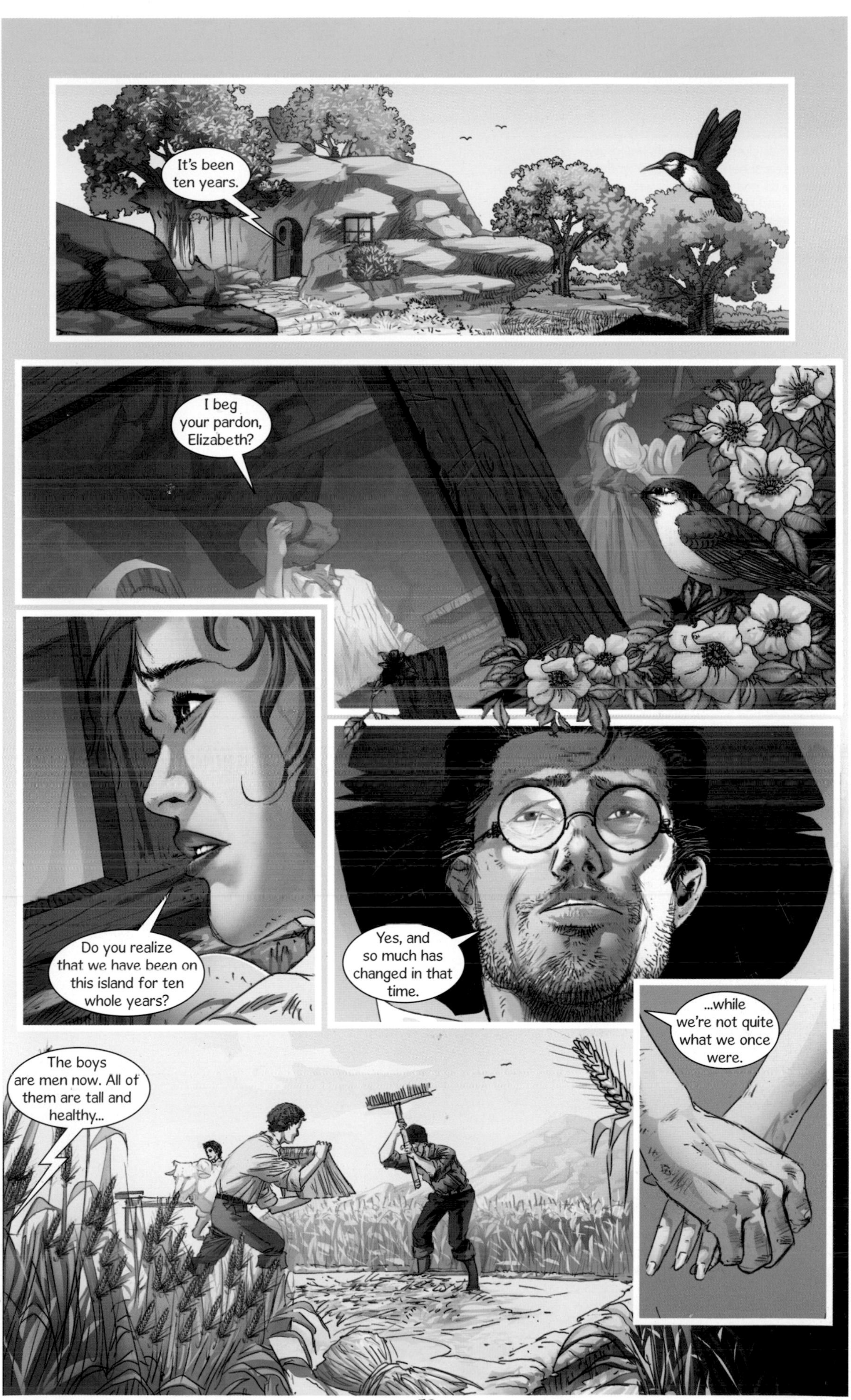
It's been ten years.
I beg your pardon, Elizabeth?
Do you realize that we have been on this island for ten whole years?
Yes, and so much has changed in that time.
The boys are men now. All of them are tall and healthy...
...while we're not quite what we once were.

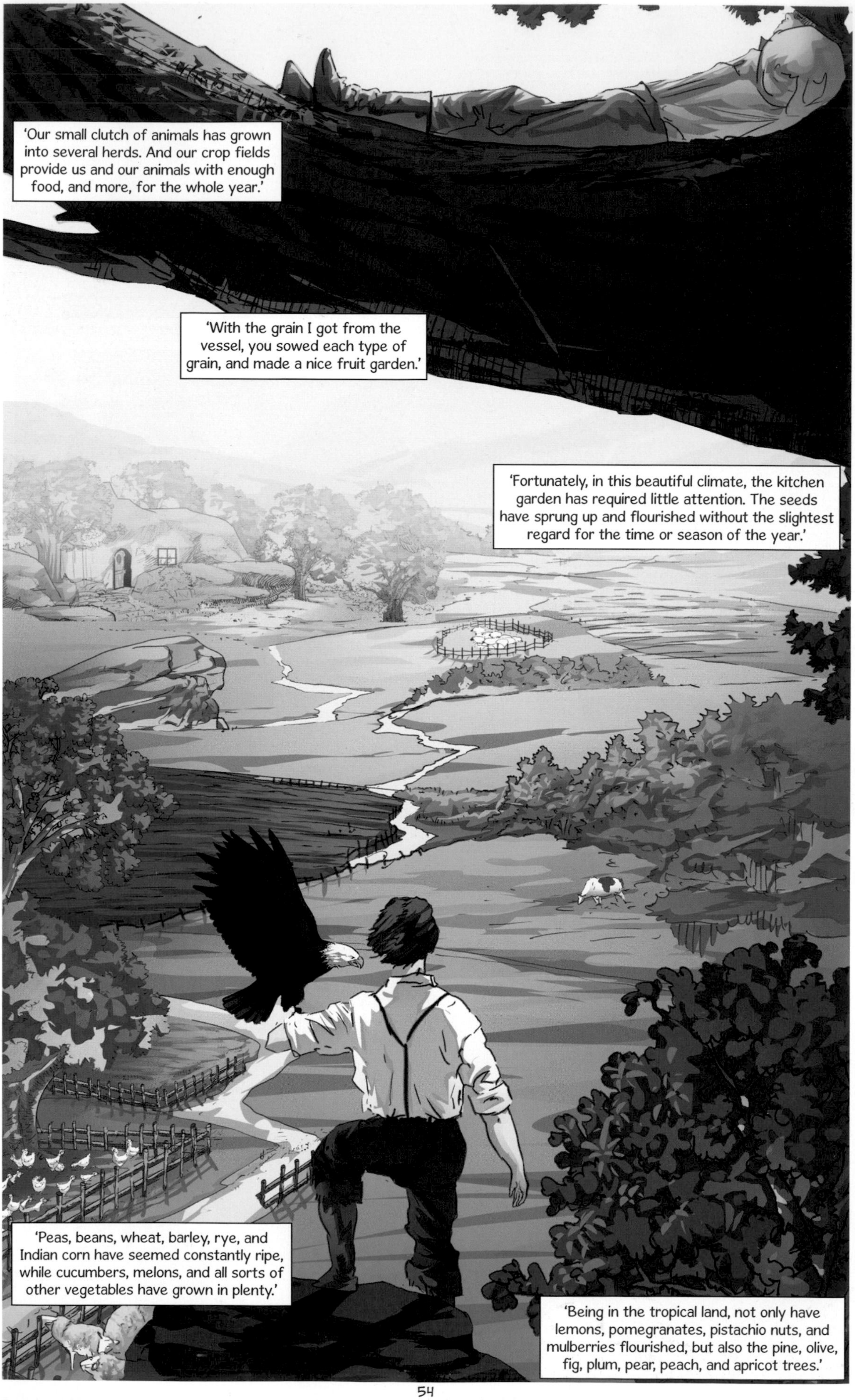
'Our small clutch of animals has grown into several herds. And our crop fields provide us and our animals with enough food, and more, for the whole year.'
'With the grain I got from the vessel, you sowed each type of grain, and made a nice fruit garden.'
'Fortunately, in this beautiful climate, the kitchen garden has required little attention. The seeds have sprung up and flourished without the slightest regard for the time or season of the year.'
'Peas, beans, wheat, barley, rye, and Indian corn have seemed constantly ripe, while cucumbers, melons, and all sorts of other vegetables have grown in plenty.'
'Being in the tropical land, not only have lemons, pomegranates, pistachio nuts, and mulberries flourished, but also the pine, olive, fig, plum, pear, peach, and apricot trees.'

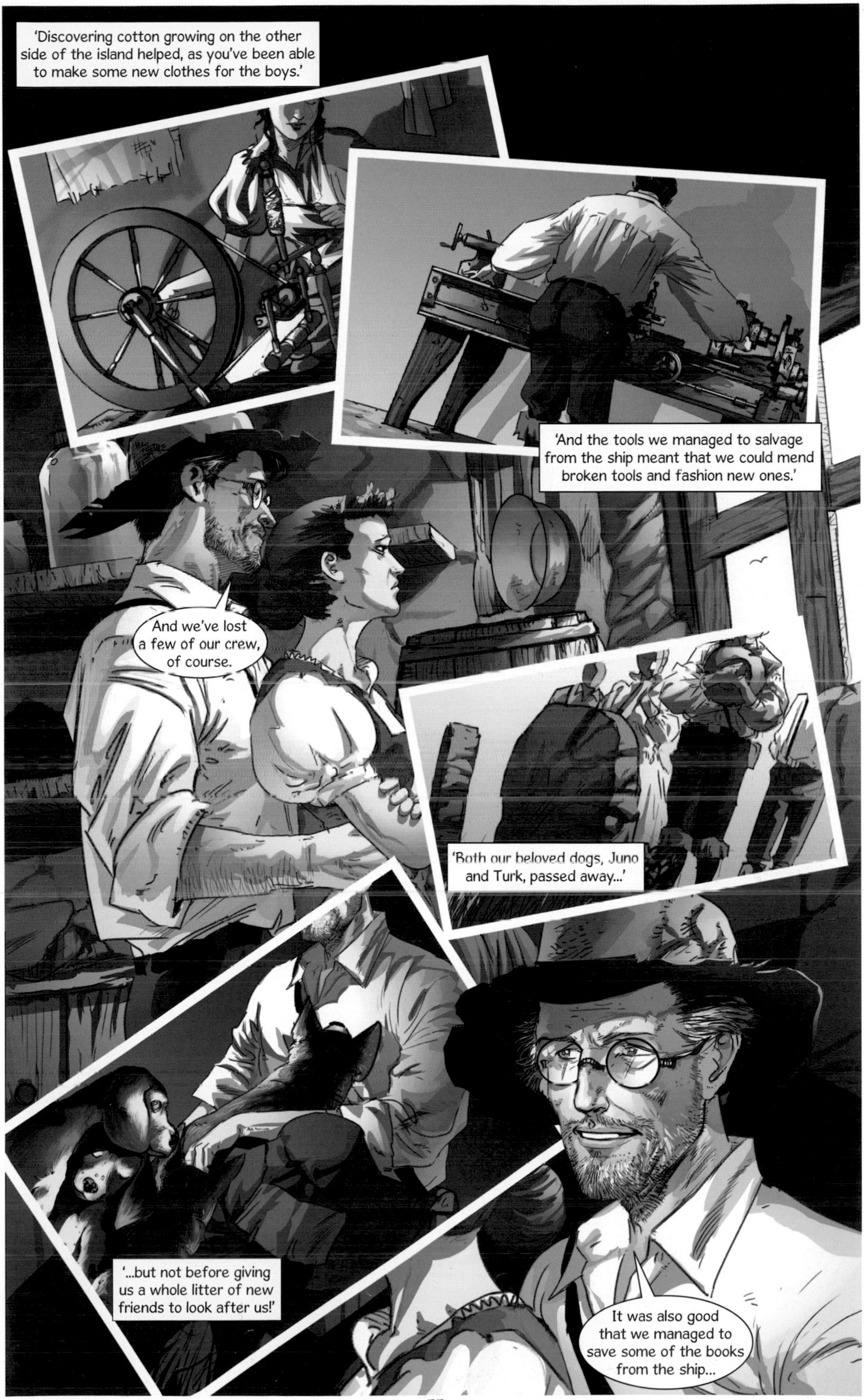
'Discovering cotton growing on the other side of the island helped, as you've been able to make some new clothes for the boys.'
'And the tools we managed to salvage from the ship meant that we could mend broken tools and fashion new ones.'
And we've lost a few of our crew, of course.
'Both our beloved dogs, Juno and Turk, passed away...'
'...but not before giving us a whole litter of new friends to look after us!'
It was also good that we managed to save some of the books from the ship...

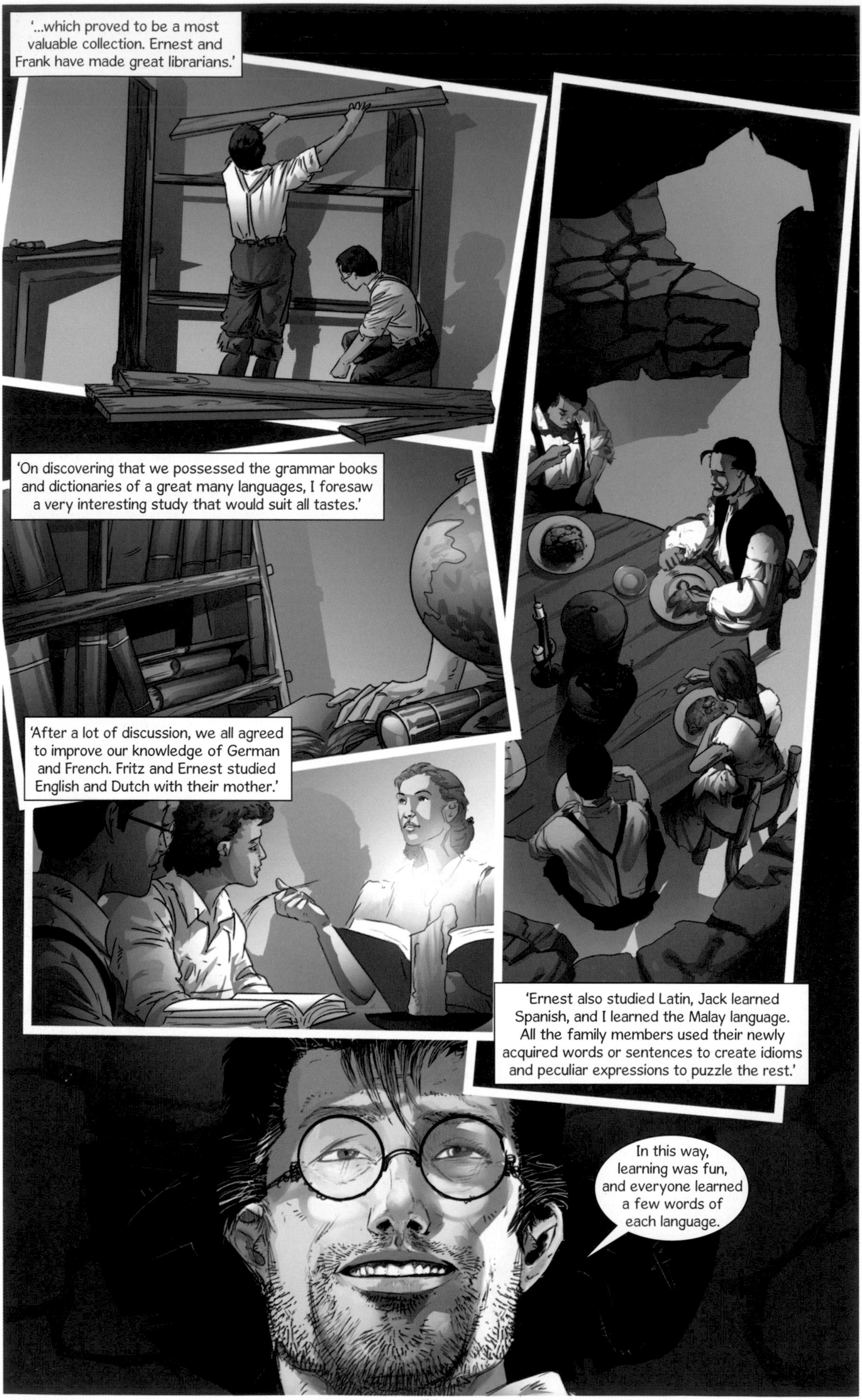
'...which proved to be a most valuable collection. Ernest and Frank have made great librarians.'
'On discovering that we possessed the grammar books and dictionaries of a great many languages, I foresaw a very interesting study that would suit all tastes.'
'After a lot of discussion, we all agreed to improve our knowledge of German and French. Fritz and Ernest studied English and Dutch with their mother.'
'Ernest also studied Latin, Jack learned Spanish, and I learned the Malay language. All the family members used their newly acquired words or sentences to create idioms and peculiar expressions to puzzle the rest.'
In this way, learning was fun, and everyone learned a few words of each language.

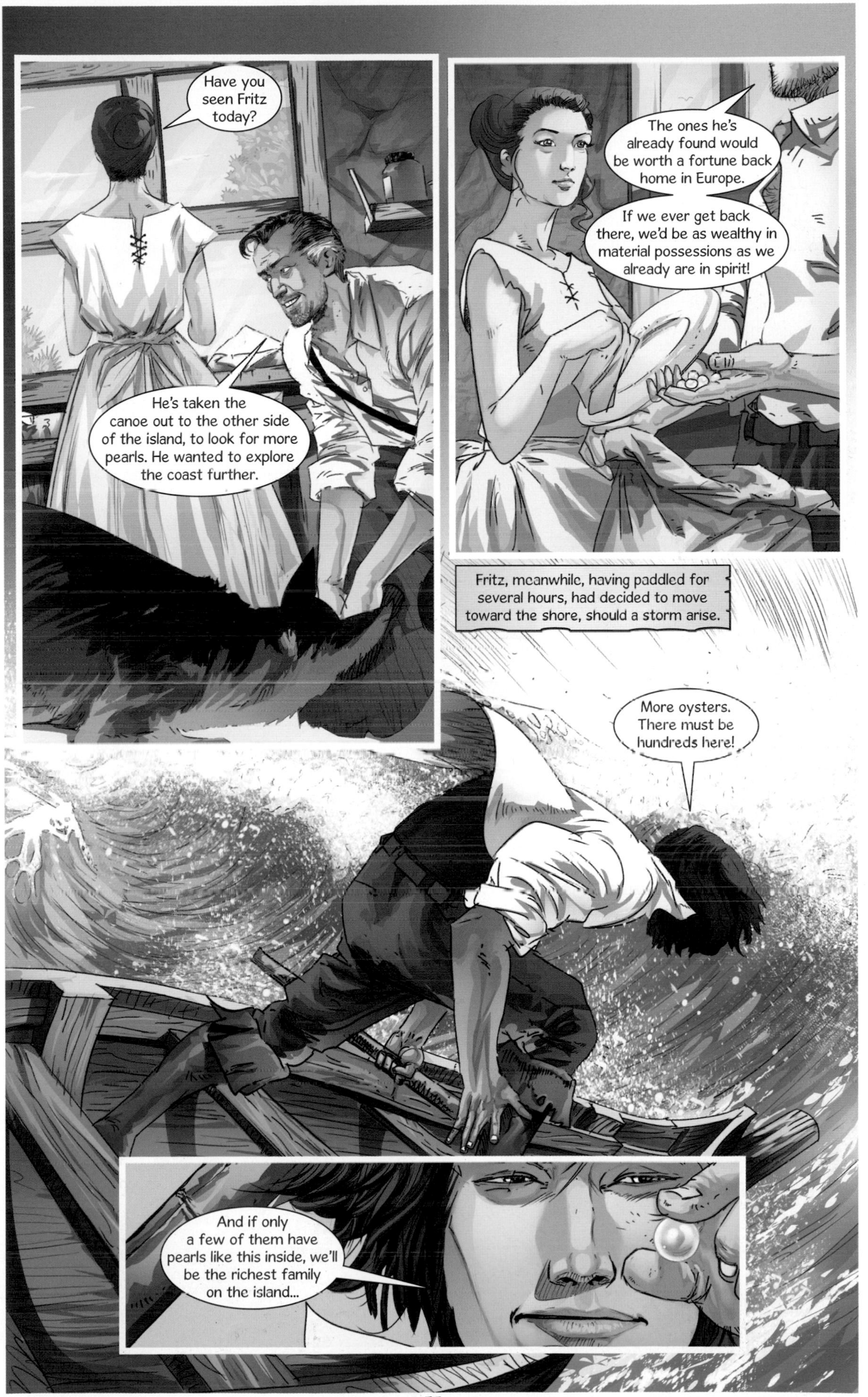
Have you seen Fritz today?
He's taken the canoe out to the other side of the island, to look for more pearls. He wanted to explore the coast further.
The ones he's already found would be worth a fortune back home in Europe.
If we ever get back there, we'd be as wealthy in material possessions as we already are in spirit!
Fritz, meanwhile, having paddled for several hours, had decided to move toward the shore, should a storm arise.
More oysters. There must be hundreds here!
And if only a few of them have pearls like this inside, we'll be the richest family on the island...

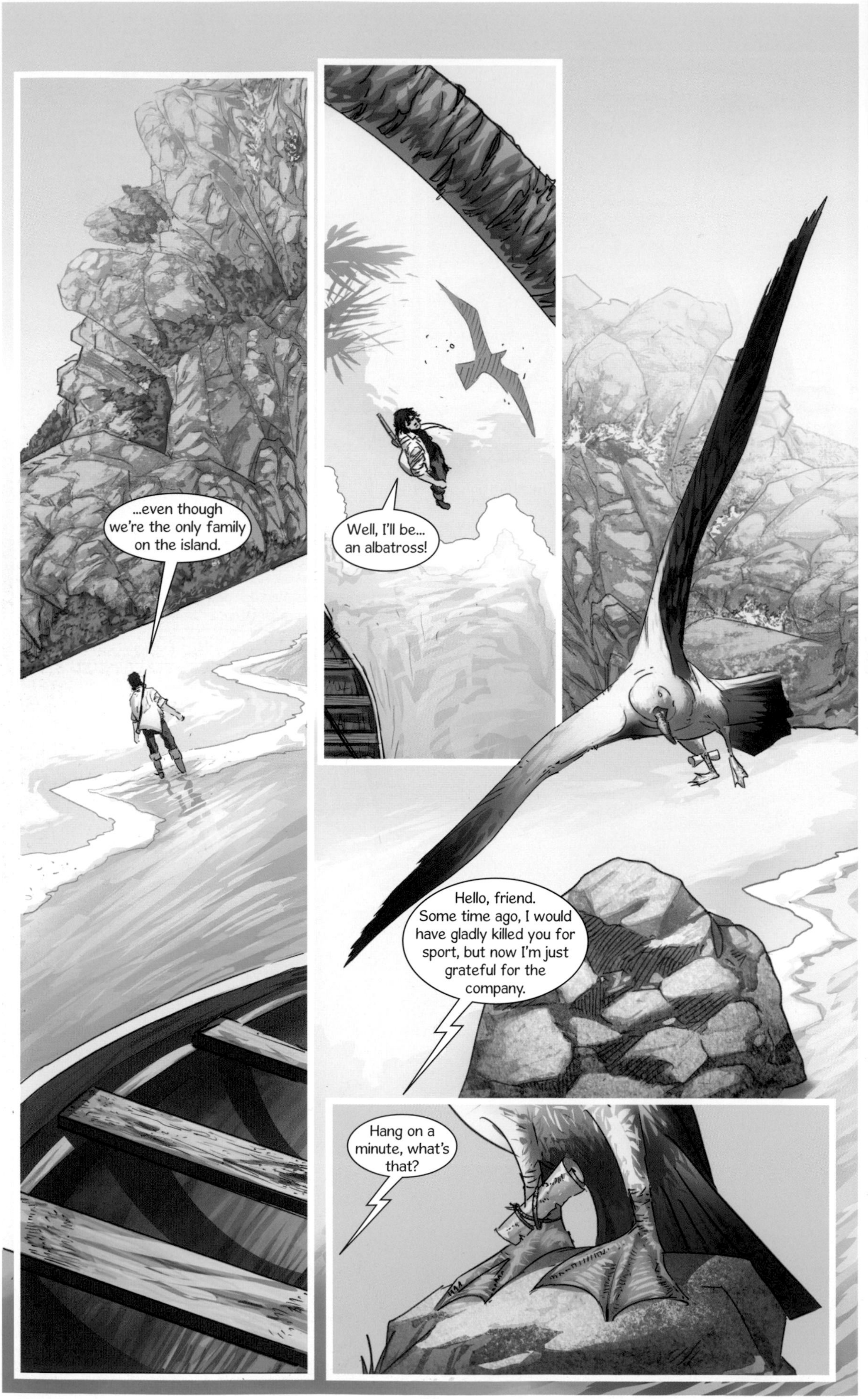
...even though we're the only family on the island.
Well, I'll be... an albatross!
Hello, friend. Some time ago, I would have gladly killed you for sport, but now I'm just grateful for the company.
Hang on a minute, what's that?

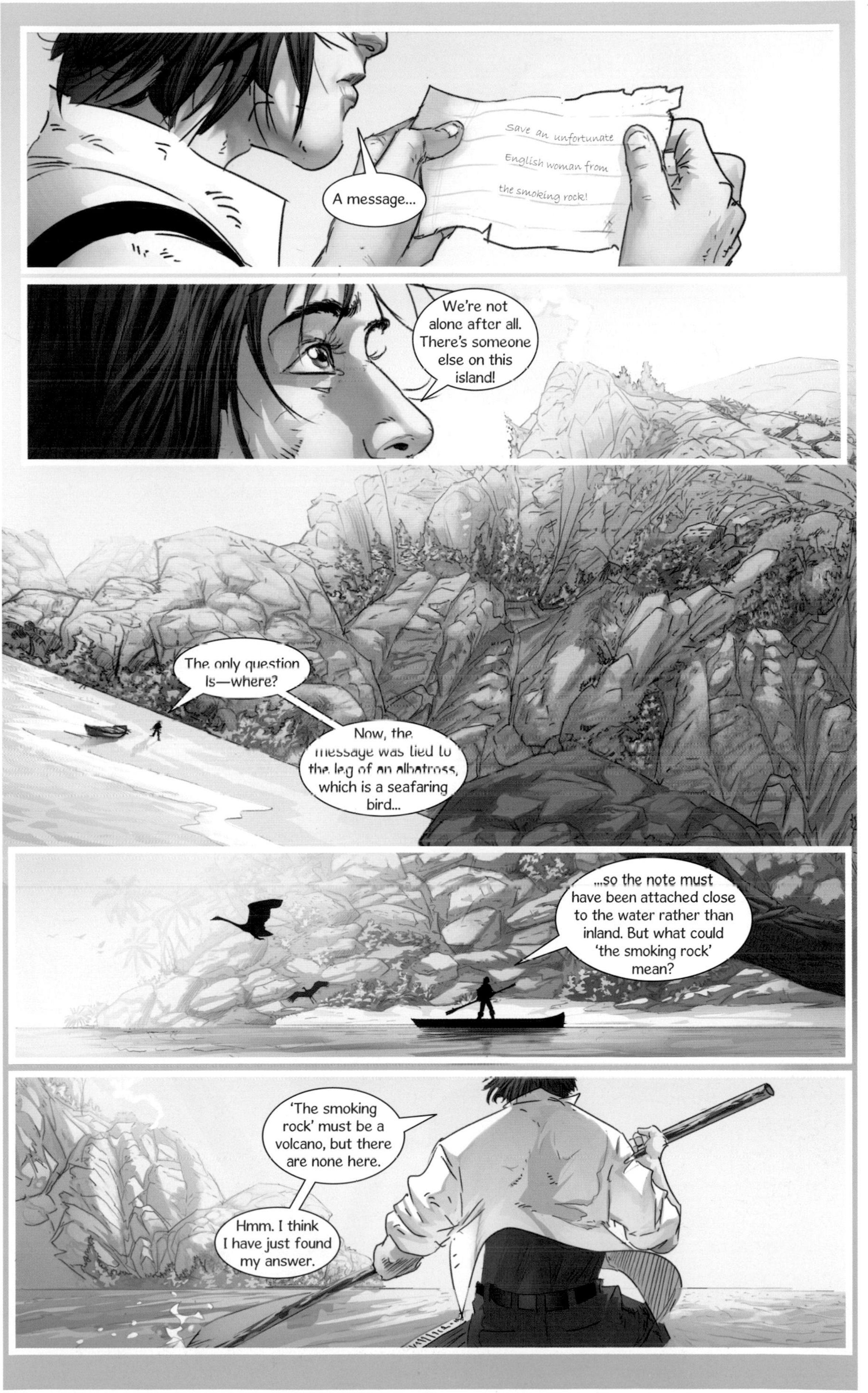
Save an unfortunate English woman from the smoking rock!
A message...
We're not alone after all. There's someone else on this island!
The only question is—where?
Now, the message was tied to the leg of an albatross, which is a seafaring bird...
...so the note must have been attached close to the water rather than inland. But what could 'the smoking rock' mean?
'The smoking rock' must be a volcano, but there are none here.
Hmm. I think I have just found my answer.

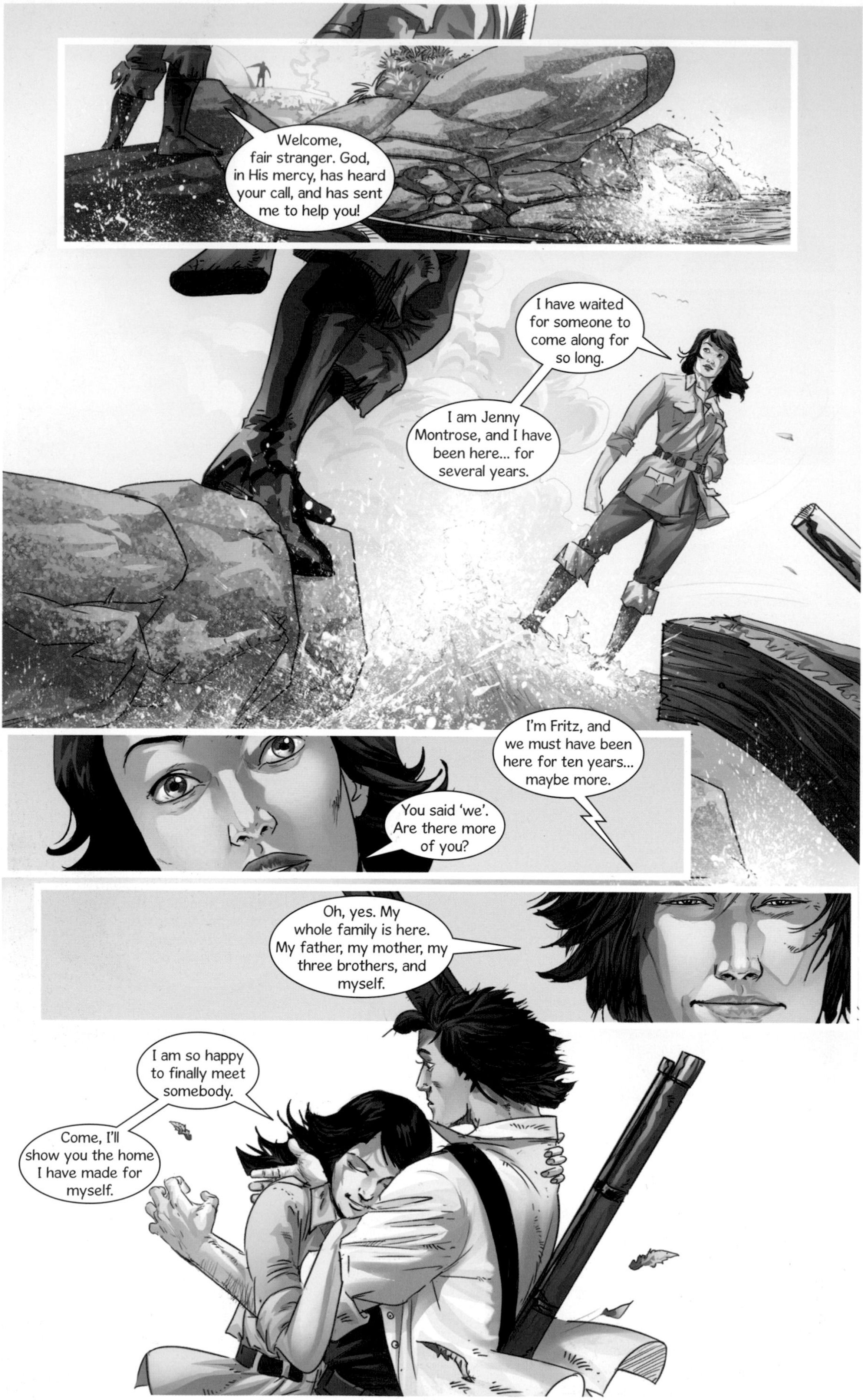
Welcome, fair stranger. God, in His mercy, has heard your call, and has sent me to help you!
I have waited for someone to come along for so long.
I am Jenny Montrose, and I have been here... for several years.
I'm Fritz, and we must have been here for ten years... maybe more.
You said 'we'. Are there more of you?
Oh, yes. My whole family is here. My father, my mother, my three brothers, and myself.
I am so happy to finally meet somebody.
Come, I'll show you the home I have made for myself.

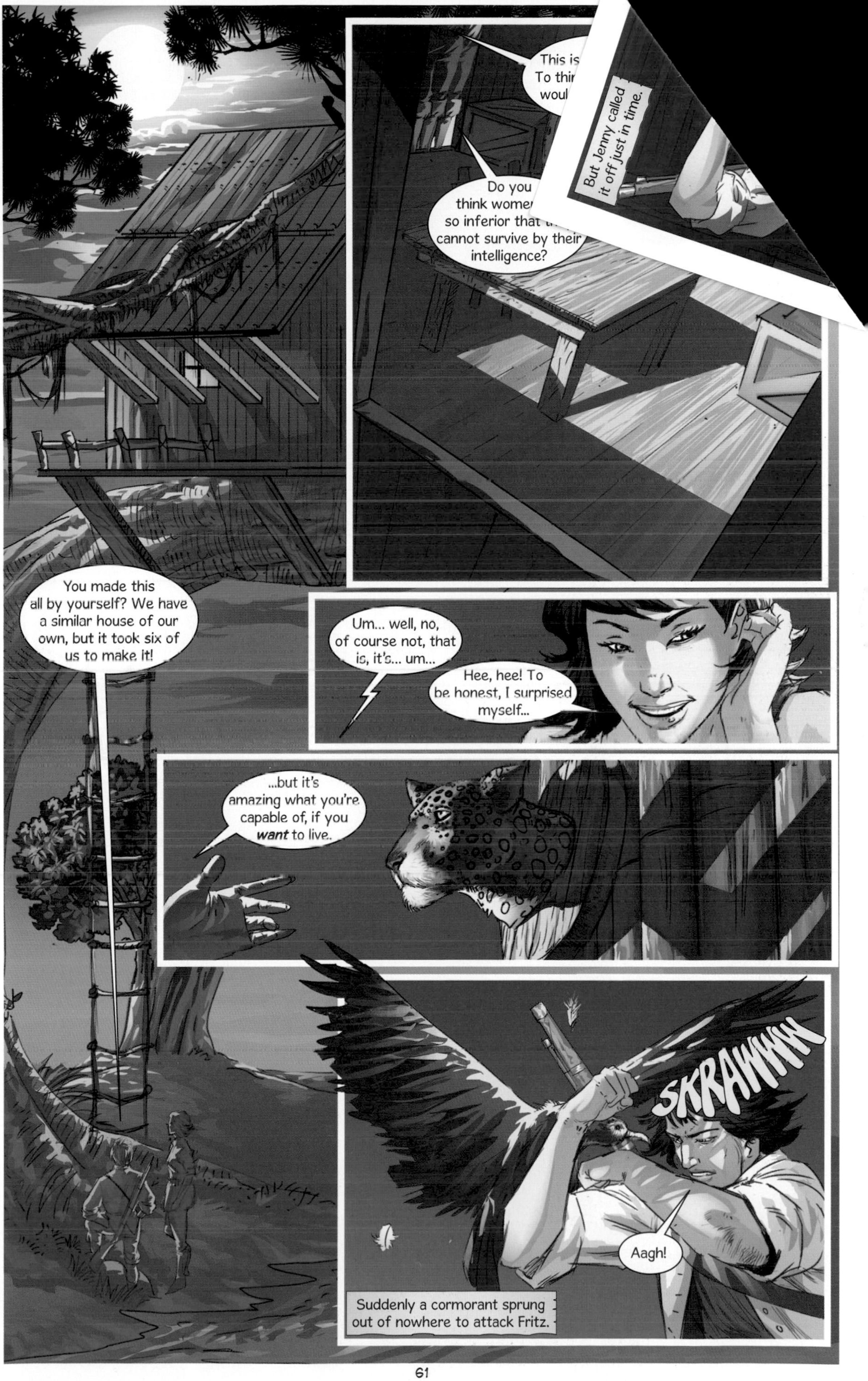

This is
To thir
woul
Do you
think womer
so inferior that t
cannot survive by their
intelligence?
But Jenny called it off just in time.
You made this all by yourself? We have a similar house of our own, but it took six of us to make it!
Um... well, no, of course not, that is, it's... um...
Hee, hee! To be honest, I surprised myself...
...but it's amazing what you're capable of, if you *want* to live.
SKRAWWW
Aagh!
Suddenly a cormorant sprung out of nowhere to attack Fritz.

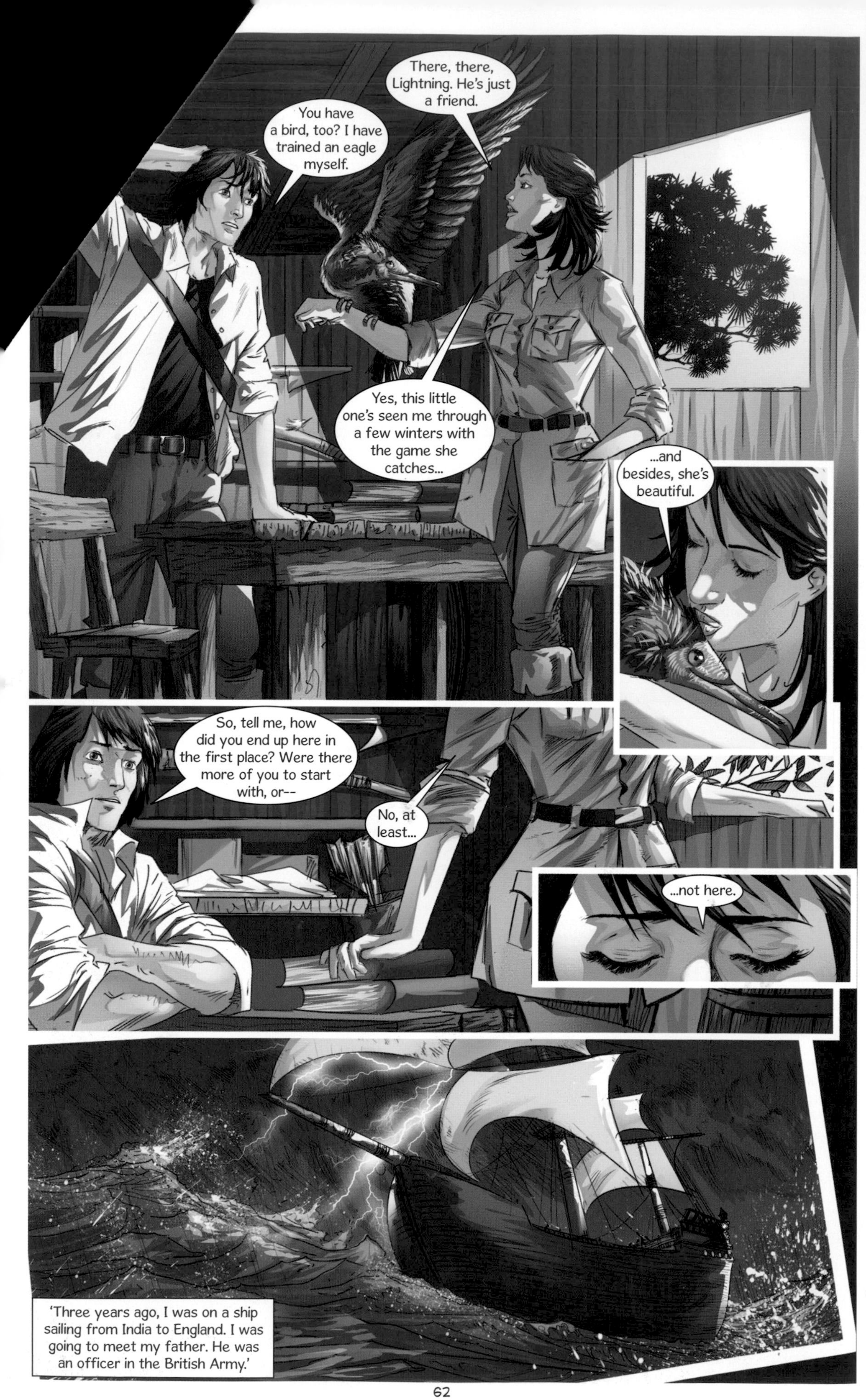

You have a bird, too? I have trained an eagle myself.
There, there, Lightning. He's just a friend.
Yes, this little one's seen me through a few winters with the game she catches...
...and besides, she's beautiful.
So, tell me, how did you end up here in the first place? Were there more of you to start with, or--
No, at least...
...not here.
'Three years ago, I was on a ship sailing from India to England. I was going to meet my father. He was an officer in the British Army.'

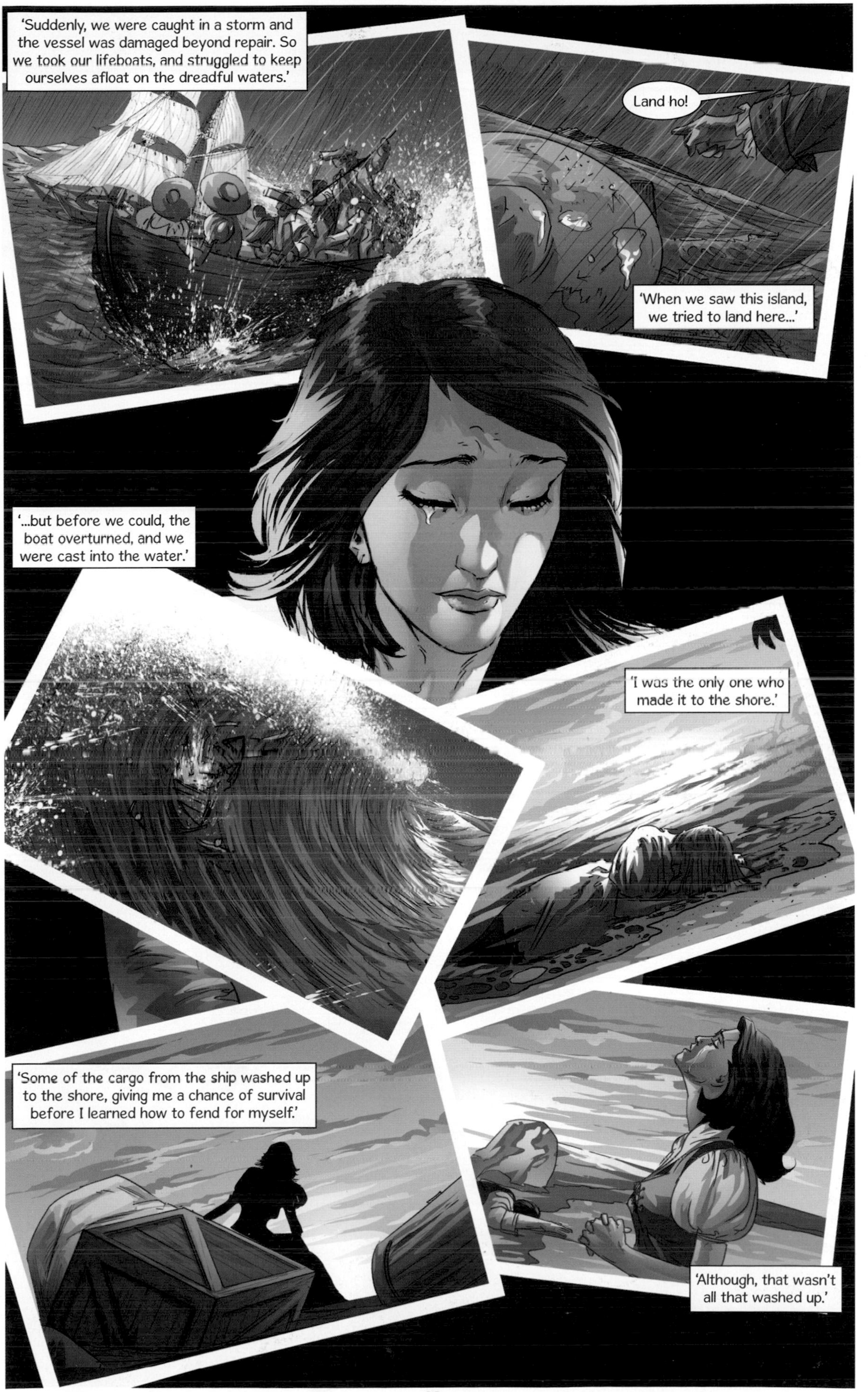
'Suddenly, we were caught in a storm and the vessel was damaged beyond repair. So we took our lifeboats, and struggled to keep ourselves afloat on the dreadful waters.'
Land ho!
'When we saw this island, we tried to land here...'
'...but before we could, the boat overturned, and we were cast into the water.'
'I was the only one who made it to the shore.'
'Some of the cargo from the ship washed up to the shore, giving me a chance of survival before I learned how to fend for myself.'
'Although, that wasn't all that washed up.'

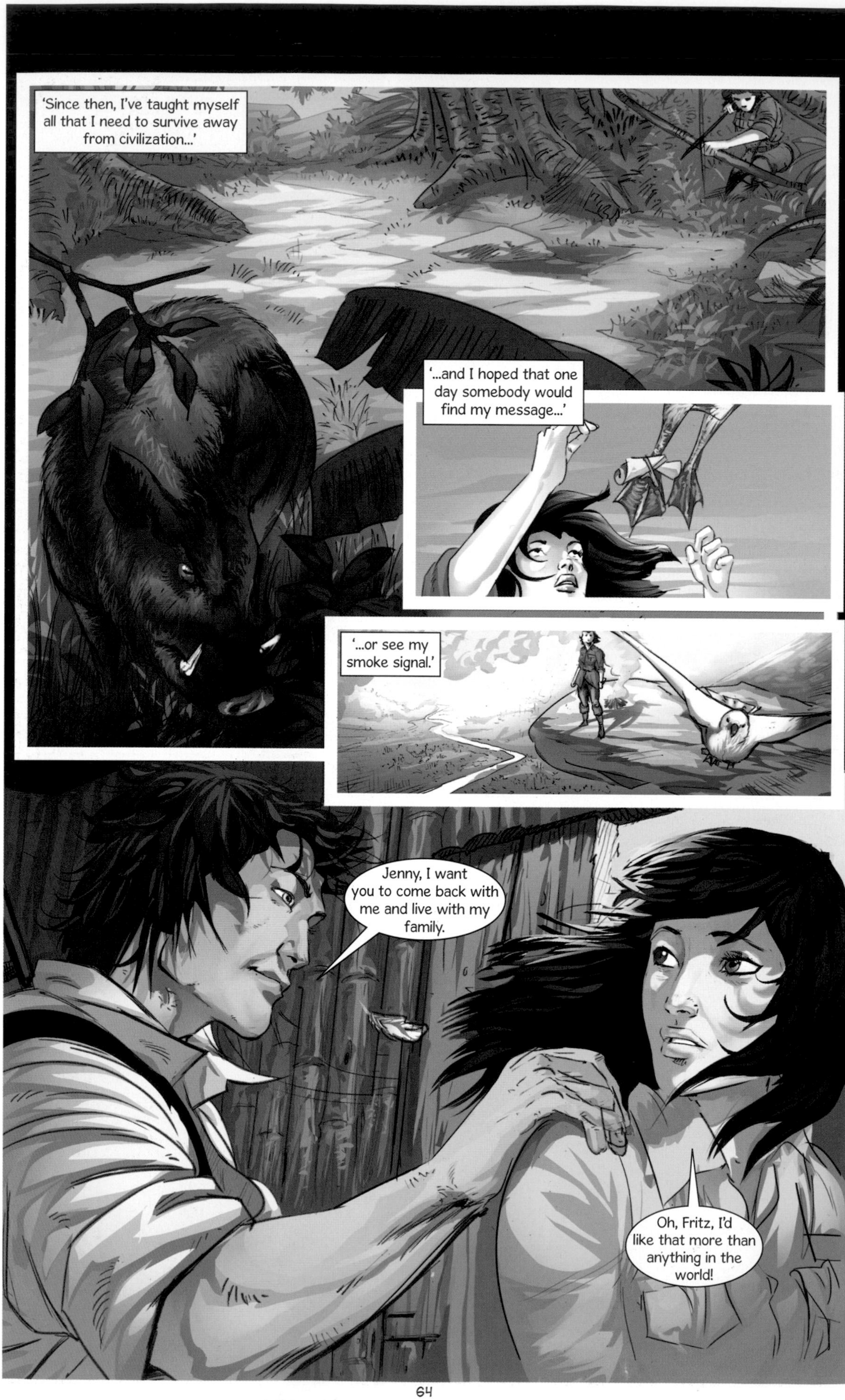
'Since then, I've taught myself all that I need to survive away from civilization...'
'...and I hoped that one day somebody would find my message...'
'...or see my smoke signal.'
Jenny, I want you to come back with me and live with my family.
Oh, Fritz, I'd like that more than anything in the world!

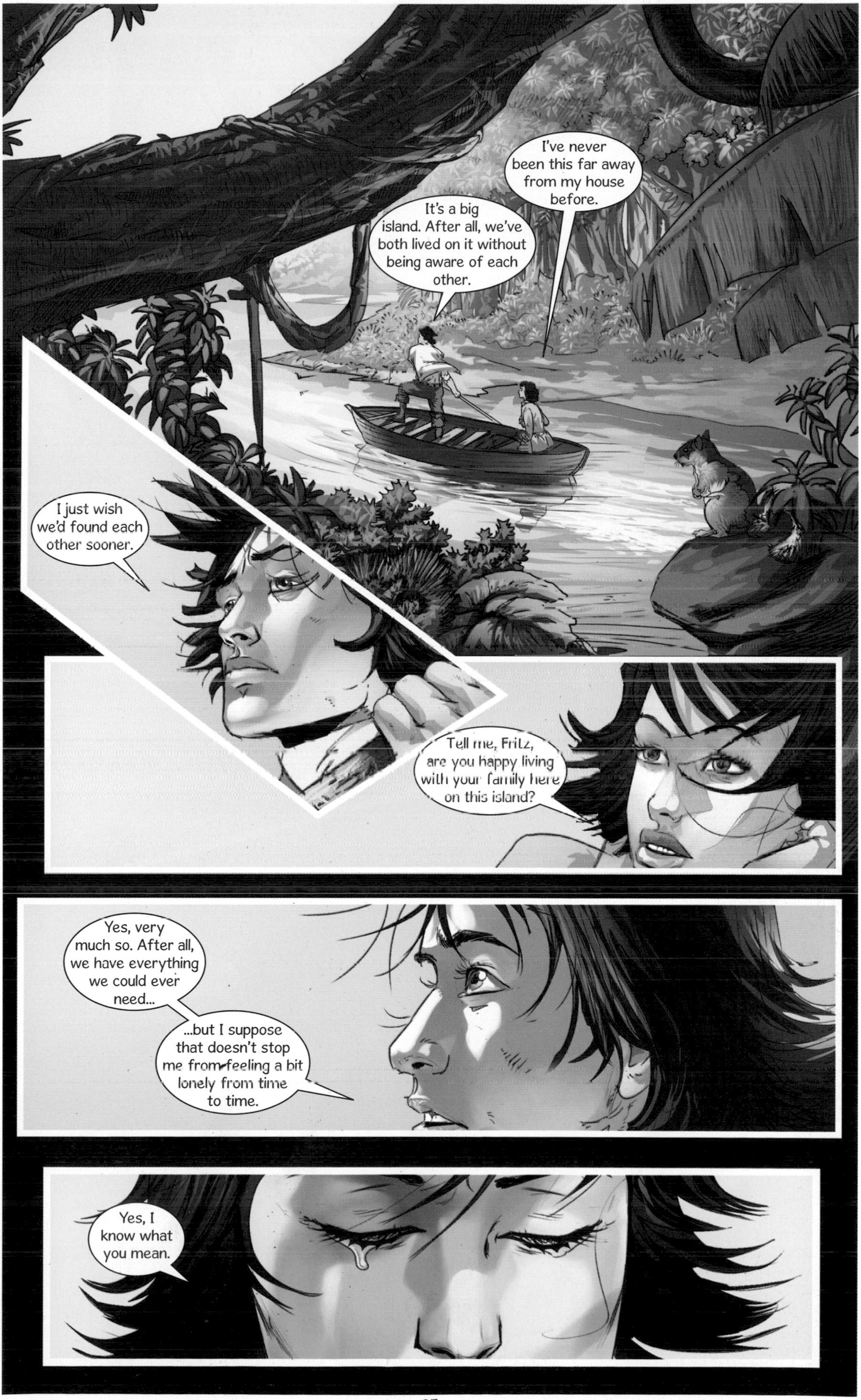
It's a big island. After all, we've both lived on it without being aware of each other.
I've never been this far away from my house before.
I just wish we'd found each other sooner.
Tell me, Fritz, are you happy living with your family here on this island?
Yes, very much so. After all, we have everything we could ever need...
...but I suppose that doesn't stop me from feeling a bit lonely from time to time.
Yes, I know what you mean.

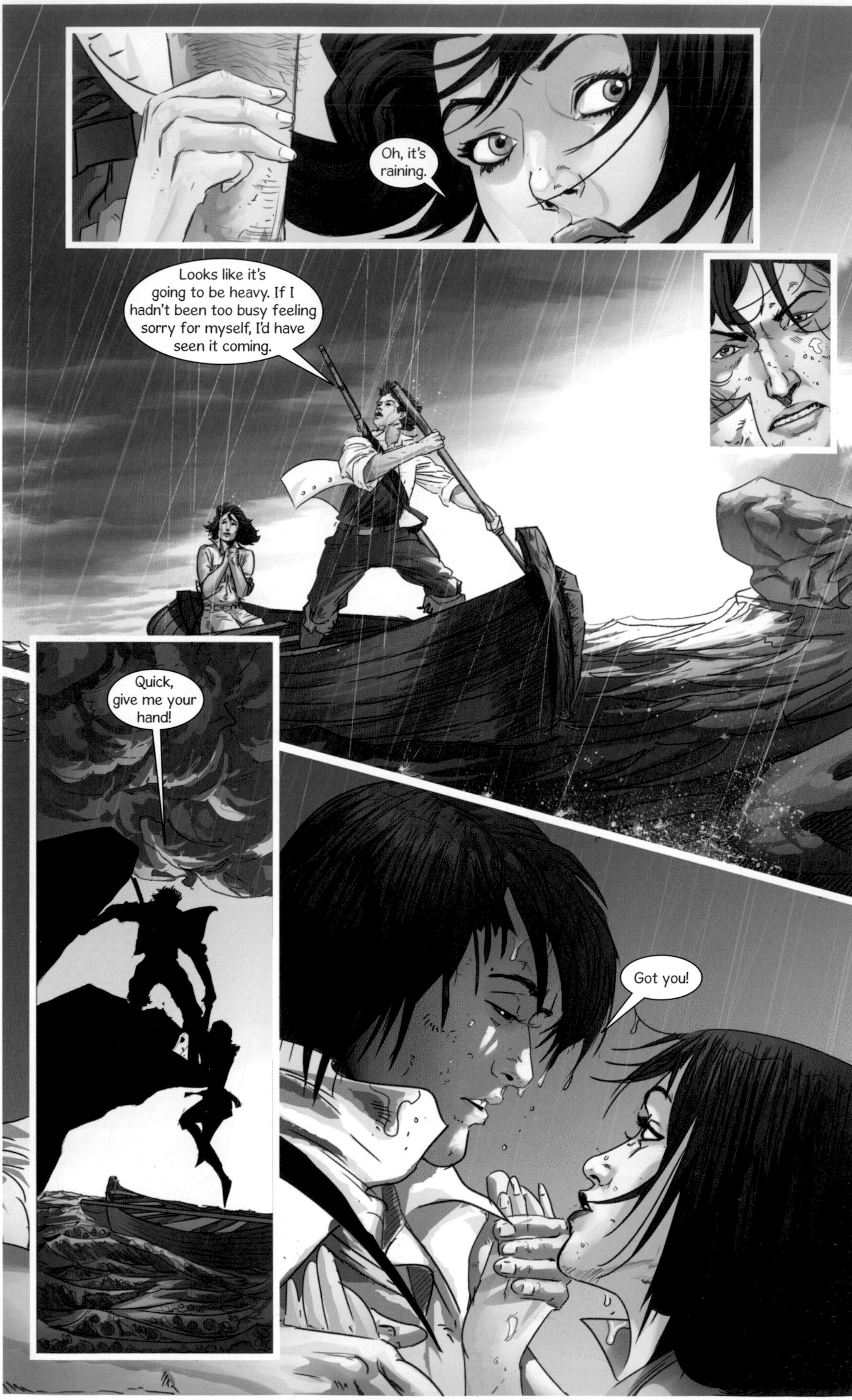
Oh, it's raining.
Looks like it's going to be heavy. If I hadn't been too busy feeling sorry for myself, I'd have seen it coming.
Quick, give me your hand!
Got you!

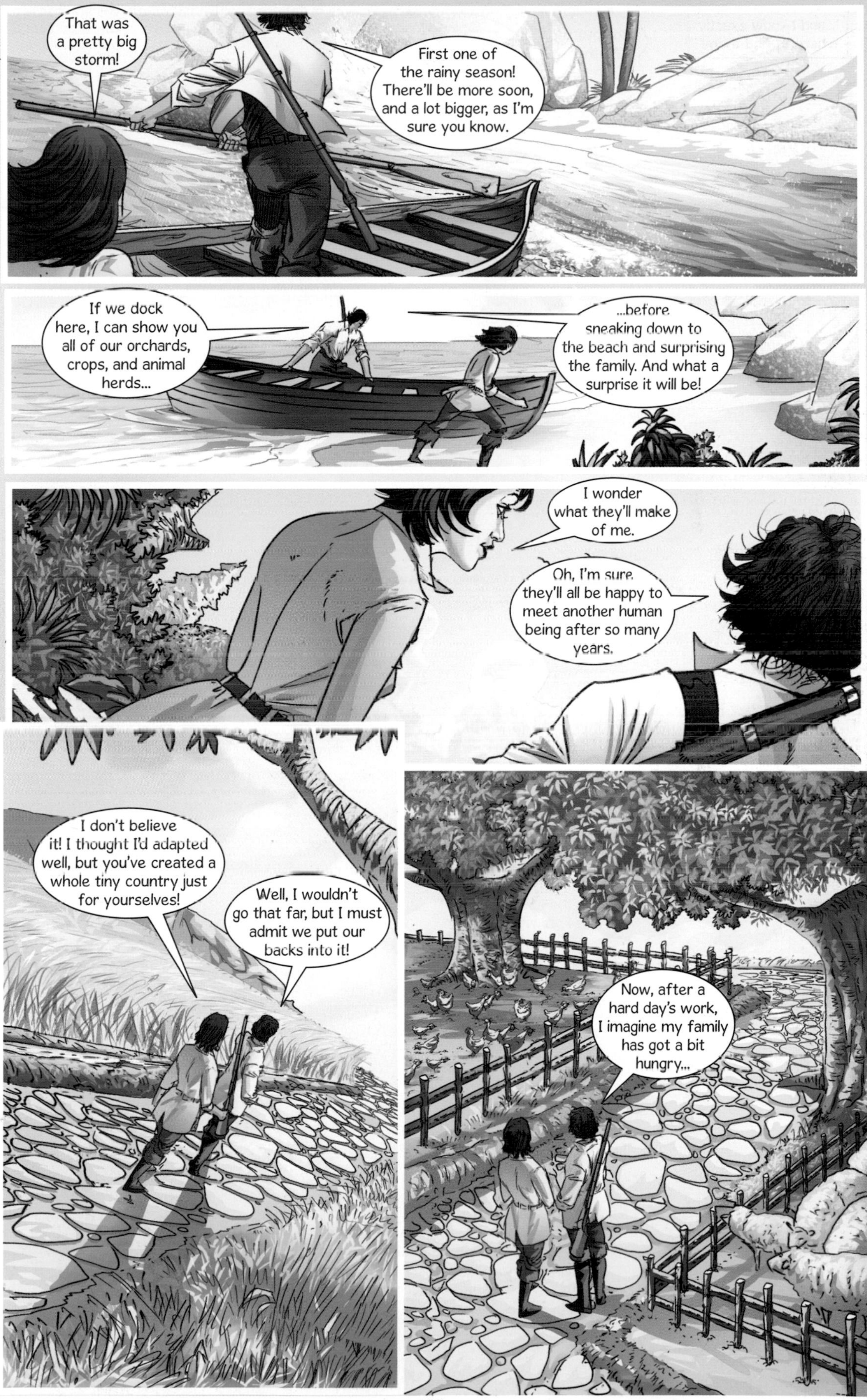
That was a pretty big storm!
First one of the rainy season! There'll be more soon, and a lot bigger, as I'm sure you know.
If we dock here, I can show you all of our orchards, crops, and animal herds...
...before sneaking down to the beach and surprising the family. And what a surprise it will be!
I wonder what they'll make of me.
Oh, I'm sure they'll all be happy to meet another human being after so many years.
I don't believe it! I thought I'd adapted well, but you've created a whole tiny country just for yourselves!
Well, I wouldn't go that far, but I must admit we put our backs into it!
Now, after a hard day's work, I imagine my family has got a bit hungry...

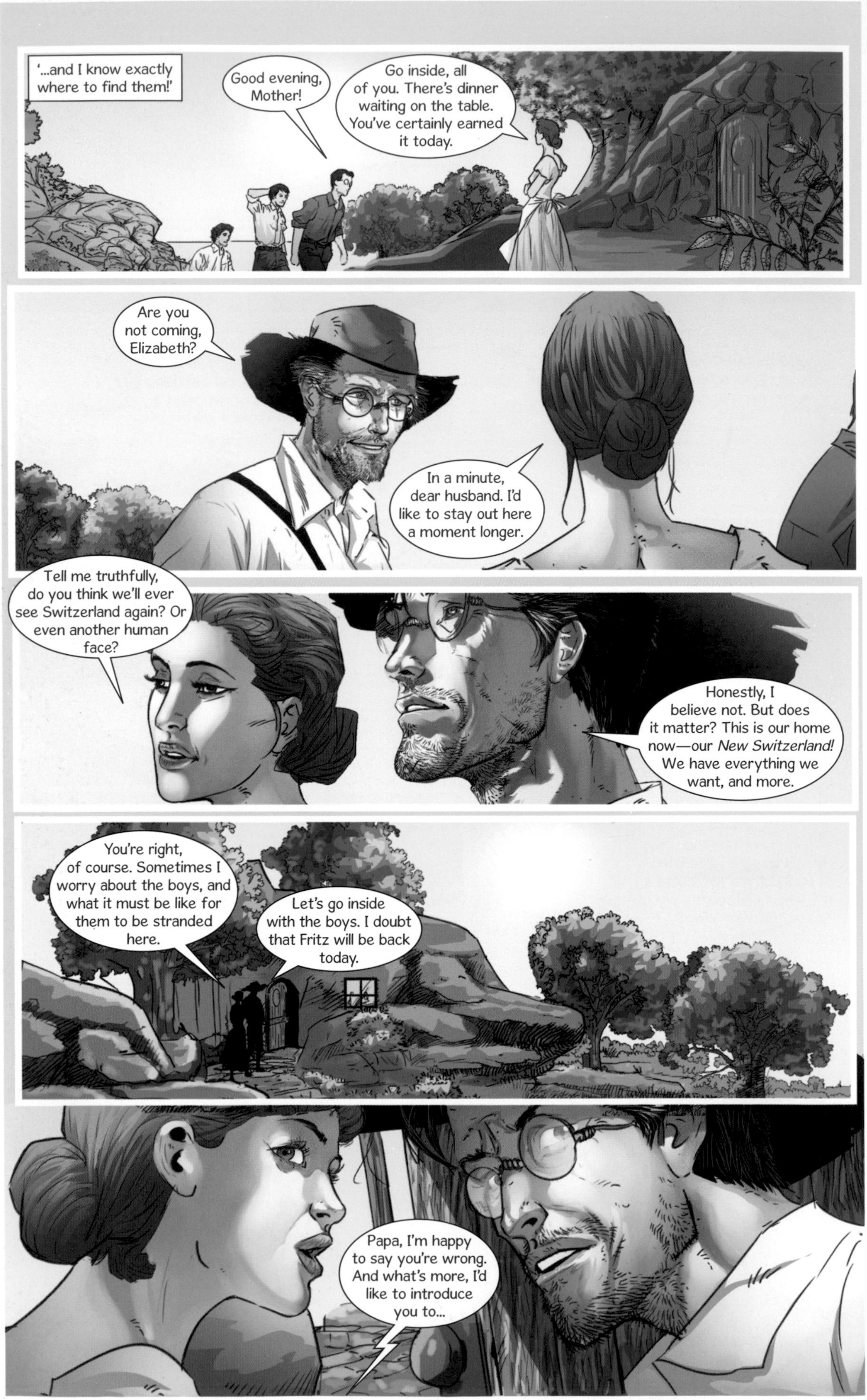
'...and I know exactly where to find them!'
Good evening, Mother!
Go inside, all of you. There's dinner waiting on the table. You've certainly earned it today.
Are you not coming, Elizabeth?
In a minute, dear husband. I'd like to stay out here a moment longer.
Tell me truthfully, do you think we'll ever see Switzerland again? Or even another human face?
Honestly, I believe not. But does it matter? This is our home now—our *New Switzerland!* We have everything we want, and more.
You're right, of course. Sometimes I worry about the boys, and what it must be like for them to be stranded here.
Let's go inside with the boys. I doubt that Fritz will be back today.
Papa, I'm happy to say you're wrong. And what's more, I'd like to introduce you to...

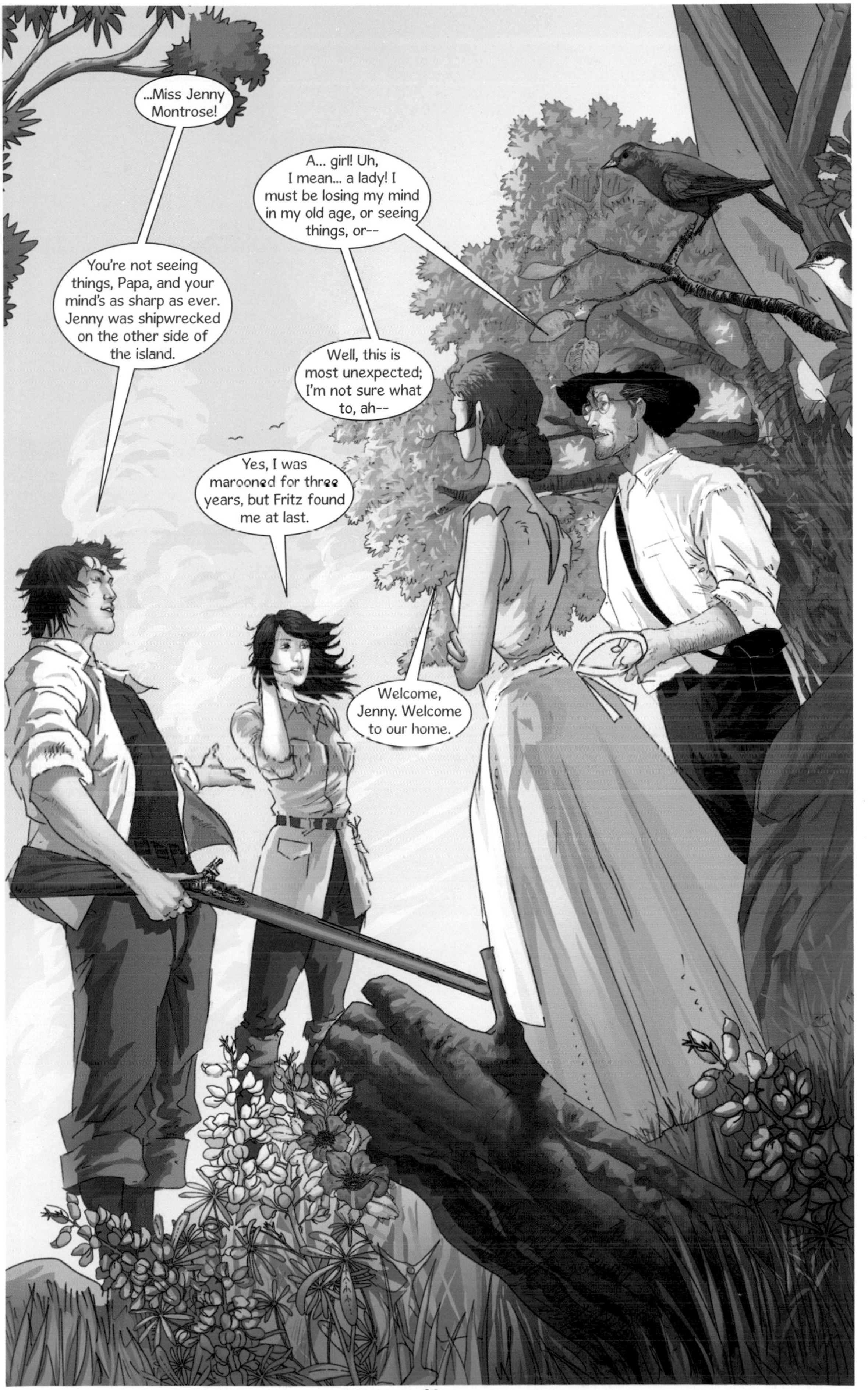
...Miss Jenny Montrose!
You're not seeing things, Papa, and your mind's as sharp as ever. Jenny was shipwrecked on the other side of the island.
A... girl! Uh, I mean... a lady! I must be losing my mind in my old age, or seeing things, or--
Well, this is most unexpected; I'm not sure what to, ah--
Yes, I was marooned for three years, but Fritz found me at last.
Welcome, Jenny. Welcome to our home.

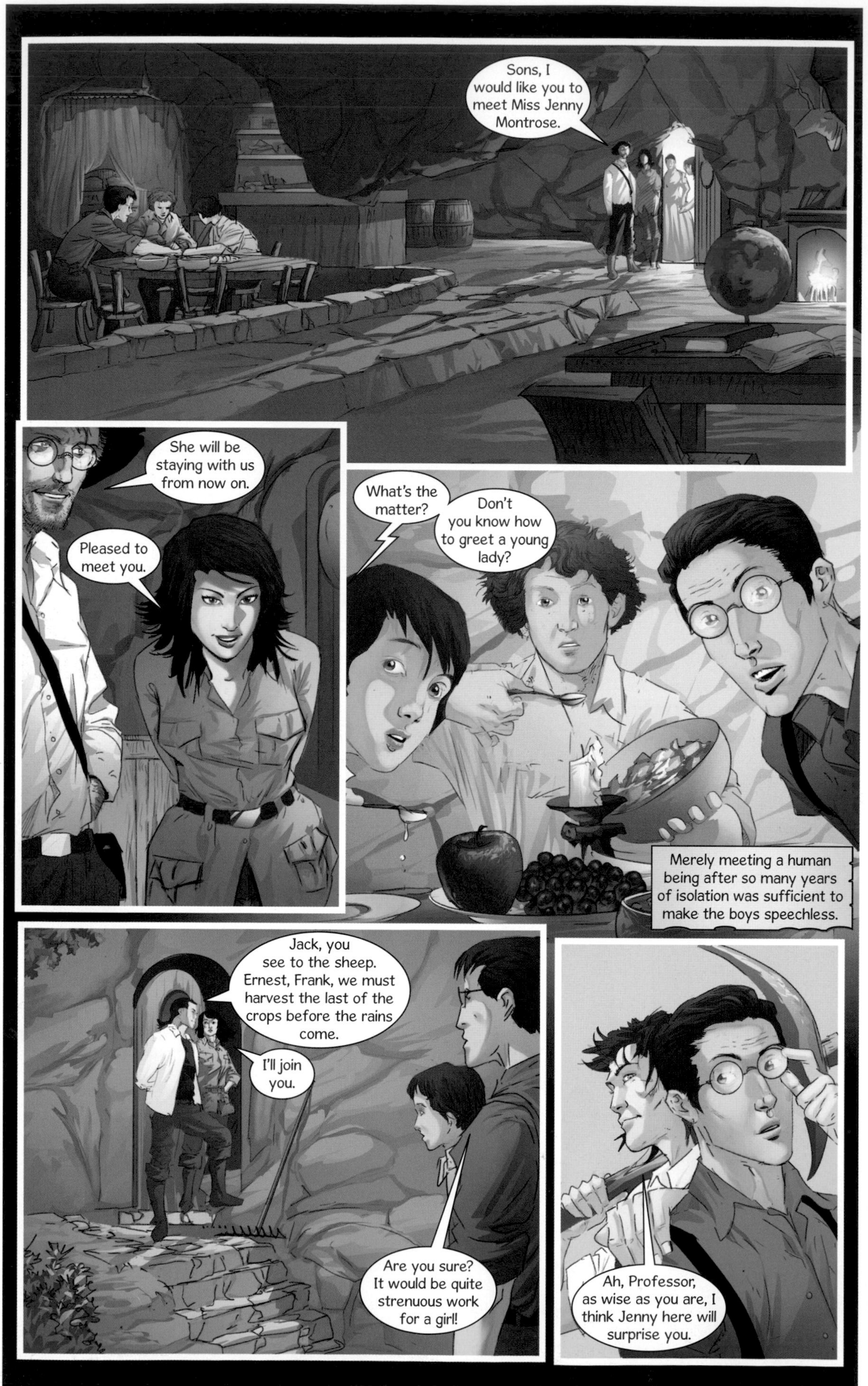
Sons, I would like you to meet Miss Jenny Montrose.
She will be staying with us from now on.
Pleased to meet you.
What's the matter?
Don't you know how to greet a young lady?
Merely meeting a human being after so many years of isolation was sufficient to make the boys speechless.
Jack, you see to the sheep. Ernest, Frank, we must harvest the last of the crops before the rains come.
I'll join you.
Are you sure? It would be quite strenuous work for a girl!
Ah, Professor, as wise as you are, I think Jenny here will surprise you.

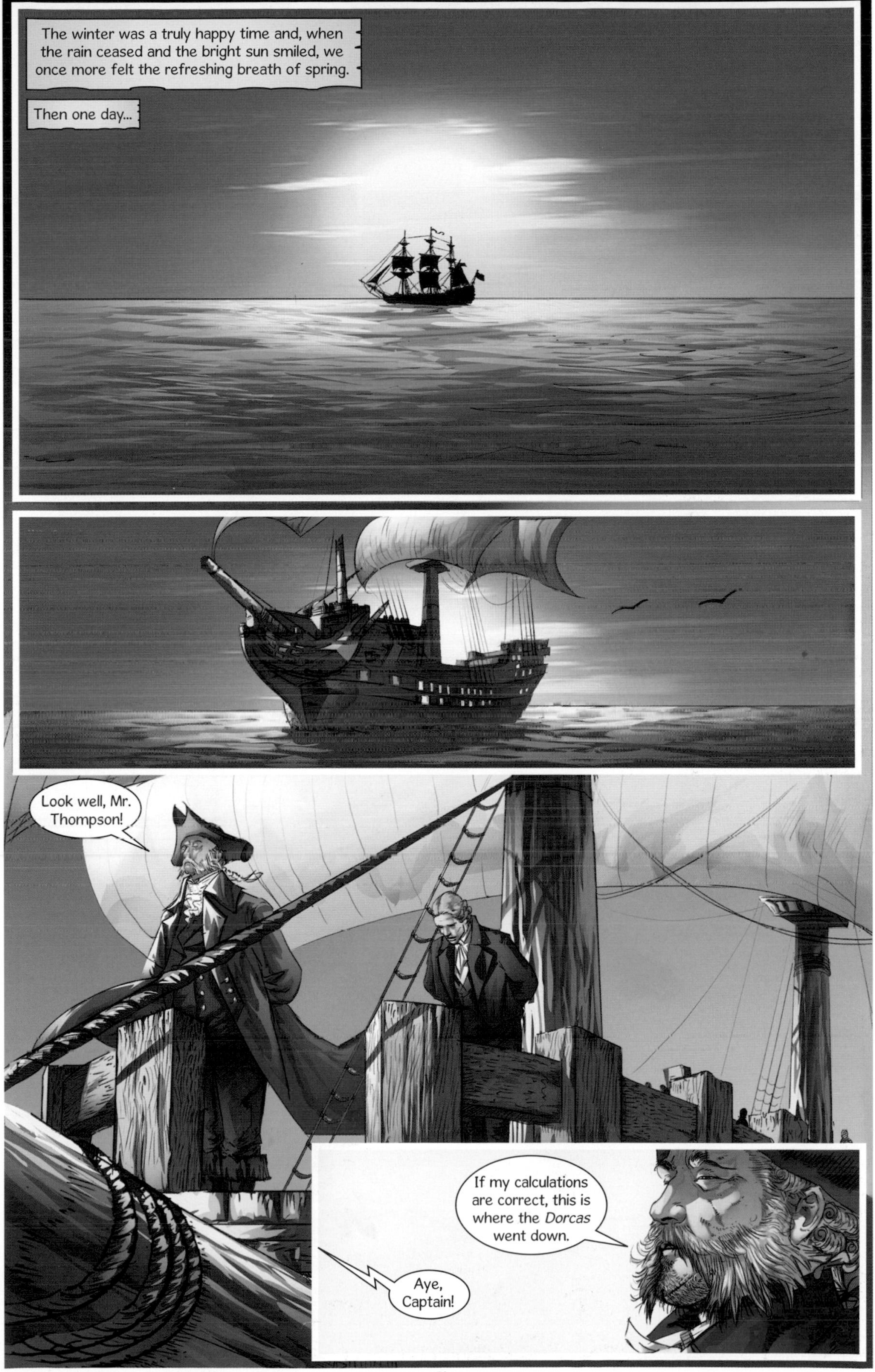
The winter was a truly happy time and, when the rain ceased and the bright sun smiled, we once more felt the refreshing breath of spring.
Then one day...
Look well, Mr. Thompson!
If my calculations are correct, this is where the *Dorcas* went down.
Aye, Captain!

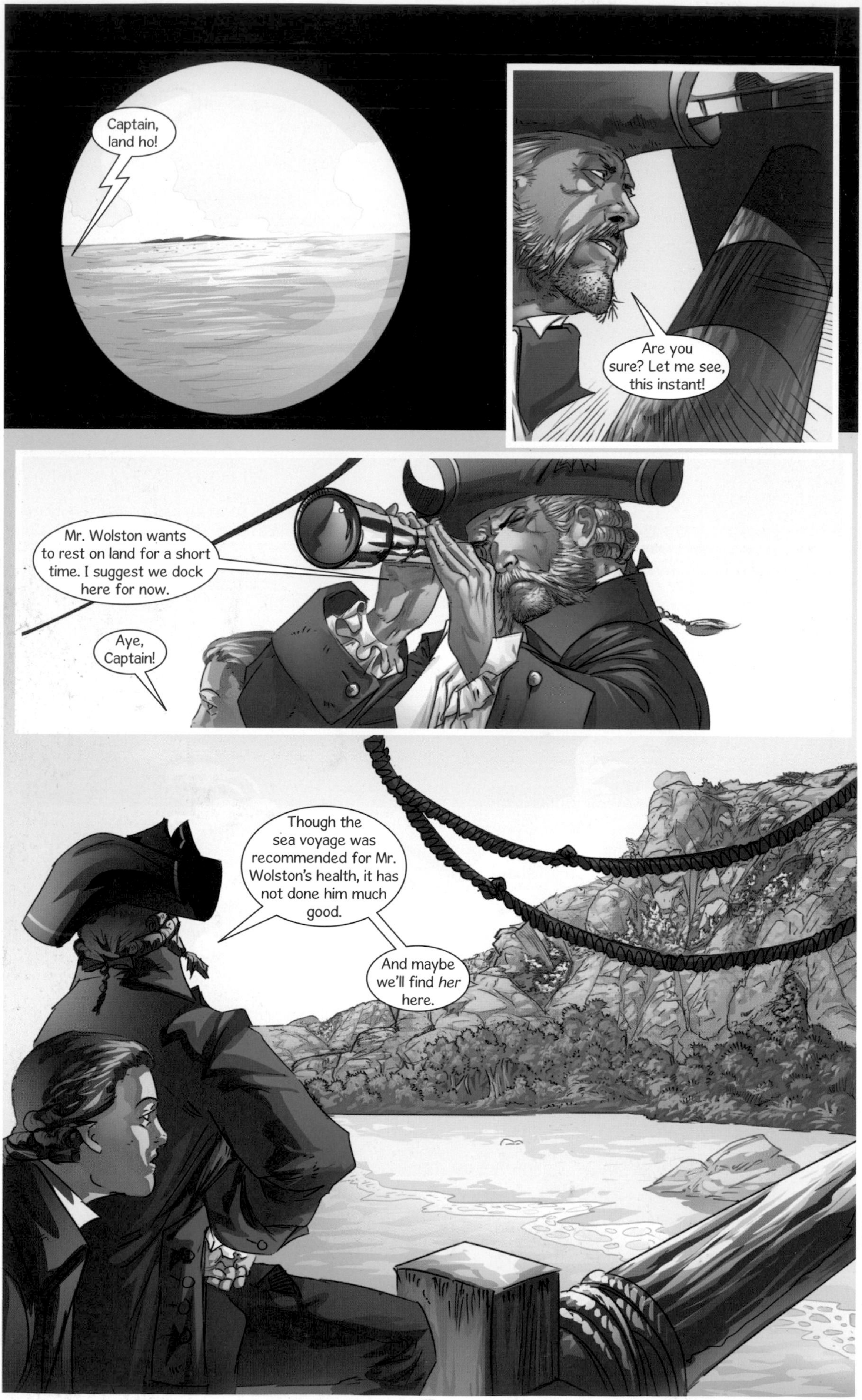
Captain,
land ho!
Are you sure? Let me see, this instant!
Mr. Wolston wants to rest on land for a short time. I suggest we dock here for now.
Aye, Captain!
Though the sea voyage was recommended for Mr. Wolston's health, it has not done him much good.
And maybe we'll find *her* here.

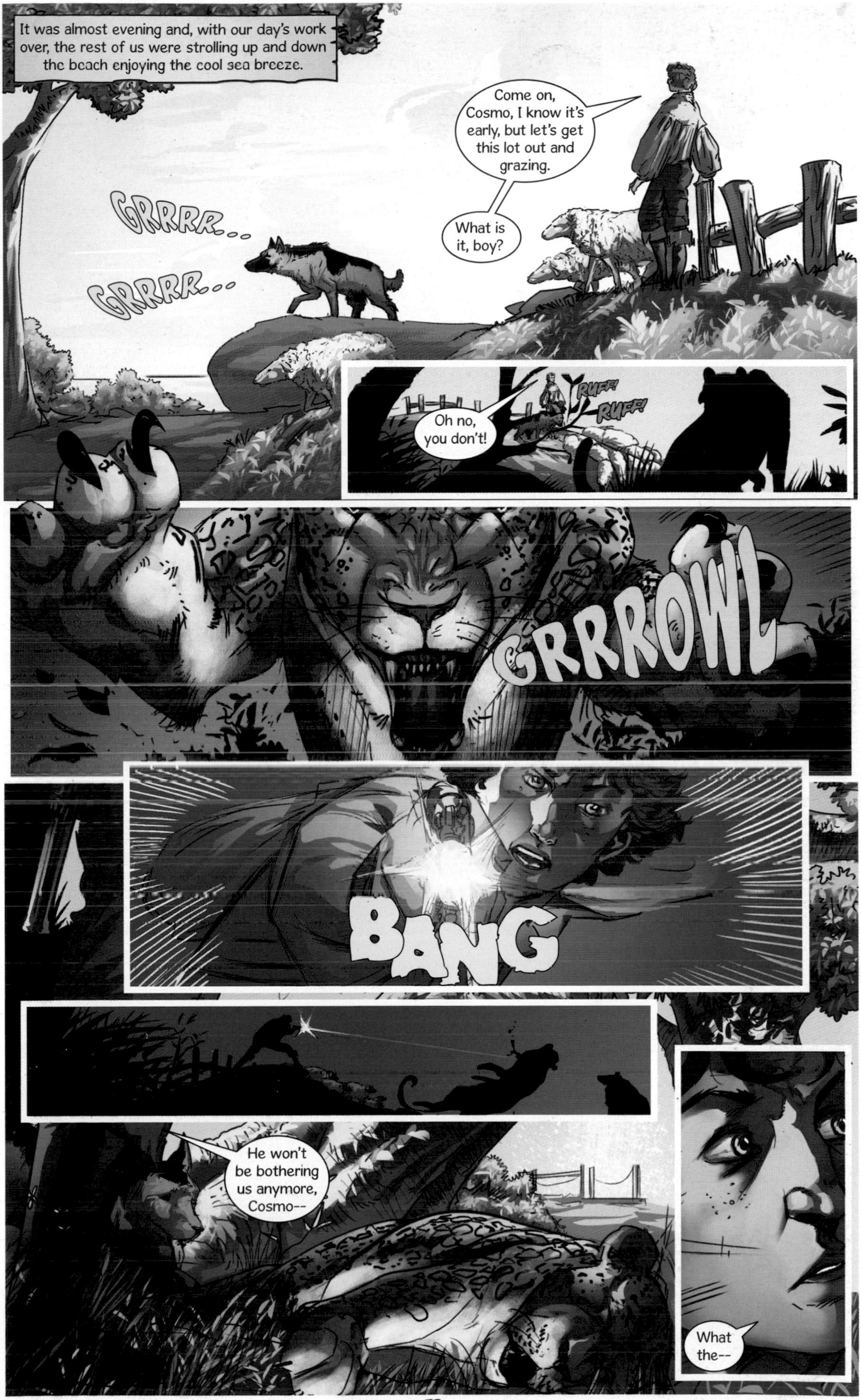

It was almost evening and, with our day's work over, the rest of us were strolling up and down the beach enjoying the cool sea breeze.
Come on, Cosmo, I know it's early, but let's get this lot out and grazing.
What is it, boy?
GRRRR...
GRRRR...
RUFF!
RUFF!
Oh no, you don't!
GRRROWL
BANG
He won't be bothering us anymore, Cosmo--
What the--

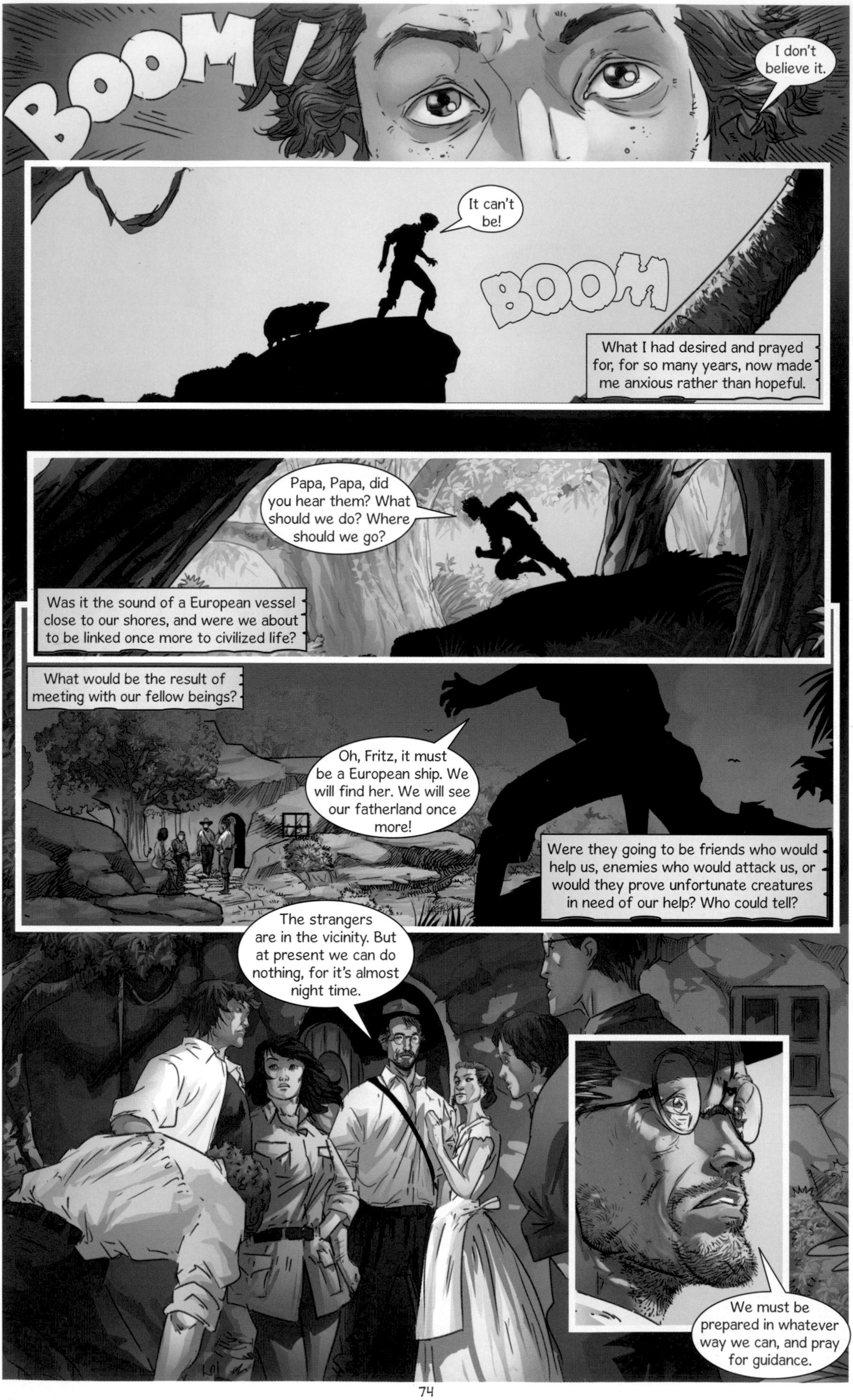
BOOM!
I don't believe it.
It can't be!
BOOM
What I had desired and prayed for, for so many years, now made me anxious rather than hopeful.
Papa, Papa, did you hear them? What should we do? Where should we go?
Was it the sound of a European vessel close to our shores, and were we about to be linked once more to civilized life?
What would be the result of meeting with our fellow beings?
Oh, Fritz, it must be a European ship. We will find her. We will see our fatherland once more!
Were they going to be friends who would help us, enemies who would attack us, or would they prove unfortunate creatures in need of our help? Who could tell?
The strangers are in the vicinity. But at present we can do nothing, for it's almost night time.
We must be prepared in whatever way we can, and pray for guidance.

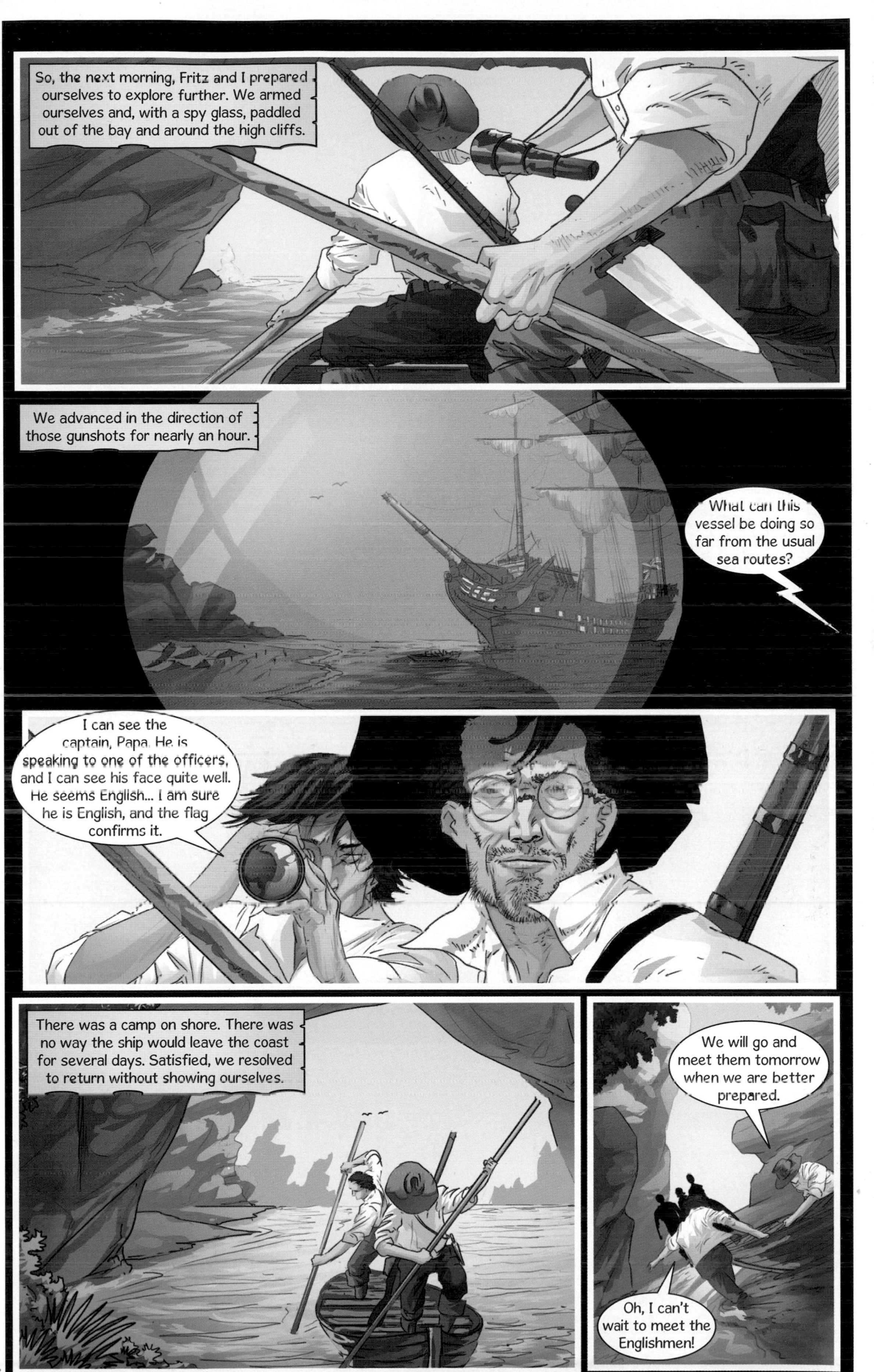
So, the next morning, Fritz and I prepared ourselves to explore further. We armed ourselves and, with a spy glass, paddled out of the bay and around the high cliffs.
We advanced in the direction of those gunshots for nearly an hour.
What can this vessel be doing so far from the usual sea routes?
I can see the captain, Papa. He is speaking to one of the officers, and I can see his face quite well. He seems English... I am sure he is English, and the flag confirms it.
There was a camp on shore. There was no way the ship would leave the coast for several days. Satisfied, we resolved to return without showing ourselves.
We will go and meet them tomorrow when we are better prepared.
Oh, I can't wait to meet the Englishmen!

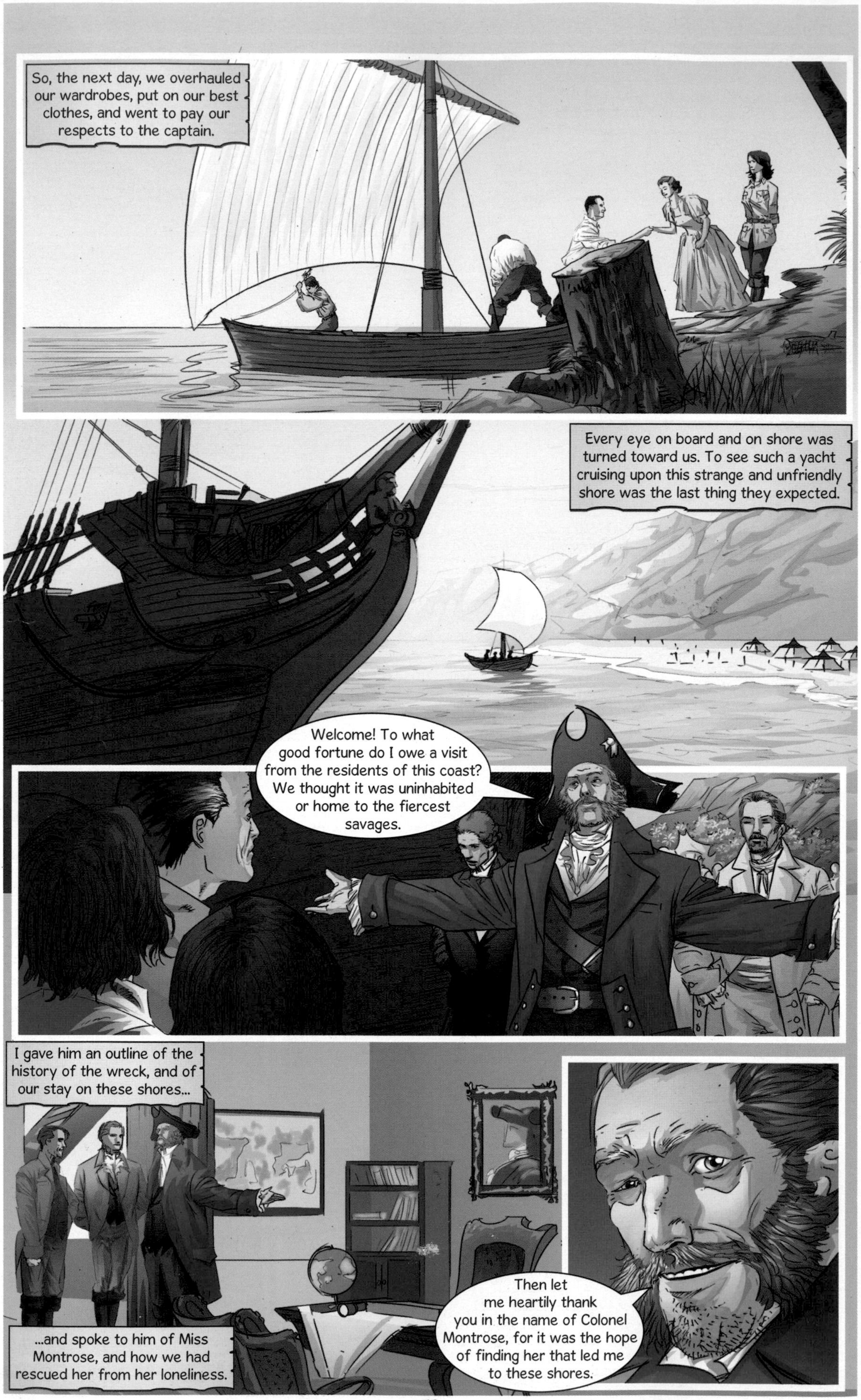
So, the next day, we overhauled our wardrobes, put on our best clothes, and went to pay our respects to the captain.
Every eye on board and on shore was turned toward us. To see such a yacht cruising upon this strange and unfriendly shore was the last thing they expected.
Welcome! To what good fortune do I owe a visit from the residents of this coast? We thought it was uninhabited or home to the fiercest savages.
I gave him an outline of the history of the wreck, and of our stay on these shores...
...and spoke to him of Miss Montrose, and how we had rescued her from her loneliness.
Then let me heartily thank you in the name of Colonel Montrose, for it was the hope of finding her that led me to these shores.

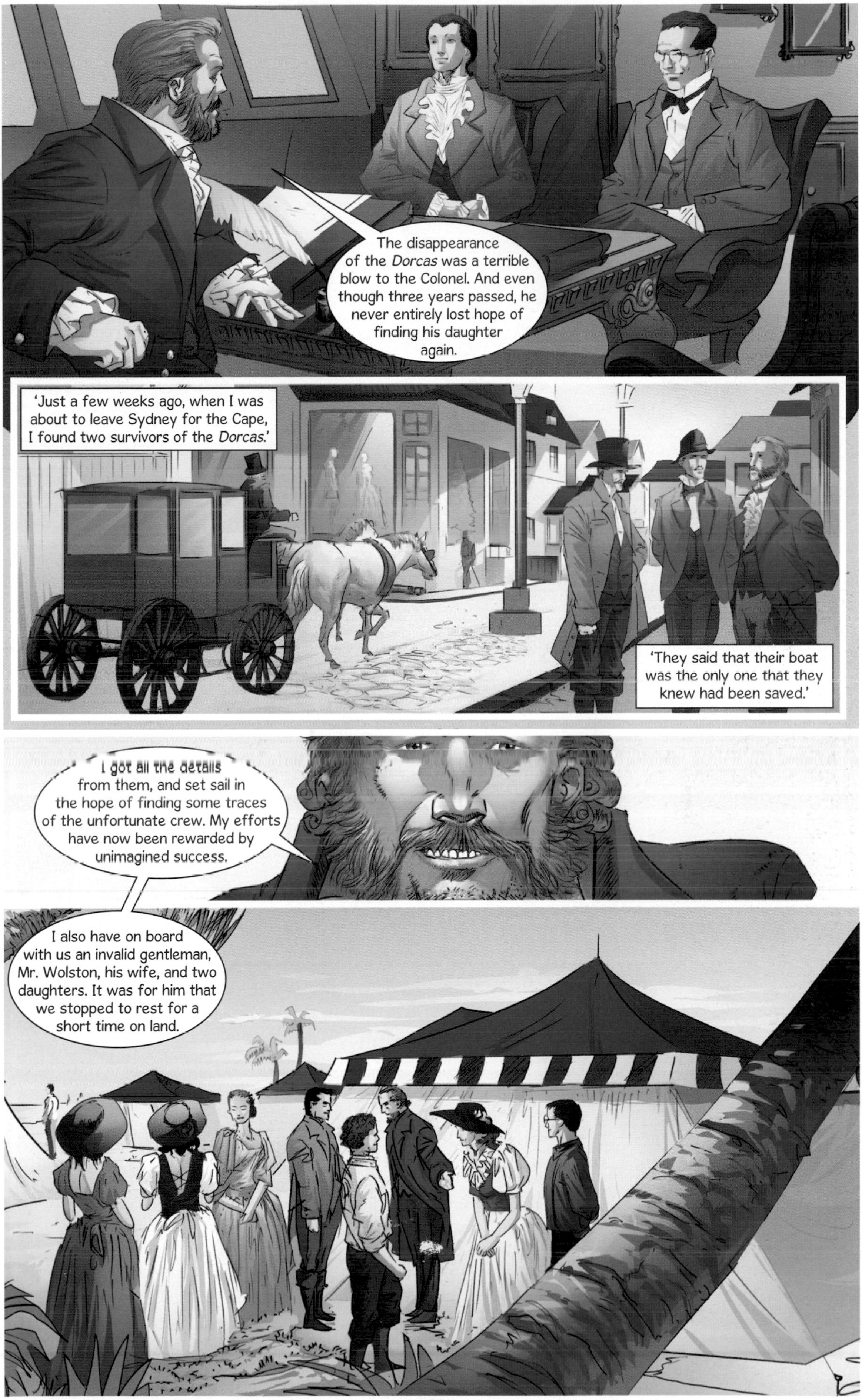
The disappearance of the *Dorcas* was a terrible blow to the Colonel. And even though three years passed, he never entirely lost hope of finding his daughter again.
'Just a few weeks ago, when I was about to leave Sydney for the Cape, I found two survivors of the *Dorcas*.'
'They said that their boat was the only one that they knew had been saved.'
I got all the details from them, and set sail in the hope of finding some traces of the unfortunate crew. My efforts have now been rewarded by unimagined success.
I also have on board with us an invalid gentleman, Mr. Wolston, his wife, and two daughters. It was for him that we stopped to rest for a short time on land.

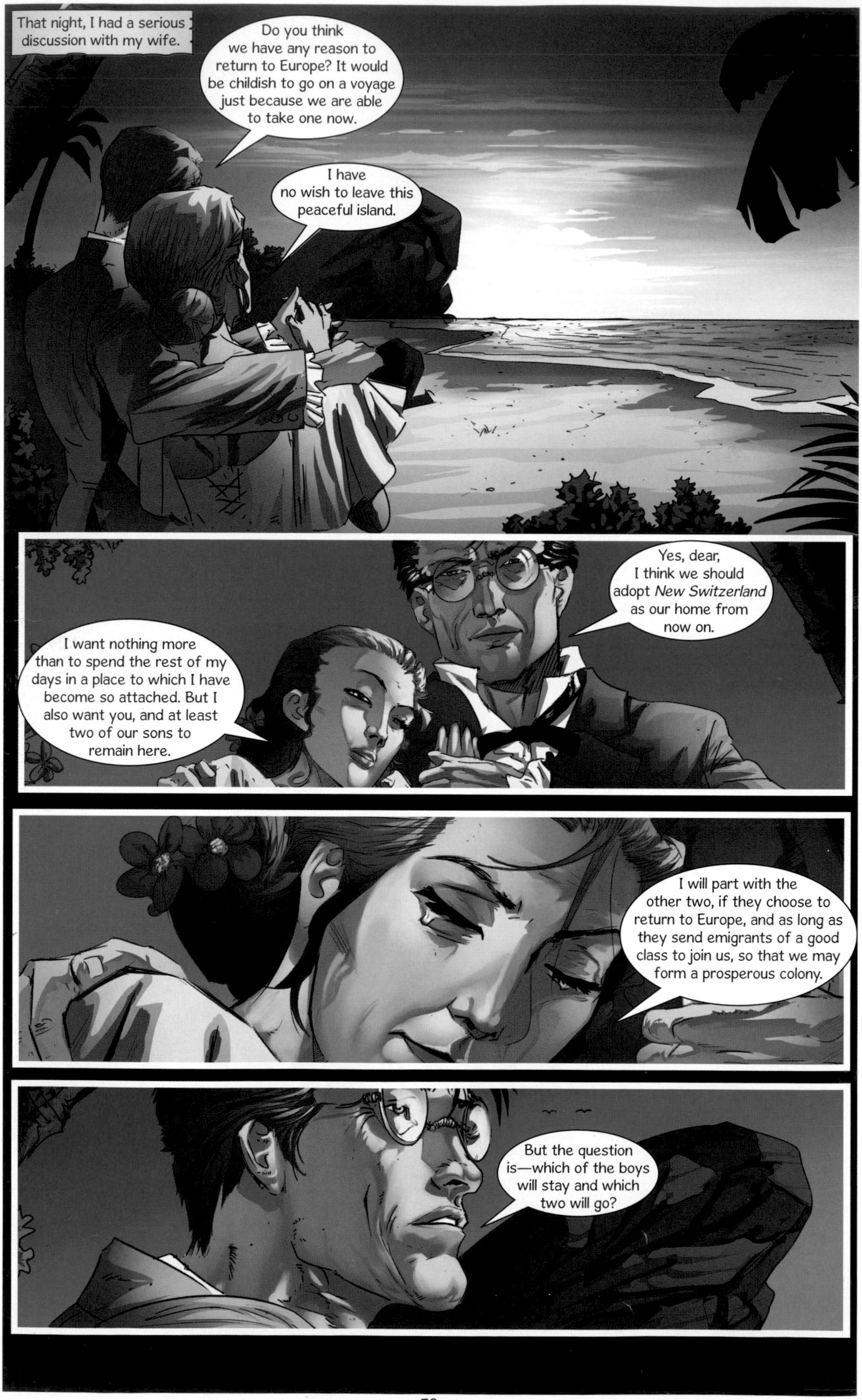
That night, I had a serious discussion with my wife.
Do you think we have any reason to return to Europe? It would be childish to go on a voyage just because we are able to take one now.
I have no wish to leave this peaceful island.
Yes, dear, I think we should adopt *New Switzerland* as our home from now on.
I want nothing more than to spend the rest of my days in a place to which I have become so attached. But I also want you, and at least two of our sons to remain here.
I will part with the other two, if they choose to return to Europe, and as long as they send emigrants of a good class to join us, so that we may form a prosperous colony.
But the question is—which of the boys will stay and which two will go?

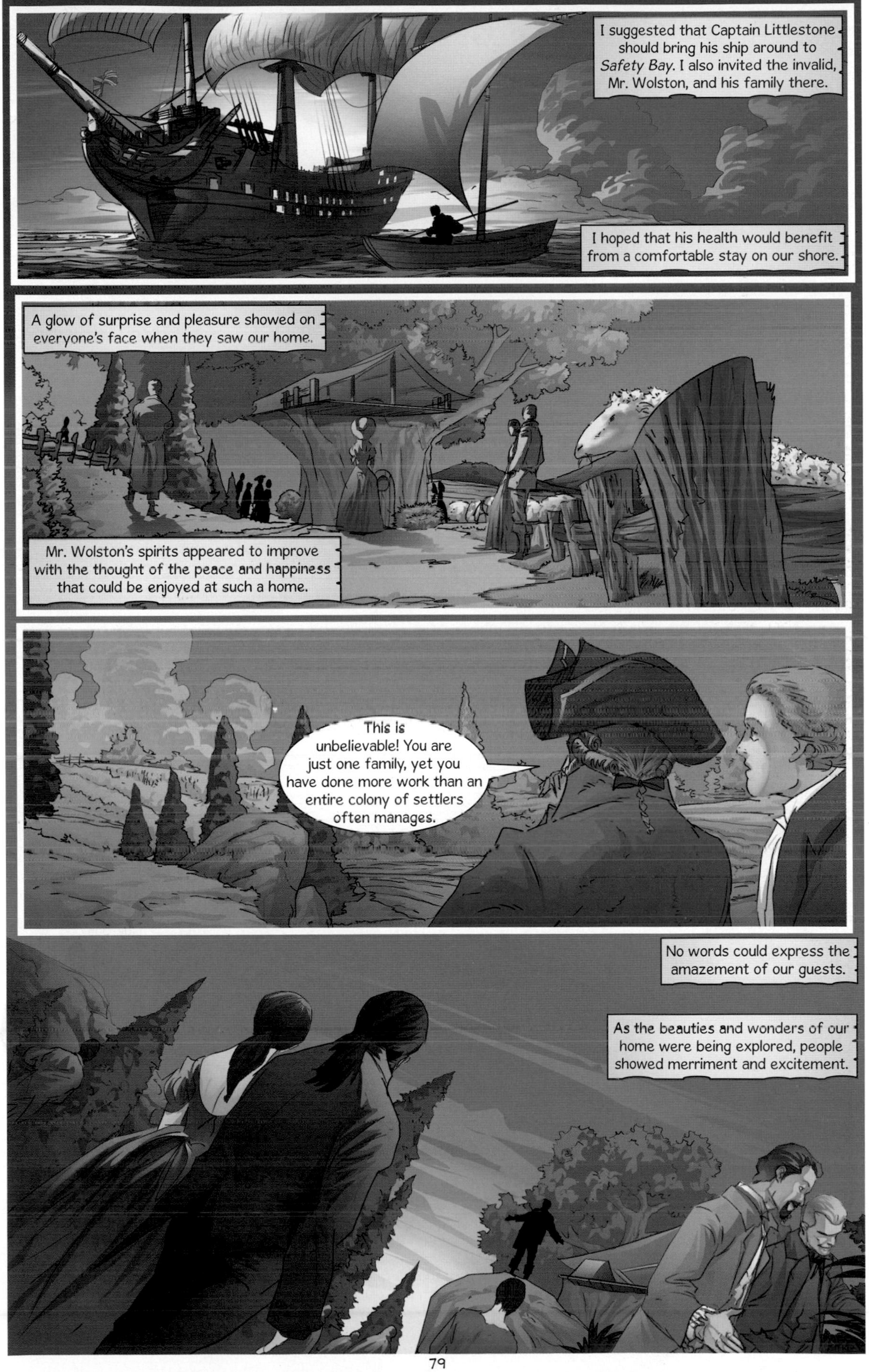
I suggested that Captain Littlestone should bring his ship around to *Safety Bay*. I also invited the invalid, Mr. Wolston, and his family there.
I hoped that his health would benefit from a comfortable stay on our shore.
A glow of surprise and pleasure showed on everyone's face when they saw our home.
Mr. Wolston's spirits appeared to improve with the thought of the peace and happiness that could be enjoyed at such a home.
This is unbelievable! You are just one family, yet you have done more work than an entire colony of settlers often manages.
No words could express the amazement of our guests.
As the beauties and wonders of our home were being explored, people showed merriment and excitement.

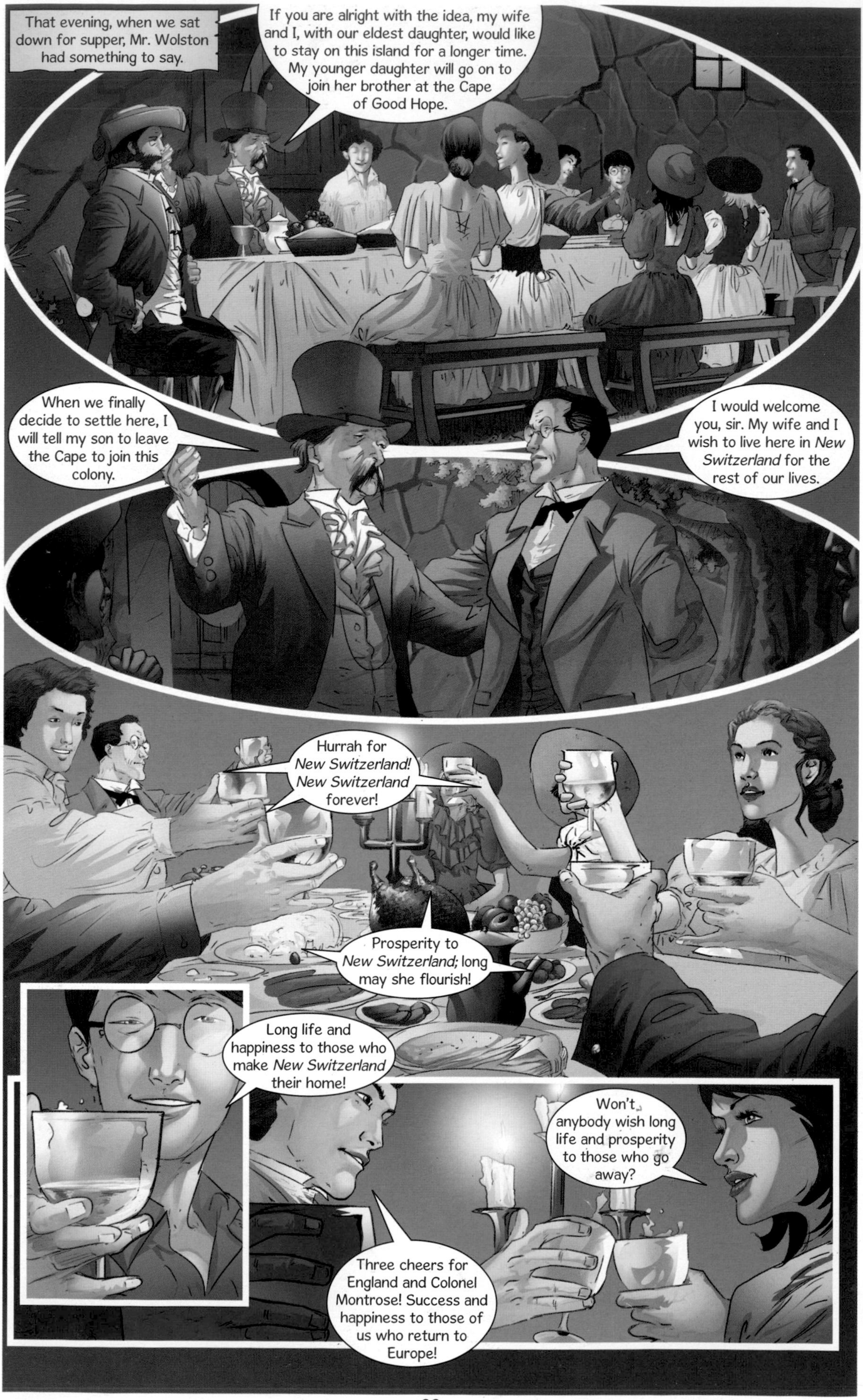

That evening, when we sat down for supper, Mr. Wolston had something to say.
If you are alright with the idea, my wife and I, with our eldest daughter, would like to stay on this island for a longer time. My younger daughter will go on to join her brother at the Cape of Good Hope.
When we finally decide to settle here, I will tell my son to leave the Cape to join this colony.
I would welcome you, sir. My wife and I wish to live here in *New Switzerland* for the rest of our lives.
Hurrah for *New Switzerland! New Switzerland* forever!
Prosperity to *New Switzerland;* long may she flourish!
Long life and happiness to those who make *New Switzerland* their home!
Won't anybody wish long life and prosperity to those who go away?
Three cheers for England and Colonel Montrose! Success and happiness to those of us who return to Europe!

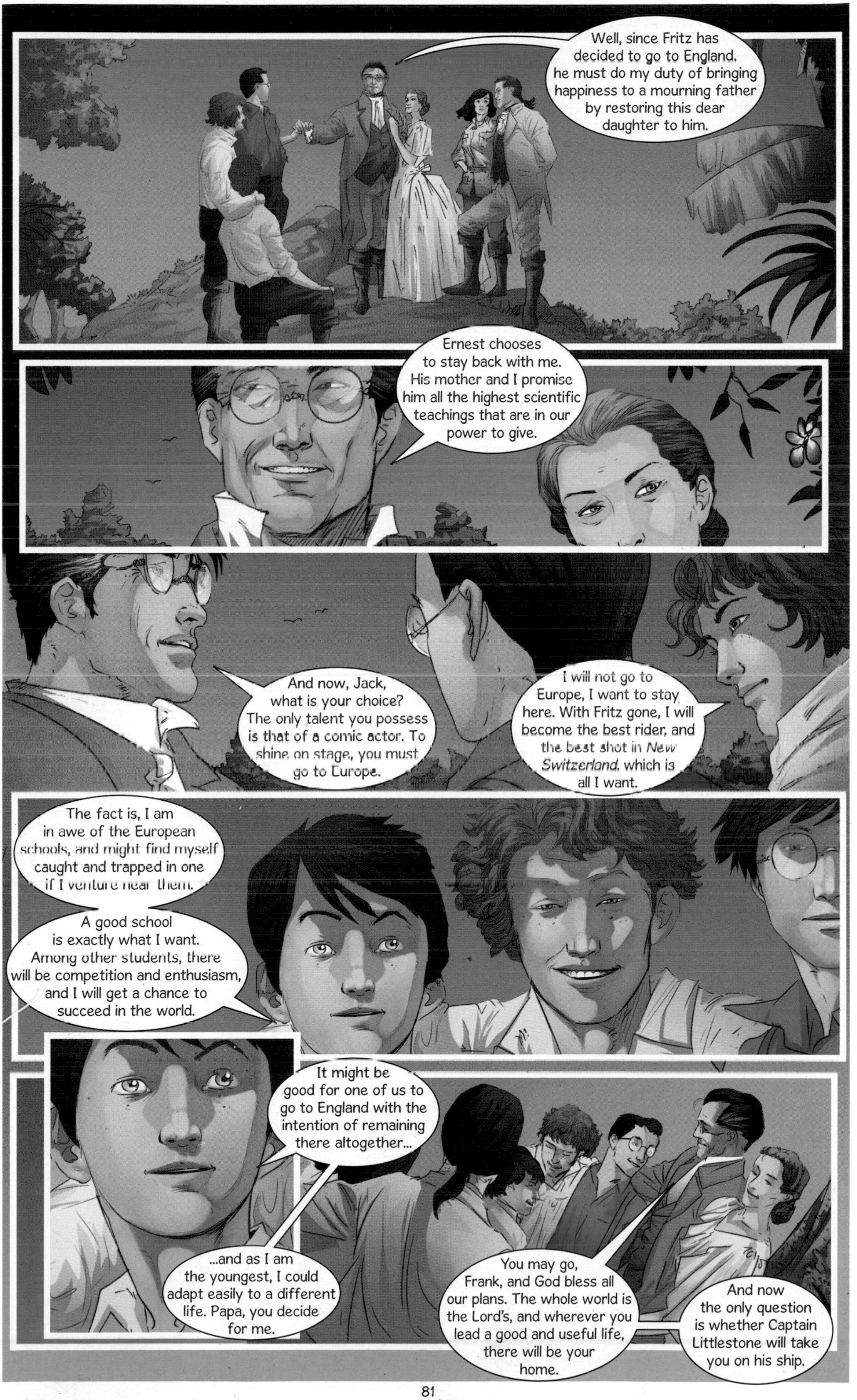
Well, since Fritz has decided to go to England, he must do my duty of bringing happiness to a mourning father by restoring this dear daughter to him.
Ernest chooses to stay back with me. His mother and I promise him all the highest scientific teachings that are in our power to give.
And now, Jack, what is your choice? The only talent you possess is that of a comic actor. To shine on stage, you must go to Europe.
I will not go to Europe, I want to stay here. With Fritz gone, I will become the best rider, and the best shot in *New Switzerland*, which is all I want.
The fact is, I am in awe of the European schools, and might find myself caught and trapped in one if I venture near them.
A good school is exactly what I want. Among other students, there will be competition and enthusiasm, and I will get a chance to succeed in the world.
It might be good for one of us to go to England with the intention of remaining there altogether...
...and as I am the youngest, I could adapt easily to a different life. Papa, you decide for me.
You may go, Frank, and God bless all our plans. The whole world is the Lord's, and wherever you lead a good and useful life, there will be your home.
And now the only question is whether Captain Littlestone will take you on his ship.

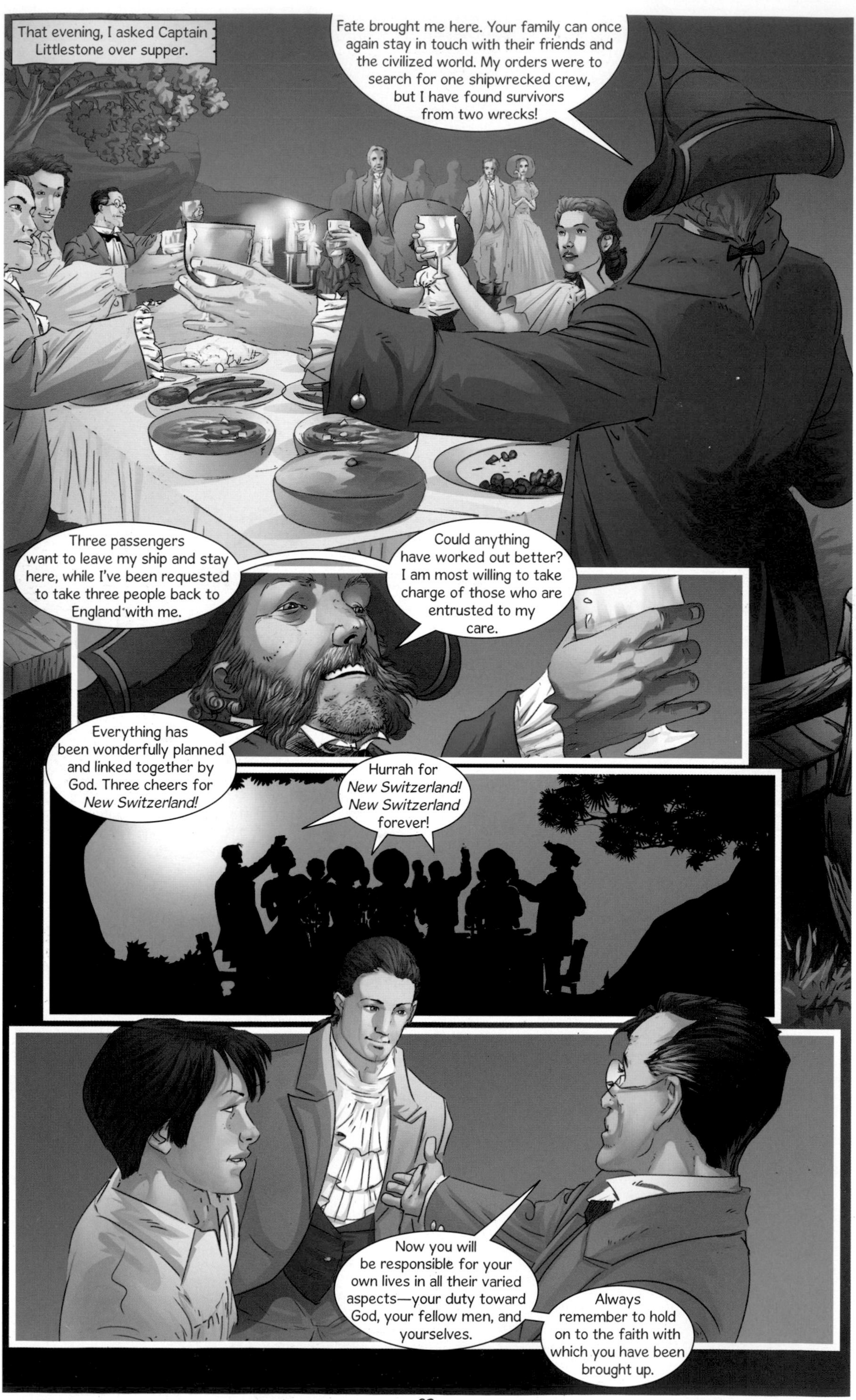
That evening, I asked Captain Littlestone over supper.
Fate brought me here. Your family can once again stay in touch with their friends and the civilized world. My orders were to search for one shipwrecked crew, but I have found survivors from two wrecks!
Three passengers want to leave my ship and stay here, while I've been requested to take three people back to England with me.
Could anything have worked out better? I am most willing to take charge of those who are entrusted to my care.
Everything has been wonderfully planned and linked together by God. Three cheers for *New Switzerland!*
Hurrah for *New Switzerland! New Switzerland* forever!
Now you will be responsible for your own lives in all their varied aspects—your duty toward God, your fellow men, and yourselves.
Always remember to hold on to the faith with which you have been brought up.

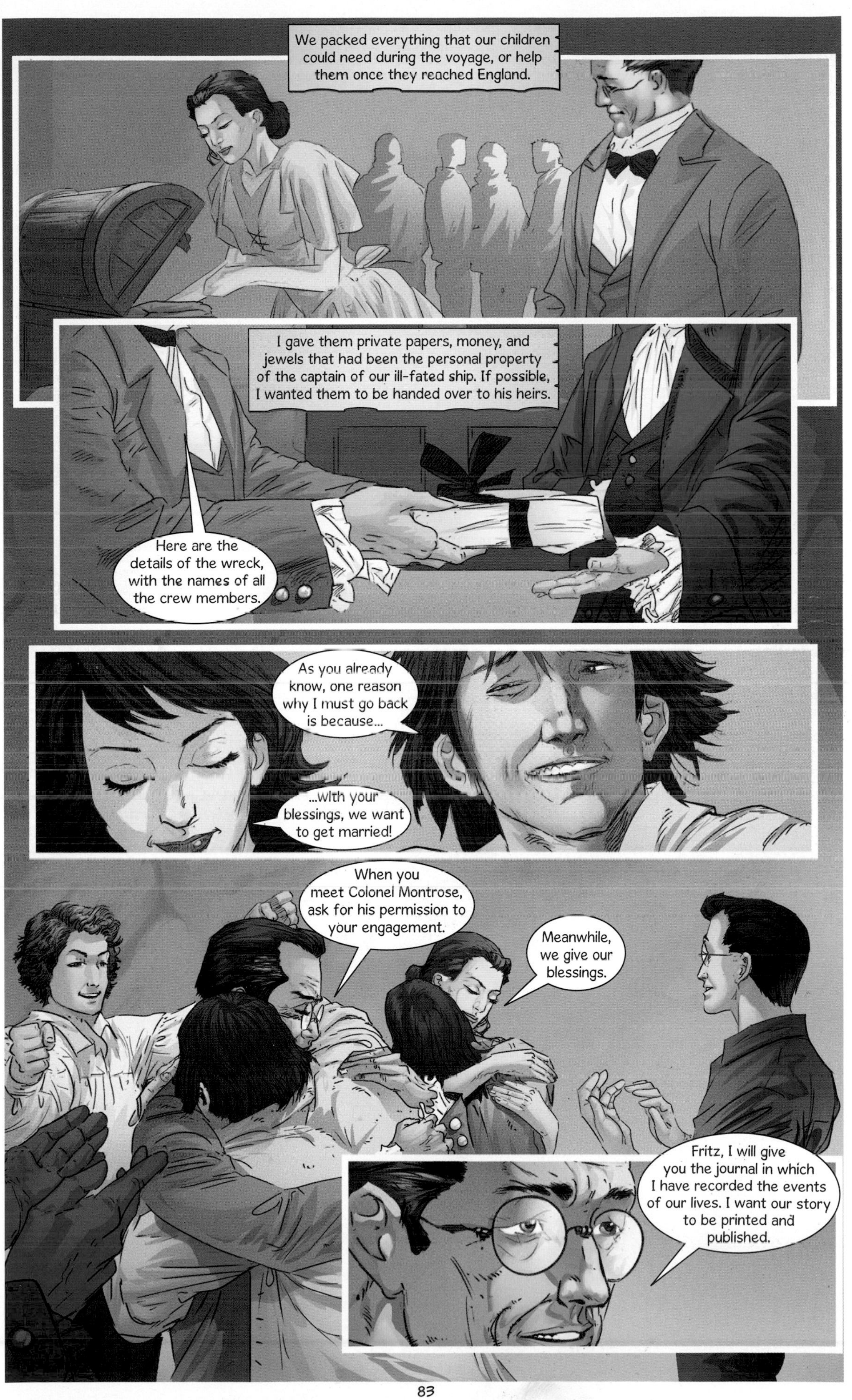
We packed everything that our children could need during the voyage, or help them once they reached England.
I gave them private papers, money, and jewels that had been the personal property of the captain of our ill-fated ship. If possible, I wanted them to be handed over to his heirs.
Here are the details of the wreck, with the names of all the crew members.
As you already know, one reason why I must go back is because...
...with your blessings, we want to get married!
When you meet Colonel Montrose, ask for his permission to your engagement.
Meanwhile, we give our blessings.
Fritz, I will give you the journal in which I have recorded the events of our lives. I want our story to be printed and published.

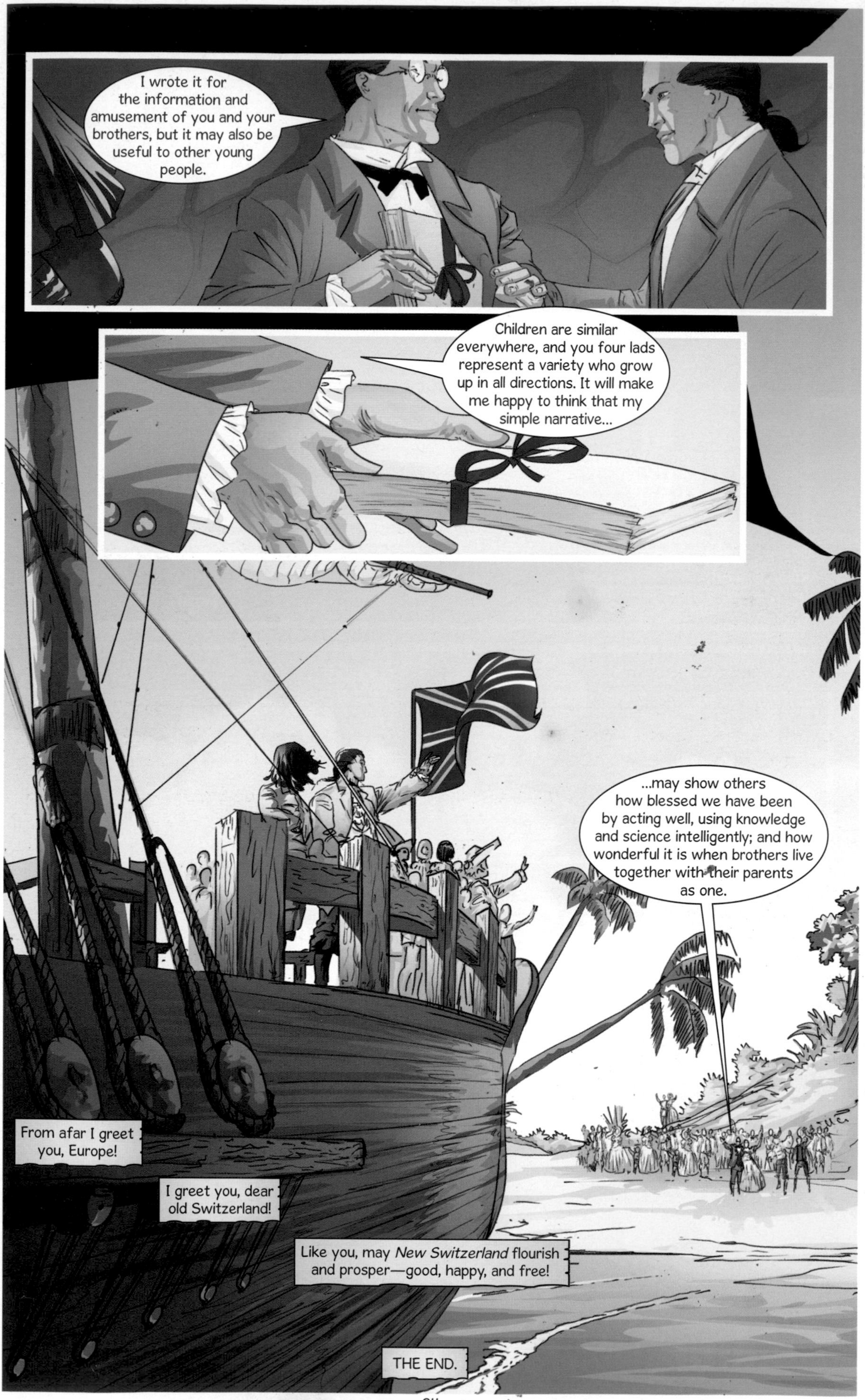

I wrote it for the information and amusement of you and your brothers, but it may also be useful to other young people.
Children are similar everywhere, and you four lads represent a variety who grow up in all directions. It will make me happy to think that my simple narrative...
...may show others how blessed we have been by acting well, using knowledge and science intelligently; and how wonderful it is when brothers live together with their parents as one.
From afar I greet you, Europe!
I greet you, dear old Switzerland!
Like you, may *New Switzerland* flourish and prosper—good, happy, and free!
THE END.

CAMPFIRE
Mythology
RYAN FOLEY
STOLEN HEARTS
THE LOVE OF
EROS AND PSYCHE
ILLUSTRATED BY
SANKHA BANERJEE

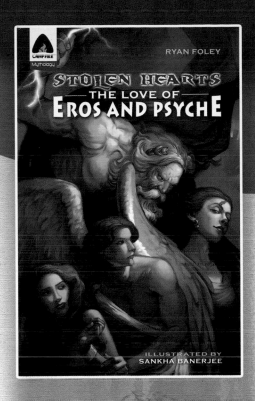

STOLEN HEARTS
THE LOVE OF EROS AND PSYCHE

WRITTEN BY RYAN FOLEY
ILLUSTRATED BY SANKHA BANERJEE

Absorb yourself in this heart-wrenching love story peppered with intrigue and the ambition of Greek goddesses.

In the time of myths and legends...

...Aphrodite, the Greek goddess of beauty, has grown jealous of a young girl named Psyche. She is envious of the praise being heaped upon the mortal girl for her splendor. The goddess decides to dispatch her mischievous son Eros, the god of love, to perform a nasty trick.

When the trick goes awry, Eros finds himself falling in love with Psyche. Unable to resist her allure, he whisks her away to a palace in the sky. Wanting Psyche to fall in love with him for who he is and not for his name or looks, Eros hides his true identity from her and forbids her to see him in the light.

Persuaded by her two jealous sisters, Psyche plots a way to see him by lamplight. Her plan backfires and, feeling spurned and betrayed, Eros abandons her. Psyche sets out on a quest to regain the trust of her one true love.

This is a wonderful story of true love, redemption, and the conquering of impossible odds during the golden age of mythology.

BRRAADOOOOM

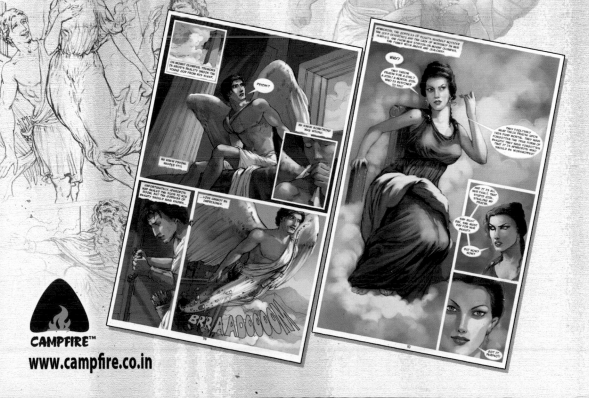

THE DARK AND THE DEEP

**The Swiss Family Robinson make a cave their winter home.
Let's learn a few interesting facts about these dark chambers.**

FORMATION OF LIMESTONE CAVES

Caves are formed in many different ways. However, most caves are made of
limestone. Let's see how they are formed.

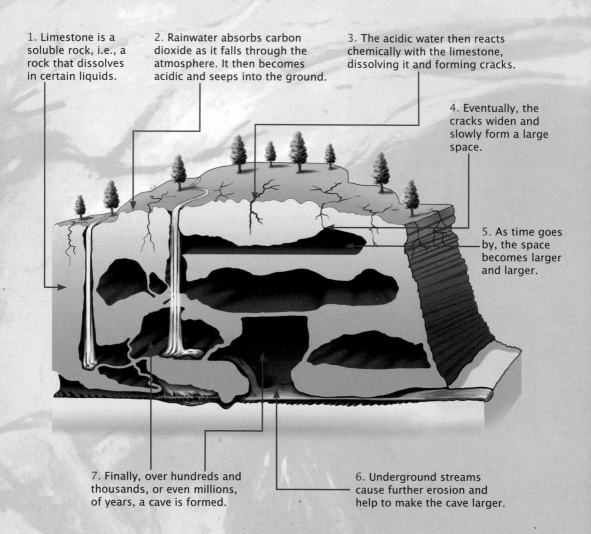

1. Limestone is a soluble rock, i.e., a rock that dissolves in certain liquids.

2. Rainwater absorbs carbon dioxide as it falls through the atmosphere. It then becomes acidic and seeps into the ground.

3. The acidic water then reacts chemically with the limestone, dissolving it and forming cracks.

4. Eventually, the cracks widen and slowly form a large space.

5. As time goes by, the space becomes larger and larger.

6. Underground streams cause further erosion and help to make the cave larger.

7. Finally, over hundreds and thousands, or even millions, of years, a cave is formed.

CAVES OF THE WORLD

THE WORLD'S LONGEST CAVE

The longest cave in the world is the Mammoth Cave System in America. It is about 587 kilometers long, and has two lakes, several rivers, and a number of waterfalls inside it!

THE WORLD'S DEEPEST CAVE

The Krubera Cave in Georgia is the deepest cave in the world. Its total depth has been measured at 7,188 feet. And, if that's not deep enough, recent expedition teams believe parts of it could be even deeper!

THE WORLD'S LARGEST UNDERGROUND CHAMBER

The largest cave in the world is the Sarawak Chamber in the Gua Nasib Bagus cave in Malaysia. Its floor area is around 23,000 square feet— about the size of three soccer fields put together!

CAVE CREATURES: TROGLOBITES

Imagine living in dark caves your entire life! Troglobites are creatures that do so. What is most fascinating about them is how they are equipped for life in total darkness. Troglobites have heightened senses of smell, taste, and vibration detection, that help them survive in the dark. At the same time, they do not have features like eyes, which would be quite useless without light. Two interesting troglobites are:

OLM

A very strange–looking creature, the olm is also called 'cave salamander' or 'white salamander'. Pinkish–white in color, it grows up to eight inches long. It lives entirely underwater in the pools and rivers found in caves. Though it has no eyes, like most troglobites, it is believed that if an olm is reared outside its natural habitat, it can develop basic ones. A long-living creature, it can live up to the age of 58 years. And here is the most interesting fact—the olm can apparently survive up to 10 years without food!

ALABAMA CAVE SHRIMP

Not very easy to find, this extremely tiny creature lives in pools in caves. It feeds on fungi, algae, and other organic matter found in the groundwater in caves. Less than an inch in size, and almost transparent, the Alabama Cave Shrimp is found in only two cave systems in the entire world. It was first found and studied in 1958. Very difficult to spot because of their lack of color and size, only 25 of these shrimps have been observed in the last two decades. They are listed as a highly endangered species.

EXTRAORDINARY USES OF CAVES

We all know that caves have been used for shelter, burial, storage, and also for religious purposes. Now read on to see what some caves have been turned into:

A CAVE SCHOOL

How would you like to study in a cave? Well, children in China's Guizhou province do study in one. A huge cave formed inside a mountain is used as a primary school, and includes basketball courts, teaching rooms and small buildings.

CAVE HOTELS

If you ever visit Cappadocia in Turkey, you can live like a modern caveman. The numerous lava caves in the area have recently been turned into cave hotels of all shapes and sizes. Most of them are located deep inside the mountain cliffs, and are a treat for any cave lover. One is even called the Flintstones Cave Hotel!

CAVE CITY

This may sound unbelievable, but it's true. During the First World War, British soldiers created a unique hideout in the French town of Arras. It was a secret underground city right beneath the unsuspecting enemy (the Germans)! Engineers linked hundreds of underground caves to create a secret city that housed 25,000 soldiers in 1917. This city included chapels, canteens, power stations, and a fully functional hospital!

DID YOU KNOW?
- The sport of exploring caves is called *spelunking*.
- The scientific study of caves is called *speleology*.

ALSO AVAILABLE FROM
CAMPFIRE GRAPHIC NOVELS

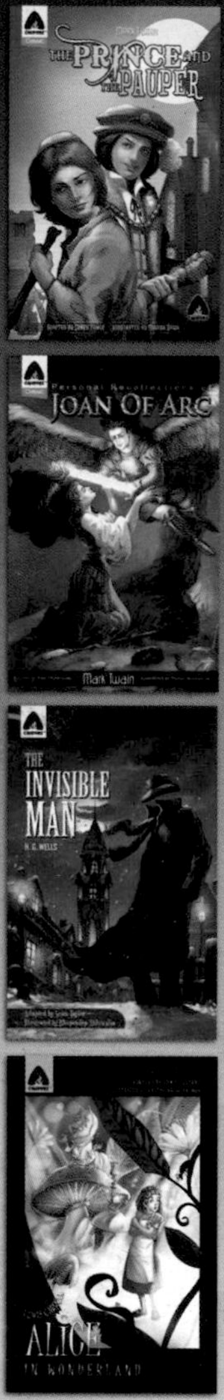
THE PRINCE AND THE PAUPER
JOAN OF ARC
Mark Twain
THE INVISIBLE MAN
H. G. WELLS
ALICE IN WONDERLAND

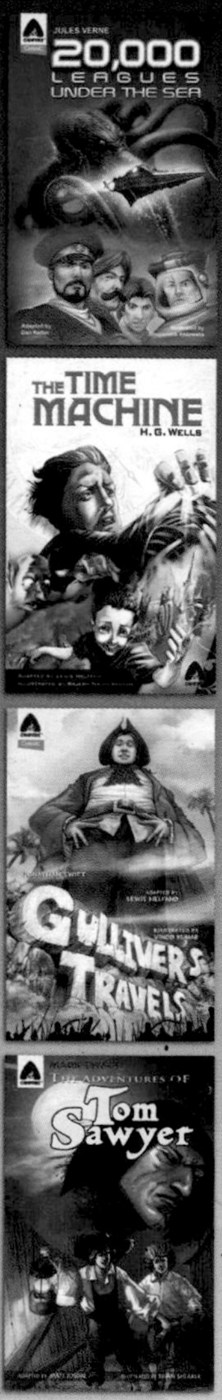
JULES VERNE
20,000 LEAGUES UNDER THE SEA
THE TIME MACHINE
H. G. WELLS
GULLIVER'S TRAVELS
THE ADVENTURES OF Tom Sawyer

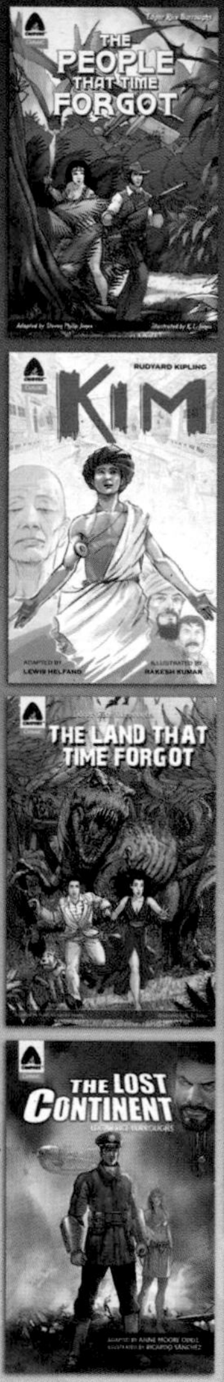
THE PEOPLE THAT TIME FORGOT
RUDYARD KIPLING
KIM
ADAPTED BY LEWIS HELFAND
ILLUSTRATED BY RAKESH KUMAR
THE LAND THAT TIME FORGOT
THE LOST CONTINENT

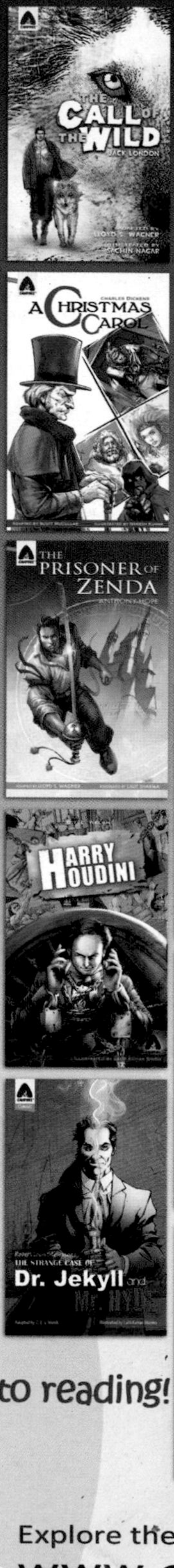
THE CALL OF THE WILD
JACK LONDON
LLOYD S. WAGNER
SACHIN NAGAR
CHARLES DICKENS
A CHRISTMAS CAROL
THE PRISONER OF ZENDA
HARRY HOUDINI
THE STRANGE CASE OF Dr. Jekyll and Mr. Hyde

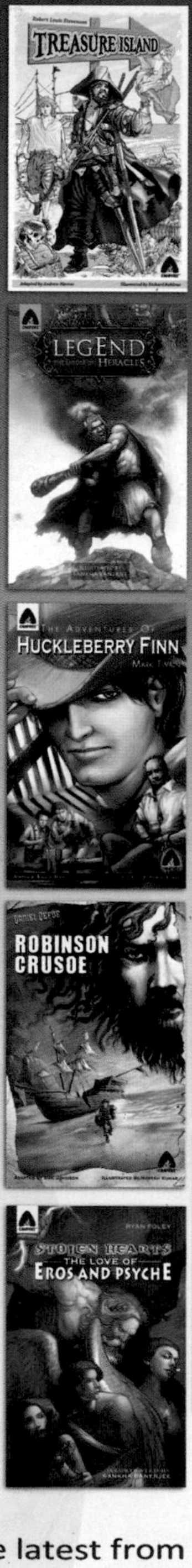
TREASURE ISLAND
LEGEND
THE ADVENTURES OF HUCKLEBERRY FINN
ROBINSON CRUSOE
STOLEN HEARTS
THE LOVE OF EROS AND PSYCHE

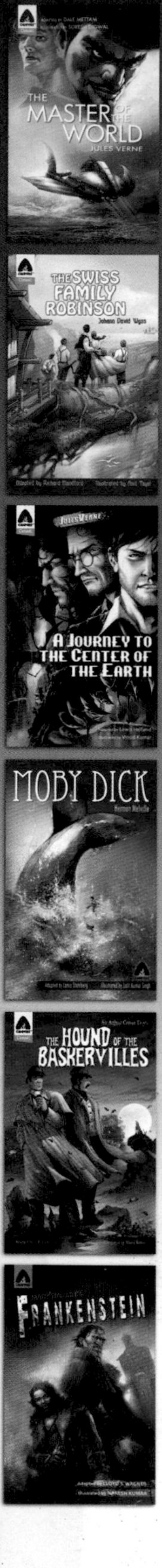
THE MASTER OF THE WORLD
JULES VERNE
THE SWISS FAMILY ROBINSON
JULES VERNE
A JOURNEY TO THE CENTER OF THE EARTH
MOBY DICK
Herman Melville
THE HOUND OF THE BASKERVILLES
FRANKENSTEIN

Putting the fun back into reading!

Explore the latest from Campfire at
www.campfire.co.in